Enchanting the Elf

ELLE STERLING

MONSTERS OF ALBERAD

Enchanting the Elf

PAPERBACK ISBN: 979-11-988262-3-7
HARDCOVER ISBN: 979-11-988262-4-4

COVER ART: MON REYES
COVER DESIGN & INTERNAL FORMATTING: COLETTE RHODES
DEVELOPMENTAL EDITING: STEPH AT RAWLS READS EDITS
LINE EDITING: ADRIENNE LEE SEO

Dedication

TO ALL THOSE WHO DISLIKE
CONFLICT AND CHOOSE TO SEE THE
BEST IN OTHERS.
NEVER CHANGE.
MEEKNESS DOES NOT EQUAL
WEAKNESS.

Content Warning

THIS BOOK IS ANGSTY AND SMUTTY, AND IS INTENDED FOR ADULT READERS 18+. PLEASE BE PATIENT WITH ADELBERT AND FLORENCE AS THEY WORK FOR THEIR HEA. I PROMISE IT'S WORTH IT.

SHOULD YOU HAVE ANY SPECIFIC QUESTIONS ABOUT TRIGGERS, PLEASE DON'T HESITATE TO REACH OUT TO ME AT ELLE@ELLESTERLING.COM FOR MORE DETAILS.

IF ANY OF THE FOLLOWING ELEMENTS MAKE YOU UNCOMFORTABLE, PLEASE PROCEED WITH CAUTION:

STRONG LANGUAGE
EXPLICIT SEX
MENTION OF DECEASED FAMILY MEMBER
(BRIEF AND OFF-PAGE)
EMOTIONALLY ABUSIVE RELATIONSHIPS
(NOT BETWEEN MAIN CHARACTERS)

1

Florence

sn't it the most enchanting sight?" I ask my sister as she joins me by the water's edge. The listless waves of the Caribbean Sea lick at my feet while my gaze stays riveted on the most spectacular sunset I've seen in my life.

Salmon pink and lemon yellow tinge the sapphire-blue sky, casting a million sparkles across the ocean's surface and making my heart sing at the beauty.

"You want to thread paint it, don't you?" Dede asks, referring to my career as a landscape embroidery artist. She digs her toes into the sugary sand and slips her hand into mine.

I turn to Dede and squeeze her hand, grateful that I have a sister who understands me so well. We've always been close—Cece and Dede, Florence and Sadie, sugar and spice. We saved up all year for this weeklong summer vacation together and it has been the best bonding experience we've had to date.

"Absolutely. I want to take a picture, but also not. It won't do it justice. I keep thinking about which threads I'd have to layer to even remotely come close to capturing this. But it's captivating me."

Dede's bright blue eyes glisten with emotion and her voice is filled with sincerity. "You're such a talented artist, I'm sure you'll figure it out. Just like you did with that piece of the woman dancing in the forest. It's imprinted in my brain. Your best work yet." She rubs at her chest and lifts onto her toes. "I'm so proud of you. When I showed your website to Iris and Helena, I could literally feel my chest puffing up more with each piece they saw."

Iris and Helena are the loveliest women. We met them earlier this week at a beach bar and clicked right away. When my sister brought up my embroidery and started showing our new friends my work, my face grew so hot that my cheeks probably looked like two fresh cherries. But the way Dede spoke about me, the pride in her voice, it made my heart so full it'll be charged for months to come.

Iris organized their Caribbean vacation as a post-breakup trip for Helena, her best friend. She generously chartered a yacht for the night and invited me, Dede, and six other women to join them for a ladies' night.

Everyone has been so nice. We all met on the dock and sailed to this uninhabited island to enjoy a sunset picnic and some dancing before we'll head back to our hotels later tonight.

I preen under Dede's praise again and tuck a piece of my long hair behind my ear. Smiling broadly, I say, "That's my favorite embroidery piece I've ever done. The whole scene came to me in a vivid dream. I don't know if you noticed, but the woman dancing in the meadow looks similar to me." A blush heats my cheeks at admitting that aloud and I roll my lips between my teeth as I contemplate whether I should say more. Knowing my sister won't judge me, I decide to tell her what I've not told anyone else.

"I *know* the scene can't be real, but it *felt* real. Like it was in a past or future life. It was like I could feel the crisp fall air on my skin, even now as I recall the dream. I could smell the fresh forest air, the grass, the trees. Oh, the trees." My words drift off as the clear image from my dream replaces the ocean view in front of me. "There were shades of mustard, amber, rust, ginger, olive, brick red even..."

"Do you still have it?" Dede asks.

"I haven't had the heart to sell it yet," I admit sadly, knowing I need the income from such an intricate piece, but not being willing to part with a piece of my heart.

"Well, maybe you're meant to keep it," Dede says confidently. "I love what a great artist you are and how you've developed your craft, how you can paint with thread and bring a picture to life on fabric. I'm also proud of you for being a savvy small business owner, for turning your art into a living."

Before I accidentally start crying, I wrap my younger sister in a hug, careful not to accidentally ruffle a strand of her perfectly styled blonde hair. We pour all our emotions into the hug, saying so much more than we could with just words.

Before my emotions get the best of me, I step back and cup Dede's shoulders. "Sisters by blood."

She cups my shoulders back. "Friends by choice," she finishes our mantra with a brilliant smile.

Dede scrunches up her face and closes her eyes, sending a bolt of apprehension into me for what she wants to say next. "Soooo, not to ruin this beautiful moment, but you don't suppose an uninhabited island has facilities, do you? The champagne seems to have gone right through me. Do you maybe want to come with me, just through those trees?" She opens one eye to peer at me, probably knowing I'll do anything she asks and feeling guilty for stealing me away from this amazing view.

"Dede," I sigh out with so much love.

"We'll be quick." My sister pouts her raspberry-pink lips and makes the cutest puppy dog eyes that are impossible to say no to.

"Let's go." I smile at her antics. As if I won't give up this view to ensure my sister is safe as she wanders on a desert island. "I'd like to be back in time to catch the last remnants of the rays dancing on the surface, though," I add as a specific shade catches my eye. "I have an idea to highlight the water with this very thin gold thread..."

My physical body follows Dede deeper into the jungle, but mentally I am off creating the perfect palette to capture the sunset's reflection on the waves.

"Watch out for any lurking predators!" Natalie calls with a laugh from somewhere to our right. I hadn't even noticed Dede talking to the easygoing woman with the wicked sense of humor.

We met Natalie right before boarding the yacht. Dede loves clothes and says Natalie has a "goth-chic aesthetic," but I'm more fascinated by her pretty tattoos. I remember she said she's originally from Arizona and is now backpacking around the world without a final destination in mind. I can't imagine traveling constantly without a cozy place with all your handpicked knickknacks to call home. But she seems happy, so I'm happy for her.

Dede and I make our way deeper into the jungle, but I pause when something catches my eye. Fascinated, I bend down to study one of the bright blue flowers with a nearly bioluminescent glow. A bunch of them trail deeper into the forest, and something deep inside of me is calling me to find them all.

"Aren't they beautiful?" My voice comes out thick and I glance at Dede who has remained a wary step behind me. "It looks like they're growing in some kind of path. I've never seen anything like it."

"Should we call the others to come look?" Dede asks.

For the first time in I'm not quite sure how long, I feel a little selfish. I want to share these flowers with the eight other women on the island, but not quite yet. Something keeps me from extending an invitation to them right now and beckons me to keep walking.

"Let's venture a tad farther in, and then we can get the others. I have a feeling there's something even more special waiting up ahead for us."

Adelbert

s this helping your brain switch off a little?" Edmond asks me, raising his voice to be heard above the rush of the waterfall and the boisterous laughter coming from our friends. He lowers himself onto the rock next to me and stretches out his leathery wings behind him.

In front of us, Jasper cannonballs into the natural pool then proceeds to playfully wrestle Jamie, taking care not to nick him with his long horns. The rest of our friends are chatting, laughing, or roughhousing with each other around the clearing, and my lips twitch into a small smile.

"I am not sure about switching off, but it is most definitely quieter. I needed to get away for a little while," I tell my friend and roll my shoulders back.

"It makes me happy to know you are able to relax here with us. We appreciate you offering the Caribbean Estate for our reunion and coming out here early to ward it so securely," Edmond says with absolute sincerity. He and Harvey have always been the most empathic members of our friend group, the "nice guys" as Everett calls them.

"It is no problem." I take a deep breath and add, "My father and some other elves assisted me with the warding. He wanted to ensure it was done *properly*."

"Nithard Alberad actually left Germany to 'help'?" The surprise in Edmond's voice amuses me and I scoff at the notion that my father would do such a thing.

"I would not call it 'help' as much as ensuring I don't fuck it up."

Edmond's long tail flicks out in agitation. "That seems very on-brand for your father. But let's not talk about him. He ruined enough fun while we were at school. How's your research coming on? The final presentation is this fall, if I'm not mistaken?"

I nod and my shoulders tense at the reminder. "It is coming along fairly well. However, I would prefer not to talk about it right now."

Edmond stretches out a hand toward me in what I'm sure is meant to be a comforting gesture, but quickly retreats because he knows elves don't welcome physical touch.

"I know leaving Germany must be hard at this point when you are under such immense pressure. Whenever, *if* ever, you would like to talk, I am here. We all are."

"I appreciate that," I say and really mean it, though the prospect of me sharing my research with anyone at this point is highly unlikely.

An odd sense of home seeps into my chest and my heart rate suddenly ratchets up. A wind whips past me and my eyes scan the clearing for its source, finding all the leaves still.

"Did you feel that?" I ask Edmond, my voice holding a nearly breathless quality to it.

"Feel what?" Edmond sits up straighter and his eyes dart around the pool, the waterfall, and the trees surrounding us, searching for a threat.

"Where's Everett?" I ask when I can't see or sense him, then realize it's him who must have zoomed past us. "Please excuse me. I'm going to see where he's gone off to."

"Sure." Edmond tries to look casual but his body remains

on high alert as I stand up. "Shout if you need anything."

My feet lead me toward the wall of foliage where the sound ward extends up to, a strange sensation bubbling deep within me and propelling me forward. My hands grow clammy and my heart beats faster and faster until my whole body vibrates with nervous energy.

I reach forward and part the curtain of leaves. Then, my heart nearly stops beating all together.

In front of me is the most beautiful woman I have ever laid eyes on. Long pearly hair meets her lithe waist and glimmers in the evening light. Her eyes, alight with kindness, blink at me. They're an unforgettable shade of blue, the same shade as the cornflowers that pepper my favorite meadow in the summer.

There's something soft and graceful about her and, instead of fear or shock marring her expression, there's a serene smile painted on her rosy lips.

I steel my spine and square my shoulders, ignoring the odd itch on my ribs and swallowing down all the unwelcome emotions the human woman is stirring up in me. Only then do I notice my closest friend and another woman partially hidden behind him.

"Everett, who are these women?" I ask him.

"I was just coming to get you to figure out how they were able to penetrate the wards. I've been trying to get some answers out of them, but they're not being particularly cooperative." He shoots a pointed look over his shoulder at the woman in the pink dress. Though, there is nothing stern about the expression, it seems rather playful. He likes her.

How long have they been out here while I was relaxing by the waterfall, oblivious of our wards being penetrated by humans? My father will never let me hear the end of this if he finds out.

Something tightens in my chest at the thought of the two women being frightened of us and I do my best to soften my features and project calmness. Everett and I are two of the most human-looking among our friends, though both of us possess monstrous qualities I hope the women have not yet noticed.

"We were merely following the flowers," the woman with ethereal beauty says. Why does even her voice have to sound sweet?

I sweep my gaze around the clearing and tilt my head to the side to get a better look at the foreign flowers. They grow in a trail from the edge of the ward down toward the beach.

A loud gasp comes from behind Everett's back and the woman in pink whispers, "Are you like a faerie or something?"

My eyes instantly flick from her to the woman in front of me, expecting some kind of negative reaction. I am surprised to find her demeanor still calm, if not curious as she studies my pointed ears. Her smile is like sunshine that pierces through a stormy cloud and I suck in a breath before schooling my features again.

The one behind Everett keeps babbling, and I arch my brows at her.

Raising her hands, the talkative one says, "But I promise you, we won't say anything. Seriously. We'll just be on our way and—"

"Enough!" My voice comes out harsher than I intended, though I appreciate the efficiency with which it halts her speech. "I can sense that there are other humans on this island. I have no idea how that is possible, but we cannot allow you to leave until we have the answers as to how you were able to sneak this far onto the island. Especially without me detecting it." Realizing I might be scaring them more, I gentle my voice. "We mean you no harm. But since we are unsure of what forces are at play here, it is for your own safety that I request you and your companions come with us up to the manor, and then I'll answer some of your questions."

The talkative one steps out from behind Everett and, with more attitude than I care to deal with, asks, "How can you 'sense' the others? If only my sister and I saw you, don't you have to be concerned about only us? The others don't even know anything."

Everett points toward the beach. "The 'others' are actually headed this way as we speak."

The woman in pink turns in the direction he pointed and tries to see what he means, as if her human senses could pick up anything from this distance.

"I can't see anything," she says.

"I can hear them approaching. They're quite... rowdy. Sounds like a fun party." Only Everett would see that as a positive and crack jokes at a time like this when the secrecy of monsters could be at stake.

We go to great lengths to ensure our safety from humans. I have studied warding and magic for years in order to keep the mere existence of monsters hidden.

"More like an assault to the senses," I mutter and glance back at the pretty sister who has been standing quietly watching the scene unfold.

"There you are! We were wondering where you ran off to," a woman calls. I presume she must be the leader of the group as seven others trail behind her.

"Who are these guys?" another woman asks. Distrust rolls off her in waves and hits me square in the chest. I am glad to see there is someone with a sense of danger in the group.

Needing to reassure all ten of the women that we mean no harm, I step forward and place my hand on my chest. "Ladies, please allow me to introduce myself. My name is Adelbert Alberad. My family owns this island and, by proxy, I am therefore responsible for your safety. It has come to our attention that you have inadvertently breached our security measures, and I would like to ascertain how that may have come about. If you would be so kind as to follow me up to the manor, then we can discuss this matter further, and possibly alleviate any concerns you might have."

No one says anything for a couple of seconds and then laughter bursts forth as they talk over each other, making it clear they do not intend to follow us anywhere.

My eyes bounce between the women, trying to figure out a way to make them see sense. I swallow hard and run a hand through my hair as nerves claw up my throat.

How did they even get onto the island? How am I going to fix this?

Just when I think it cannot get any worse, I turn, only to see Harvey's curved horns parting the curtain of leaves behind me and bursting into the clearing, soon followed by the rest of the group.

Florence

gasp as beings I thought were only fictional come through the foliage behind us. My hand flies to my mouth and my eyes round, not wanting to look away from the different species entering the clearing.

My eyes register horns, wings, tails, and fur, but my mind can't make sense of any of it.

"Oh, fuck. Shit just got interesting, don't you think, sparkles?" the man called Everett says to Dede. He smirks, and a hint of a fang pokes out.

I step closer to the man with the pointy ears and platinum-blond hair. I think he said his name is Adelbert. The stress radiating from him is almost palpable and my hands ache to comfort him. He doesn't look like the type to easily accept hugs from strangers though, so I'll just lend him some silent support.

The men—magical creatures?—don't scare me. They have a boisterous kindness to them that is evident in how quickly they stop when they notice all of us.

The two groups pause and watch each other—human women on one side, magical creatures on the other—no one daring to make a move.

Just when I think the tension might snap someone in half,

Everett says loudly, "Now it looks like a party."

Taking the lead, Adelbert steps into the middle with his hands raised in a nonthreatening gesture. I can't help but notice his long, elegant fingers and an unbidden lustful thought enters my brain when I think about how they would feel on my body.

I'm not an inexperienced woman, but never before have I felt such an instant, visceral attraction to someone. I blink the thought away just as Adelbert starts to speak.

"I apologize for the abrupt appearance of my brethren. Please do not fret. Though their monstrous appearance may startle you at first glance, I can assure you they mean you no harm. I can attest to the sound character of each."

My heart twists at how sincere he is, but the formal speech is not going to calm anyone. I want to step up and help but speaking in front of so many people is not something I am able to do.

"Ladies," Everett drawls in a voice I'm sure has got Dede swooning. I look over at my sister, and I see verifiable hearts in her eyes.

Everett proceeds to translate Adelbert's words into a more palatable manner that the women seem slightly more receptive to.

A muscle ticks in Adelbert's jaw but he nods stiffly at Everett to continue, most probably acknowledging that Everett might have a smoother way of convincing the ladies to trust them.

My eyes sweep over the many interesting features on the different species, but for some reason, my gaze keeps drifting back to Adelbert. His body is so rigid I'm afraid he's going to hurt himself. I have this weird urge to either hold his hand and tell him it's going to be okay, or nibble on his ear until he giggles.

One by one, the men head off to the manor, giving the women some breathing room to hear Adelbert and Everett out who remain behind with us. They try their best to explain that none of the men pose any threat to the safety of the women. They just want to get to the bottom of why we were able to get on the island.

After some serious deliberation, the women cautiously

decide to follow them, making Adelbert's shoulders visibly sag in relief.

His silver eyes catch mine. A sensation I can't place wells up in my chest and spreads outward to the tips of my fingers and toes. Blissfully unaware of the effect he is having on me, he gestures for me to walk in front of him.

"Thank you." My voice comes out more timid than I'd like. I gather the skirt of my dress so I don't trip on it in the dim light, then clear my throat. "I'm Florence."

I glance over my shoulder to see Adelbert inclining his head. "Adelbert."

"I guess you don't meet many women like this?" I try to joke. Despite my shyness, I have this awkward sense of humor that always makes an appearance when I'm nervous.

"Never," Adelbert answers seriously. "You are the first to have crossed the wards. No human has ever set foot on this island. Until now."

"Oh." I'm not sure how to follow that, and we lapse into silence.

I can't make out what Dede and Everett are saying, but they are chatting nonstop, chemistry almost popping between them. I hope she gets his number and that they can stay in touch.

I chew on my lip, trying to think what I can say to ease the tension between me and Adelbert when a good idea springs to mind.

"Adelbert, what do you call a cow that plays the guitar?"

"Cows do not play guitar," he scoffs.

"I know, silly goose. Just play along." I shrug, then try again. "What do you call a cow that plays the guitar?"

"I don't know," Adelbert says flatly.

"A moooo-sician," I draw out the word then giggle at my own joke, but Adelbert's brows only furrow deeper.

Okay, not a fan of corny jokes. Or maybe it's not the right time.

"Do you live here?" I ask, hoping a plain question is simpler to answer.

"No. I live in Germany. Everett lives in Las Vegas. The others are spread out around the world. We came together for our reunion this weekend."

"What kind of reunion is it?" I prod, trying to find the question that'll ignite conversation. There's something about him that makes me curious, like I want to know more about him—everything about him.

Adelbert lets out a long sigh and my cheeks flush with embarrassment. I roll my lips between my teeth to keep myself from speaking until he asks me something instead.

Surprising me, Adelbert explains, "We attended Alberad School for the Supernatural in Germany. It has been ten years since all of us have been together in one place. We would have met there, however, some preferred a tropical vacation. This island has been specially warded with extra magic to keep humans from stumbling upon it. Now, it is my duty to figure out *how* and *why* you were able to make landfall."

Before I ask another question, I let all that information seep into my brain so I can sort through it. He introduced himself as "Adelbert Alberad" and if the school is "Alberad School for the Supernatural" then he is most probably like school royalty. Before Adelbert arrived, Everett told us that the Alberad family owns this island too. That must put *a lot* of pressure on him. I hope the others can help him figure it all out.

"I'm sorry," I offer weakly, my feet slowing automatically with the apology. Even though I know I didn't crash their party on purpose, I feel bad for ruining what was probably a lot of fun.

Adelbert accepts my apology with a nod and matches my pace. "You do not seem to possess any magic of your own, so you would not have been able to undo the wards. I am certain there is an explanation for this. We are approaching another ward now. Please tell me if you experience any odd sensations."

I ignore the joke about "sensations" that is on the tip of my tongue. Instead, I focus on the placement of my feet on the footpath.

Not being able to help my curiosity, I venture to ask, "Could you tell me how the wards work? How we would've been able to pass through them?"

A line forms between Adelbert's brows and I almost reach up to smooth it away but catch myself in time.

"There is a repulsion charm around the entire island, meant to keep people from *wanting* to step foot on it. Then, there is a sound ward that extends to where we met. The strongest wards are placed around the manor to keep it shielded from view. The combination of these wards make the island look uninhabited."

I swallow and then offer Adelbert a small smile. "I seriously had no idea. Sadie and I only met the other women earlier tonight when we got on the boat. We sailed around before stopping for a picnic on the beach."

"You are oddly calm for someone who is on an island full of monsters," Adelbert says and gives me a strange look. I'd like to say I detect concern in his gaze but it might only be curiosity.

"Before I got on the boat tonight, I said it was time I step out of my comfort zone," I explain. In a quieter voice, I add, "Also, I can't explain why, I know it doesn't make sense, but I feel safe around you."

Adelbert tilts his head and looks at me with a sudden intensity, making a single butterfly take flight in my stomach. "Do you always trust this easily?"

I give that some thought, watching my feet as we weave deeper into the jungle, steadily climbing toward the center. Despite my meek nature, I am not a pushover nor am I naive.

I shake my head. "Nope. Guess you're special," I say brightly and shrug one shoulder.

It's dark by the time we make it to the manor and Adelbert asks us to take a seat in the living room. He heads over to a group of men standing in the corner. One of them hands him a ring and, right before my eyes, I watch Adelbert's pointy ears round to a more human shape.

I study the men a little closer and realize they were the ones from the clearing, but they all have a more human look now. No more fur, no horns, no tails. This must be how they blend into society and go unnoticed by us.

"Saved you a seat," Natalie calls. Dede and I join her and Diana on their cream-colored couch just as Adelbert steps into the center of the room.

Conversations taper off and the tension ratchets up. Next to me, Sadie slips on her mask of unaffectedness and I lean in a little closer, brushing my shoulder against hers to lend her my silent support.

Clasping his hands in front of his body, Adelbert straightens his spine and addresses the room. "Welcome to the Alberad Caribbean Estate. I shall get straight to the point. Your presence on this island is highly disturbing to me. It defies all the laws of our magic. This residence has been in my family for many generations, and our wards have never been breached. The supernatural beings of the world prefer to keep our existence concealed." His brows contract and something in my chest smarts when he adds in a low voice, "Humans are... unpredictable at best."

I don't know what happened in the past to make Adelbert say that, but I know it must be serious. You don't go to these lengths to keep your whole existence a secret for no reason. I feel awful that we have unwittingly added to their burdens.

The room is charged with nerves, no one daring to say anything as his words hang in the thick air. There's something pivotal in this moment, like what he'll say next has the power to alter our lives.

I reach over for Dede's hand, needing my sister's touch to anchor me, and she laces her fingers with mine.

Adelbert attempts to arrange his expression to look more relaxed, but the tight set to his shoulders and the way the corners of his mouth pull down give away how much stress he carries. "Our secrecy is both for your benefit as well as ours. It is, therefore, imperative that we determine how you were able to make landfall upon this island. Until this is concluded, I must insist you all remain here... as my guests, of course."

Everett steps forward and takes over talking, but I can't hear him over the rushing in my ears. I sit, completely frozen, as my mind flits through what this could mean.

How long would we have to stay here? What about Sadie's job? What about everyone else's jobs?

The men all look friendly enough, but is it wise to stay with strangers—monsters, as they call themselves?

I snap back into the moment as Adelbert runs a hand through his hair, making the silky strands messy with the action, and his other hand flexes next to his thigh.

Adelbert looks each woman directly in the eye and I see so much sincerity in his gaze. "We mean you no harm. I vow by the fates that you are safe in this house with us," he says, imploring us to trust them.

A deep-seated need to help ease his stress skitters through the cells of my body. I gather all my courage and, to my own disbelief, my hand lifts into the air to catch Adelbert's attention. "Maybe you can tell us a little about yourselves? I think that will help everyone feel more comfortable," I suggest.

The look of sheer relief and gratitude on Adelbert's face makes speaking up in front of everyone worth it. He gives me a small smile and nods vigorously.

"That is a splendid notion, Florence."

Adelbert lines all the males up—not men—and introduces each to us. He is an elf, Harvey is a minotaur, Edmond a gargoyle, Daehan a grim reaper, Jamie a leprechaun, Jasper a krampus, Erik a selkie, Sawyer a bear shifter, and Rollo is a wolf shifter.

After Everett introduces himself as a dhampir, I stare out the window, letting the sliver of the moon's reflection shimmering on the dark ocean entrance me.

So much has happened in such a short span of time, and there's way too much information to take in, so I quietly sit and run through the names again and match them to their species. There isn't much I can control in the chaos of this situation, but I can attempt not to accidentally offend someone by calling them the wrong name later.

Jamie suddenly blinks into existence in the center of the room with blood streaming from his nose. I didn't even notice he had left.

What could possibly have happened now?

I gasp at the sight and reach toward him, wanting to help him but not knowing how. My fingers curl back as I look around the room, searching for tissues or anything to stem the flow.

"So, that didn't quite go according to plan. I swear, I don't usually have performance issues," Jamie says with an uncomfortable chuckle.

Adelbert steps in front of Jamie and helps him while

someone starts giggling. I still don't understand what happened, but the laughter spreads and soon even Jamie joins in with bright pink staining his cheeks.

Next to me, Natalie shifts the hem of her miniskirt and studies the tattoos on her thigh. With a deep frown and cherry-red pursed lips, she tilts her head from side to side, and runs her fingers along the pretty overlaid sun, moon, and star design.

"So, not to alarm anyone or anything, but this is new," Natalie says, pointing to her tattoo.

I look to Adelbert for some kind of explanation, only to find all the color drained from his face and his eyes the size of saucers. My heart starts galloping in my chest at what this could possibly mean.

The women and males pick up on the strangeness of the situation and frantically search their bodies, marking their findings one by one.

Jasper prances over to Natalie with a giant smile lighting up his face.

"Well, will you look at that? Twinsies!"

Adelbert steps into the center of the room once again and raises his voice to be heard. "Could each of you be so kind as to please voice if you have discovered a new marking and said marking's location? I would like to ascertain if a counterpart could be paired."

Subconsciously, my hand goes to my ribs where I had the oddest itch earlier this evening, and I instinctively know I'll find the same tattoo there. I glance up to find Adelbert's gaze already fixed on me. His right arm is crossed over his chest, resting on his left side, right where mine is. I pull my bottom lip into my mouth, suddenly feeling very shy, and blood warms my cheeks up to the tips of my ears.

Adelbert nods at me and my lips quirk into a timid smile, silently acknowledging what it means.

5

Adelbert

I am unsure why it surprises me that Florence would be the one to have my matching mark. The moment I saw her, I knew there was something different about her. Some would go as far as saying "special." However, that is not a thought I can entertain—neither now, nor ever. My future is set in a heavy stone that I carry on my shoulders at all times. It constantly reminds me of my father's expectations for my life and my lack of choices.

I am an Alberad. It is my responsibility to solve whatever has occurred tonight—on my family's property—and to send everyone back to their homes posthaste. It is my responsibility to not shame the Alberad name. It is my responsibility to keep everyone safe. It is my responsibility to ensure vows of secrecy are given, before we never see the women again.

I clear my throat and the room's attention turns to me. "It seems that most of us have found a tattoo partner. I am unsure as to the meaning of this, but I shall head to the library to commence research pertaining to this unique predicament and find a means to dissolve the markings that have appeared. I apologize for the inconvenience. Please help yourselves to some refreshments while the males prepare your accommodations. We shall return shortly to take you to your wing. I apologize once again, but I will do my utmost to make sure you are as comfortable as possible while we figure this out."

My eyes dart around the room, trying to reassure each person present, instead of settling on Florence, who they seem to gravitate toward.

The leader of the group, Iris, stands up and thrusts her hands on her hips. "Lovely speech, Adelbert. And not to knock the wind out of your sails, but before all the males leave, I would like to know what the captain said about us not returning. I hope he understood and is not sending out a search party or anything."

Fuck. I had already forgotten that we sent Jamie to check on the boat and that he had not yet reported on his findings. I curse myself for getting so distracted. Even though I would like to blame someone, anyone, for my lapse, I cannot.

I chance a glance at Florence, wondering if I will find judgment in her eyes, but those big blue pools are only filled with compassion. She is *too* nice for this world. I would ruin her. Better to stay as far away from her as possible.

Averting my gaze, I tune into the last part of Jamie's explanation. "When I went to teleport, I smashed into a barrier of some kind. It's never happened before. Usually, if I try to go too far, I have a stretching sensation before reaching my limit. But this was just like running into a solid wall. Hence the bloody nose and sore arm."

My brows furrow as I sift through options of what this "barrier" could be. Our wards are not tangible, so it must be something else. It could possibly be connected to the symbols on our bodies.

Before I have a chance to even ask, Everett—being the helpful friend that he is—stands up and walks backward toward the door. "Bertie, let me run down to the beach real quick and see if I can find the problem."

"Thank you, Everett. That would be most kind," I say, though he zooms out so fast that my words are lost to the wind. Turning back to the room, I try to come up with a plan that will appease them. "Everyone, let's remain gathered here until the return of—"

Sadie shoots out of her seat, forcing everyone's attention to her. "What the fuck?" she says with a shaky voice.

The women swarm around her and some of the males join me as I approach her too, but it's like she's caught in her own world. Her face pales and she holds a hand to her stomach as she skids forward another foot.

My palms grow clammy and my heart rate accelerates to an uncomfortable degree. The pressure from today tightens the increasingly heavy noose of responsibility around my neck. Sweat drips down my back but I keep my face impassive as I imagine explaining this in front of the other elves, or worse, my father.

I don't know what this is. I don't know how to fix it.

I sense Everett approaching and people part for him as he strides directly for Sadie with a single-minded focus.

Placing a gentle finger under her chin, Everett tilts her head up until their eyes meet. "Are you alright?" he asks earnestly. The moment between them feels intimate and intense, so much more than should be expected between two people who only met each other today.

I look away and try to give them some privacy, everyone following suit, though confusion and concern remain on their faces. Their emotions are so strong that they scrape against my mental barriers and my anxiety ratchets up, unable to keep them all out.

All my life I strive to ensure boundaries are in place, that emotions remain personal unless voluntarily shared with me. I aim to never exert force or alter others' emotions, just as I never enjoy when it's done to me. However, when chaos ensues—like today— the ability to keep everyone from infiltrating the ice wall I have raised around my mind, is nearly impossible.

Everett covers Sadie's hand where it rests on his forearm, and addresses the room. "Can everyone please take a seat? I think I've discovered something else that might complicate our situation.

Actually, Jamie did earlier, but we got sidetracked."

Still suspended in shock, no one moves to take a seat.

Everett looks to Sadie and they share some kind of silent communication. "Oookay, um, seems like the fates have another surprise for us. If I'm not mistaken, we now have a limit to the distance we can be separated from our... tattoo partner."

Around the room, people drop into seats with various degrees of disbelief. Calling on my lifelong experience of masking my emotions, I keep my face neutral and lock my joints to keep my posture straight and unaffected.

Unable to help myself, I look to Florence to see how she is taking this information. She shares a soft smile with her sister but I don't miss the tremble in her hands where she fidgets with her hair.

I take up pacing in the hopes that it will center my thoughts and force some kind of explanation for today's events to magically appear. I ask Jamie and Everett so many questions, it feels like an interrogation, but it is imperative that I find a reason for all of this.

My teeth ache as I grit out questions, years of research flitting through my brain as I search for plausible explanations. Everett and Sadie had such a strong reaction to their distance limit, yet Jamie and Iris did not. *Why?*

I card my hands through my hair and tug on the strands. Pausing my pacing, I look to Everett, who is holding Sadie close. "Is there any reason you can think of that things would be different with you and Sadie? Something you've done?"

The room holds its breath as I voice my question, the women leaning forward in their seats, the males tilting their heads.

Everett looks to Sadie before speaking to everyone else. "I don't know if this could be it, but we have physically touched. When I grabbed her wrist back in the forest and touched her skin for the first time, it was like a jolt went through my body. She felt something too."

"Oh yeah, Iris and I haven't touched... yet." The salacious tone in Jamie's words and his ability to make jokes at a time like this irks me beyond belief.

Nevertheless, I follow the line of thought pertaining to touch, and glance at the males scattered around the room. "Has any male here made physical contact with one of the women, except for Everett and Sadie?"

Of their own accord my eyes move to Florence first, though, I redirect my gaze, knowing we have not so much as brushed clothing against each other.

One by one, the males shake their heads. I don't miss the muted desire in Edmond's eyes as he looks at Sylvia, nor the flare of Sawyer's nose as he looks at Louisa.

Jasper's eyes darken when he meets Natalie's equally as hungry gaze. He bites his lip and says, "Not yet."

The pheromones pumping through the air are suffocating and I rub at my brow in an effort to focus. "How far would you estimate this distance limit to be, Everett?"

"I'd say about a hundred yards."

I grab the back of my neck and catch the bead of sweat rolling down before folding my arms across my chest while my neutral mask remains firmly in place. Then, I unintentionally thank the elvish custom of suppressing emotions and letting logic take the lead at all times.

From what I can deduce, none of this was planned by anyone, thus leading me to believe the fates have intervened in tonight's events. I will need to search all resources we have on the estate referencing the fates so we can separate from our partners as soon as possible.

I will not fret. I will find a way to dissolve this distance limit. I will not have a stranger bound to remain within a hundred yards of me.

Voice edging on panic, Helena asks, "So what you're telling us is that we now have a hundred-yard limit from the matchy tattoo?"

I take a deep breath in through my nose and on my

exhale, answer truthfully. "It would seem that we can conclude that, yes." Speaking to everyone, I say. "The fates have presumably intended for us to meet and orchestrated some of tonight's events, placing various obstacles in our way to dissuade our separation. I shall promptly start my research to find the means to sever these connections as fast as the fates would allow. Please refrain from making any physical contact with your partner unless you also wish to be in a similar predicament as Everett and Sadie. I hope to have found a resolution by morning."

Florence's hands still their motion through her wavy strands. Her hair looks so soft, I wonder what it would feel like to glide my fingers through them, or wrap them around my fist.

No! There is no time for lascivious thoughts.

There is a crisis currently unfolding and as the sole heir to Alberad, I am responsible for solving it. All thoughts of Florence—and her hair—need to be firmly locked away, never to be revisited again.

With the kindest eyes and a pale pink dusting her cheeks, Florence says, "Thank you for your hospitality. Is there anything we can do to help you with your research?"

Why does she have to be so nice? So beautiful?

I answer stiffly, "No, thank you. It would be most convenient for everyone to get settled for the evening. Ladies, please help yourself to some refreshments in the dining room before retiring to the east wing. If you need anything, please don't hesitate to ask one of the males, or you could approach me in the library on the second floor of the main building. Once again, please refrain from making any physical contact for the time being."

Harvey steps into my line of sight and holds up a hand. "Excuse me, Bert. If I may make a suggestion?"

I incline my head toward Harvey, signaling for him to continue and knowing the women are in good hands with his gentle, caring nature, then I silently slip out of the room and head to the library.

I don't dare to look back to see Florence's expression.

6

Adelbert

trudge through the house and push open the heavy door to the library. Though only a fraction of the size of the official Alberad library in Germany, I hold a certain amount of hope that I will be able to find a way to rid ourselves of these strange markings.

I quickly scan the shelves for any books containing *Amarto* in their title, hoping the Elvish word for "the fates" might lead me in the right direction.

One by one, the rest of the males join me in the library and meticulously comb through the shelves. Harvey finds me kneeling on the floor as I trace the titles of each book on the bottom shelf, finding nothing promising in this section.

"Bertie, your Elvish is better than any of ours. How about you go take a seat at the desk and we will bring you anything we think might be relevant," Harvey suggests gently.

I look up to find a few of my friends standing over me, their faces lined with determination to assist me in my search.

"That is a kind offer," I acknowledge. "I shall start with the ones I have selected. Please bring me anything regarding the fates, unintentional pairings, or magical tattoos."

"I'll come with you," Edmond says, picking up half of the

stack of books I have selected. "I've kept up my Elvish and it will go faster if you have help."

"Thank you," I say, accepting Edmond's assistance. Walking toward the heavy desk at the back of the room, I ask him, "Is there a reason you have continued reading Elvish texts?"

"I've always been fascinated by theories behind magic and, as a hobby of sorts, I like to spend my time diving deeper into it."

We set our books on the desk and take our seats across from each other. Mine is a typical high-backed chair, and Edmond's is a specially designed low-backed chair to accommodate his wings. Prior to our reunion, I made sure a variety of seating options were delivered to the estate in order to accommodate the different species present.

Opening the first tome related to magic markings, I ask Edmond, "Have you ever considered a career in academia?"

Without looking up, I can sense Edmond's wings spreading in the way the air shifts around us. His bitterness presses against me as he says, "If schools ever accept professors of species other than elves, it would be something I'd be interested in."

That gets my attention. I look up, placing a hand on the page to keep my place. My lip curls back, and my irritation grows with every word as I say, "It is an atrocity that they do not welcome other species to instruct on various topics." My disgust for the hierarchical exclusion of other species in education makes my blood boil, and a shudder rolls down my spine. "I cannot help but feel that there is a wealth of knowledge we are missing out on by not diversifying the education field."

"Agreed. But one can only dare to dream," Edmond says with a faint smile.

Slowly, we sift through tome after tome, modern ones and ancient ones, no closer to finding any answers. Time coils tighter around my windpipe with every tick of the clock. My hope to find anything withers away as the minutes pass.

"I think I've found something here. Anyone else have any

luck?" Everett asks.

Without the tiniest spark of optimism, I hold my hand out for the book. "None so far. Let me see."

The title reads *Signs of Magic Through the Ages.*

I shake my head and tug on my hair. "Nothing in this one. I read the English version already."

"Bertie, it's okay," Everett says in a voice so gentle it has my head snapping up. "We'll find something. If not here, then we'll go to Alberad and search the library there."

I sat back and cross my arms over my chest. "And how will that look? A group of human women showing up with monsters who graduated ten years ago. My father would laugh at my ineptitude." I can already see the frown on ole Nithard's face.

Every conversation with my father feels like a chess game. Only difference is, I am playing blindfolded while he judges every decision I make.

The rest of the males gravitate toward the desk, and Everett asks, "What other option do we have?"

Looking each of them in the eye, I brace myself for their reactions to what I'm about to say.

"I've gone through about a hundred possibilities. Considering we have a time limit with the women having to check out of their accommodations and needing to return to their responsibilities, I've narrowed down our options to two. One really. It's a wild idea, and no one is going to like it."

Everyone is frozen, the tension building ominously as they await my pronouncement.

Edmond is the first to speak, when he says calmly, "Let's hear it, then."

Nervous energy moves through my limbs and I stand up abruptly, unable to sit still for another moment. I take a step to the left, pause, then face forward to see concerned gazes trained on me.

"I need to go to Alberad to scour more comprehensive

resources. Since I will be leaving the island, I cannot guarantee that the wards will hold as strongly with so many monsters in place without my presence. So you'll need to leave, too.

"Tomorrow morning, you'll have to talk with your partner and determine where you should go—your home, their home, or another location. I'll leave that up to you as partners to decide."

Jamie raises his hand hesitantly. "What if the women don't want to go somewhere with us?"

Already having thought of that based on Iris's opinion of him thus far, I say, "We will swear oaths to them and promise their safety. You will vow not to touch them—unless it is a consensual request. We do not want them to be any more frightened than they already are."

Nods are given around the room, everyone in agreement with my plan.

"And you?" Daehan asks.

I raise my chin. "My hope is that this will all pass quickly. I will work without cease and try my utmost to resolve this as swiftly as possible."

Daehan's face softens and his concern penetrates my shields. "We're wondering if you'll be okay. Having a stranger in your house when you're so sensitive to emotions and under so much stress with the bonds and with your presentation, that might be hard for you."

I shrug. No other ideas I have had seem feasible. "It is what it is. Do you have a different suggestion?"

We return the books and tidy the library, then head off for a couple of hours of sleep before we will break the news to the women over breakfast.

Florence

"Florence, are you awake? It is almost dawn and I would prefer for us to be off soon." Adelbert's clipped greeting comes through the door and I open it, already dressed for our mission this morning.

"Sure. All set." I offer a small smile to the handsome male and get a minor twitch of his lips in return as he assesses my embroidered jeans, white top, and canvas shoes.

He's not radiating disdain so I'll take it as approval.

"Come," Adelbert grunts and it sounds just enough like a command that I wordlessly follow him as he turns on his heel and heads to the front door.

Adelbert and I arrived at his home in the heart of the Black Forest late last night. He helped carry my bag into the house and showed me to my room, which just so happened to be on the opposite side of the house from his, but still within the magical bond's limit that we're forced to remain within.

There was no time to explore or ask questions, only a sense of urgency for morning to come so we could head to Alberad School for the Supernatural's library for him to start his extensive research and find the reason—and solution—to the bond.

Adelbert had valiantly tried to find answers while we were

in the Caribbean, scouring the estate library's limited resources. Unfortunately, he couldn't find any concrete answers, so the following morning I said goodbye to Dede as she headed off to Las Vegas with Everett, while I had to join Adelbert on the first plane back to Germany.

It's a little intimidating traveling to the other side of the world with someone you met two days ago, just after finding out monsters are real, but I remind myself that no one chose to be in this situation. The fates had intervened—for reasons yet to be known—and bonded us together.

Adelbert steps through the front door, body rigid as he holds it open for me with one elegant hand braced against the heavy wood, careful not to accidentally touch me. I incline my head in thanks as I pass him, but my feet freeze to the spot when I cross the threshold.

"Wow," I breathe as the view steals the air from me. My lungs inflate again with the fresh forest scent caressing my senses, goose bumps skittering across my arms in the brisk morning air. In front of me is a sight I'm committing to memory, my hands itching with the need to capture it with thread.

From on top of the mountain, a valley stretches out before me, the undulating slopes painted in charcoal and onyx as the first glimmer of light starts to peek over the horizon. Early morning mist hugs the treetops down below and wispy tendrils reach into the hazy sky alight with hues of dark lavender, antique mauve, and light plum.

"It's magnificent," I whisper more to myself than Adelbert, awe wrapping around my words as I bask in the beauty of the predawn sky.

"Yes, I suppose it is," Adelbert mutters, lifting his head briefly to take in the view before trudging past me.

I don't take offense to his brusque nature, it rather seems to be an inherent part of him, and it's most probably only exacerbated by everyone relying on him to solve a problem he had no part in creating.

Adelbert is equally as blameless as I am, yet I can see that he holds himself responsible for everything that transpired on the island. I can't imagine the immense pressure he is putting on himself, but I will try my best to help him and ease his burdens however I can.

Like a beacon in the dim light, Adelbert's perfectly styled platinum-blond hair beckons me to follow him down the path leading into the thick forest.

"Time is of the essence, Florence."

"Of course. Sorry." I give my head a small shake, feeling selfish for taking precious time, and hurry after him into the waking forest.

The gentle call of birds, the trickling of a small stream, and the serene whooshing of wind through the tall branches accompany my low humming as we follow the trail between the giant fir and pine trees.

"I messaged Sadie last night. Her view of the Vegas Strip from Everett's penthouse suite is so pretty. She sounds happy and like she's already enjoying herself. Have you talked to Everett yet?" I try to make small talk with Adelbert while keeping up with his brutally long strides, his long limbs eating up the distance between his home and the school.

Scarcely glancing back at me over his shoulder, his frown is firmly in place before he faces forward again.

"Nothing about anyone's status has changed since we last saw them. I will contact him when there is a reason to."

My lips press into a thin line and I give an internal sigh, mentally noting that small talk with Adelbert is fruitless. Or perhaps it's just the early morning that has him grouchy. I'll try again when the sun has properly crested the horizon.

I look up and squint my eyes at the dark branches high above to find a particular bird with a beautifully melodious song. My foot snags on an exposed root and I miss my next step. My heart drops into my stomach as I stumble, but before falling down completely, I manage to right myself, pressing a hand to my chest in the hopes that it will calm my racing heart.

"Could you please be more careful? You know I am unable to physically assist you should you injure yourself." Adelbert's tone is as stern as his face, his brows scrunched together.

My eyes catch on his fingers splayed open on either side of his hips as if reaching toward me, but he quickly curls them into fists, the veins on the back of his hands popping against his pale ivory skin.

My eyes round. "Sorry, I got distracted." My voice comes out smaller than I intended and I tuck some hair behind my ear. I don't know if I feel embarrassed for almost falling, or for drooling over his hands when there are much bigger issues to focus on.

Adelbert's scowl softens a fraction and he huffs, "For fates' sake, please don't apologize. Just... watch your step." He turns forward again and, this time, proceeds at a marginally slower pace.

I know Adelbert's not especially pleased with having a stranger in his home, but unfortunately, neither of us had much say in the situation. And despite his harsh tone, I've seen glimpses of his kindness underneath the prickly demeanor.

With that in mind, I try to break the tension with a corny joke.

"What did the horse say after it had tripped?"

Adelbert gives me a sidelong glance but doesn't reply, so I forge ahead.

"Help! I've fallen and I can't giddy up."

A laugh bubbles up in my throat, and the twitch at the corner of his mouth doesn't escape me. I don't call him out on it, though. Instead, I silently plot which joke will finally crack through his icy demeanor and have him rolling on the floor with laughter.

After covering some distance in semi-companionable silence, Adelbert is the first to speak. "I intend to find the proper resources in the library today so this... 'bond' can be resolved as soon as possible. I will gather as many books as we are able to carry back to the house and continue research in my personal study."

I trace one of the flowers I embroidered on the pocket of my jeans, and ask, "Wouldn't it be more comfortable and convenient to remain in the school's main library, though?"

"Of course it would," Adelbert answers with a bite in his tone. "But it would be difficult to explain the presence of a human on Alberad's premises."

My hands fall to my sides and a warm flush crawls across my cheeks. Naturally, Adelbert would've thought about all the angles.

Adelbert comes to a stop and turns around to look at me. "Florence," he sighs out. "There is no record of a human ever crossing Alberad's wards. Though I am still young at twenty-eight, I have studied the history of my people extensively. As the sole heir to Alberad School for the Supernatural, it is my responsibility to understand the magic of the land. Yet, you seem to defy every rule and law known to me."

My shoulders climb up to my ears. "I—"

"Please do not apologize again." Adelbert's silver eyes widen. "I am aware that you did not deliberately appear within the wards, however, it does not negate the effects."

I bristle because he can't be sure that I was going to apologize. Could he? Instead of letting any hurt show in my expression, I fix a polite smile on my face.

"You're right. Nothing about this has been deliberate. But since I'm here"—I spread my arms and gesture to the surrounding woods, the soft gilded rays of the rising sun streaking through the towering trees—"let me know if there is any way I can help you or, if you prefer, I'll leave you in peace to focus on your research in solitude."

"Thank you. I shall inform you if there is any specific thing I require," Adelbert says, not unkindly.

I remind myself that we're essentially strangers and don't owe each other anything. Living with him is temporary, and I'll most likely be back in Kentucky by the end of the week.

Why does that make me feel lonely?

While Adelbert is holed up in his study, I'll explore the forest surrounding his house—within the bond's parameters—and make the most of my first time in Europe. I wish I had my embroidery supplies to pass the time, though. I didn't pack any on my week away with Dede, since it was meant to be filled with only relaxation and sisterly bonding time.

Now, the two of us are living on opposite sides of the world for a yet-to-be-determined amount of time and my heart is longing to recreate some of the spectacular sights I've seen.

My bigger embroidery pieces sell to special collectors and it's how I make a living. A modest living, but a happy one nonetheless. But I wonder if I'll have the same level of difficulty parting with the Black Forest pieces I want to create, just like I've not been able to part from the meadow piece.

I resolve to ask Adelbert about where to buy thread if my stay extends beyond a week, but for the time being, I'll find other ways to keep busy.

A new thought occurs to me and, after a quick pep talk to myself to not be shy and to speak up, I pierce the silence with my question.

"Will I be able to enter the library or is there somewhere I should wait for you?"

A muscle ticks in Adelbert's sharp jaw.

"It would not be wise to enter the library with me. Though I am usually the only one there this early in the morning, there is a chance that staff members could be about. It would be best to have you wait outside the building at a safe distance. I know the section I want to gather resources from, so it shouldn't take too long."

I nod as I process that he's hiding me like a dirty secret. I might not like it, but his logic makes sense.

Aiming for a gentler tone, but back still rigidly straight, Adelbert continues, "I shall keep within one hundred yards so we do not upset the distance bond. Also, since I am able to sense people within certain parameters, I shall hasten to you should there be a chance of being discovered. Do you have any other questions?"

I wonder what it's like to be so goal-oriented that you forget about your emotions. Not once has Adelbert complained. He has kept a neutral mask in place since I met him and he is singularly focused on helping everyone without any assistance.

Adelbert is only two years older than me, but it feels like he has lived more lives with all the hats he wears and the responsibilities he carries.

Determined not to add to his very full plate, I straighten my spine and say cheerfully, "Nope. No questions. I'll follow your lead."

Adelbert studies me with a perceptive gaze, his silver eyes brimming with an unidentifiable emotion, then jerks his head sharply.

"We are almost to the boundary. Please stay close."

Adelbert

The presence of Florence in my home is utterly vexing, and it could not have come at a more inopportune time. I am due to give my research presentation this fall, an event where the top scholars of the supernatural community will be present.

Including my father, the head of Alberad.

I have studied, researched, and prepared for years. The result of my presentation will determine whether I will become an active professor at Alberad, the same as every other male figure in my lineage until they eventually take over the running of the school. Should I fail to impress, I will have to extend my research and present again next fall, once I have gathered sufficient results.

My father was twenty-seven when he presented his research and qualified to become a professor, a full year younger than I am now, and he will not let me forget that fact. Nor my intellectual inferiority to him, and therefore, the fate of the future of Alberad hangs in the balance because of me.

Much the same as my friends are depending on me to resolve these bonds we have been saddled with. My promise to everyone on the island that I will work as fast as I am able to in order for all to return to their normal—*separate*—lives again, weighs heavily on me.

I intend to keep my word.

My feet slow in order for Florence to catch up to me, and I quickly take a step sideways when she almost gets too close. I cannot afford for the bond to intensify like it did for Everett and Sadie. This is difficult enough as it is.

Aware that my ever-present scowl is affixed in its usual place, I try to arrange my face into something resembling friendliness. "Florence, within the next minute you will most likely feel the wards around Alberad. I am not certain how strong the effect will be since we have never had a human pass through the school's boundaries. However, you had no problem passing through the boundaries around our Caribbean estate. These should not pose a problem." I raise my brows to indicate I am attempting to elicit a response from her.

Florence's nose scrunches in what one might consider to be an adorable manner and I feel my frustration at the situation bubbling up anew. She quirks her head to the side and nibbles on her plump bottom lip. "I wish there was a way for me to not cross the wards. I don't want to get you in any trouble in case something gets triggered."

And just like that, I curse the fates again for putting this woman in my life.

She's kind and gentle and considerate. And so fucking gorgeous it almost hurts my eyes to look at her. There is no space for her in my world that's filled with routine, discipline, and harshness. I have been raised on excellence and zero emotion. Florence, in contrast, is soft and full of feelings.

She is sunshine, and I am the storm cloud threatening her warmth.

Ignoring the way the thoughts squeeze around my cold heart, I bring us to a stop in front of the invisible boundary line and say plainly, "If you feel a hint of resistance, tell me immediately. I can alter the wards and allow you passage. But first, I would like to establish if the effect here will be as minimal as it was on the island."

Florence looks up at me with an open expression and warm smile, her lustrous blonde hair cascading down her back.

"Sure, what can I do?"

I blink at her easy acceptance. For the first time in my life, I am caught off guard and left speechless. Except for my friends, everything I have said has always been challenged, needing to substantiate my opinions with facts and research. My word alone has never been enough.

I swallow against the discomfort in my throat and move my arm in an arc to indicate the light sheen of magic. "I am not sure if your human eyes can pick up the ward, but it is right in front of you."

Eyes squinting, Florence's gaze travels from the root-riddled path up to where bits of navy-blue sky peek through the branches. The corners of her mouth turn down when she comes up empty.

I do not care for her mouth in that shape. Though I know I cannot make her happy, I will try to keep that look from being a recurring feature.

Clearing my throat, I say, "I am certain that the same factors are in play here than those from the island. Even if you are unable to *see* the ward, the magic should have repelled you at this point."

"What would that feel like?" Florence asks with discomfort clear in her voice and in the slump of her shoulders.

I press my lips together for a second to stop the words of reassurance that want to escape. I must remain firm with distancing myself from her as much as possible in order to avoid her forming any sort of attachment to me.

In a neutral tone, I answer, "You would remember something you had to do and would turn back the way you came, and be disinclined from ever moving in this direction again."

Florence's cornflower-blue eyes narrow in thought. The

same blue as the flowers from the island that led her to me. The same blue that haunts me when I close my eyes.

Oblivious to my internal musings, her thoughtful expression is replaced with a soft smile and a lighthearted shrug.

"Well, I can't think of something else I'd rather be doing right now, and I definitely want to walk through this forest again. Repelling wards don't work on me. Boom. Take. That." The words are punctuated with playful fists punching at the air, inadvertently going through the barrier.

"I guess that takes care of crossing the wards," I say, unable to hide the mild amusement in my voice.

"Oh, no. Did I do something bad?" Florence's dainty hands clench into fists and she brings them to her face and hides her pinkening cheeks behind them.

"It's alright," I awkwardly try to comfort her, mirth attempting to pull my mouth into something approximating a grin, but I quickly squash it down. "You managed to punch through the barrier, but it seems there are no consequences. I cannot detect any changes to the wards."

Florence keeps her hands over her mouth as she mumbles her apology. "Honestly, I'm so sorry for my silliness. I promise I'll be on my best behavior from here on."

I acknowledge Florence's apology with a nod, ignoring the mental image of ripping her hands from her pretty lips and putting Florence on her knees, apologizing properly with my cock down her throat.

My expression darkens as I consider the sense of humor the fates have. I am not fully certain that they are to blame for this bond, but all evidence points to them.

Florence is so... pure and not someone I would choose to be sullied by me. I can only hope she will be able to leave my home unscathed by my surliness once everything has been resolved.

"On this side of the wards I require you to be as quiet as possible now that there is no sound barrier in place. Most monsters have special abilities," I remind her, "and for many that includes enhanced hearing and sight. I do not anticipate crossing paths with anyone since the students are on summer break, though, it is better to err on the side of caution."

"Sure. No talking and light, careful steps. I can manage that."

Florence raises her chin and gives herself an encouraging nod while looking down the widening path toward the school.

I refuse to find the action endearing.

"Let's go," I mutter and march ahead of her, trusting Florence to follow compliantly.

As we walk, I train my focus on finding a selection of books that could possibly dispel the bonds and the markings on our bodies, the weight of responsibility settling like a familiar mantle around my shoulders.

A week. I will grant myself a week of extensive research before I have to return to my usual studies. Before Florence has to return to her home in America. Hopefully.

With my resolve firmly in place, we round the bend and Florence lays eyes on Alberad for the first time.

Permitting myself a singular peripheral glance at her expression, I let my soul feed on the way her eyes widen, her whole being lighting up as she takes in the castle and the gardens.

Never before have I had an expression of such absolute awe on my own face.

It's going to be a very trying week.

I place my hand in front of my mouth to stop the gasp that wants to escape, the sight of Alberad castle pulling the sound right out of me.

The sunrise frames the formidable four-story classical stone building on the crest of the hill, looking like something straight out of a fairytale. Sharp gray turrets jut up proudly on each of the wings, the sandstone facade smooth and well-kept. Intricate details run above the large wood-paneled window frames, and heavy double doors lead into the maw of the castle.

The manicured garden at the foot of the hill is dreamy. Flower beds of coordinated colors run between sculpted trees and neat hedges. Roses bloom in rosettes of blush pink, lilac, and magenta. More climbing grandiflora roses are trained over archways and hugging pillars—the sunshiny yellows, creamy whites, and apricot oranges creating a color buffet for my artistic eye.

My eyes catalog each detail, trying to capture and store the hues in my mind so I can recreate them when I have access to my embroidery supplies again.

I turn to Adelbert, my eyes alight with the joy I feel, my spirit charged with the beauty I see, only to find his gaze already trained on me. His lips are slightly parted and his eyebrows squished together, his steel eyes almost soft as he studies me.

"This place *looks* magical," I whisper giddily, remembering to keep my voice low.

He blinks and replaces his expression with the harsher version I'm more familiar with, and runs a hand through his sleek hair.

"Come," he whispers back in a grim command and, with footsteps lighter than his long limbs should allow, leads me around the back of the castle.

Adelbert guides me behind a low stone wall that will obscure me from view. "You may wait here."

Underneath a lone oak tree with a gnarly bark that looks like it's witnessed thousands of stories, is a quaint bench. It's a perfect make out spot for teenagers, and I'm tempted to ask Adelbert if he's had a girl or two here.

I ignore the unexpected stab of jealousy that comes with the thought. Instead, I ask, "This is cute. Will no one find me here?"

Adelbert nods and points at a medieval-looking door.

"I do not believe so. The library is closest to that entrance and this bench is out of direct view of any windows. The dormitories are closed for the summer and the kitchen sits on the western side, therefore it is highly unlikely that anyone will come near this early."

Judging by that information, this is most definitely a make out spot. I wonder what Adelbert would do if I pulled him down with me.

No, Florence. Stop your dirty brain right there. This is not the time.

My teeth release my bottom lip from where they were nibbling away at it, and I return to more demure thoughts. "I take it that the library in this school is massive. Will you be able to remain within the hundred yards of the bond?"

Before Adelbert can answer, I rub at my chest and continue with the idea that just occurred to me, "I wish I brought my phone. Then, you could call me and tell me if I need to move closer."

"You do not need your phone. It will not work within the wards."

"But it worked at your house. I texted Sadie when we arrived last night," I counter.

Adelbert's jaw clenches. "I have tailored the wards around my house to my needs, which include allowing guests in as I please. Alberad's wards are much more... secure."

"I must be super special to be here, then. Right?" I shoot double finger guns at Adelbert, then cringe at myself.

What the hell was that? Who even makes finger guns?

Adelbert shakes his head. As he turns away from me, I swear I hear him mumble, "Looks like it."

Did he just stop using formal words? Color me intrigued. I wonder what else I can do so he'll speak more casually around me. Maybe I can even get him to let down his walls one day and we could eventually become friends.

"So, no phones..." I prompt.

Adelbert turns back to me, posture rigid once again. "There is no need to fret. Your location is a constant variable I have been conscious of since the island, and I am rather well equipped to gauge distance. Just remain on the bench and... enjoy nature." Adelbert started off so confidently, but his last two words sound more like a question, as if he's never just sat in the forest and taken in his surroundings.

I guess he hasn't.

Choosing to be mature and not remark on him saying he's "rather well equipped," I store the sentence in my memory to tell Dede about later. She'd have a ball with it.

Ball!

My smile, however, plays along my lips as I acknowledge my role this morning. "I shall keep my behind firmly placed on the bench until your return, Mr. Alberad."

Adelbert stares at me impassively, but I swear I see a flicker of amusement in his eyes as I lower myself onto the bench.

A sigh is Adelbert's only audible response, then he pivots and strides toward the back entrance.

On his way, he bends to pick up a large rock in one hand. I do not stare at his firm ass as he places the rock in front of the heavy door to prop it open. It makes sense if he's going to be carrying a bunch of books to not have to bother with door handles.

Adelbert doesn't look back at me as he disappears into the darkness of the corridor beyond.

For the first time in two days, I'm alone. Even though I slept in what is probably the loveliest bed I've ever laid down on, my sleep was fitful and insufficient. I knew we would be getting up early this morning, and I didn't want him to wait for me.

I tossed and turned most of the night, until I finally gave up on attempting to sleep. From the early morning hours, I lay awake, straining to hear any sounds coming from the other side of the house. When I heard a door click open then thud shut, I dressed quickly and waited for Adelbert to summon me.

Considering the stress of nineteen people depending on him to find a fix to this bond so we can all return to our normal lives, my heart can't help but ache for him. I wish there was something we could do to help, but no one has the resources that he has, nor would he allow anyone but me—who *had* to come—to follow him to Alberad.

Adelbert has not complained once, just taken it all in stride, and it makes me question how many burdens he carries around that this doesn't send him careening into panic.

He's a bit of a closed book and I doubt I'll have the opportunity to get to know him and have him trust me enough to tell me his deeper thoughts, but I can be a silent pillar of support while I'm here.

Because that's who I am at my core. I help where I can. I listen. I care. I empathize. And unlike my extroverted sister, I like to make as few waves as possible.

Are there things I wish I could demand more strongly? Yes,

but never at the expense of others. Not at the expense of Adelbert's peace.

Waking up early and complying with his requests while keeping my complaints to a minimum, seem like the easiest things I can do right now.

I scoot back on the bench and cross my legs as I close my eyes and bask in the tranquility of the early morning forest, my moment of solitude in nature wrapping around me in a friendly embrace.

Birds chirping, leaves rustling, and I let out a quiet sound of contentment.

A sudden humph and a weight settling on the bench beside me has my eyes flying open and a mini closed-mouthed shriek flies from me before I can catch myself.

Thankfully, it's just a cat. A wonderfully plump cuddly ginger cat looking for scratches sitting next to me on the bench.

My lips curl up in a delighted smile and, this time, it's a tiny squeal of excitement that makes it past my tightly sealed lips.

"Well aren't you the most handsomest boy in all the land," I coo gently at the cat and reach a hand forward to stroke under his chin. He looks unimpressed but allows my touch with a slight tilt to his head, intelligent sage-green eyes still locked on mine.

"You're so cute, aren't you? Are you the master of this castle?" I whisper as I keep petting and scratching him, following his lead as he shifts his body for me to reach the best spots on his back.

Seemingly pleased with the attention, he starts up a stuttering purr and moves closer, staring at my legs until I readjust so he can climb on my lap.

His sizable body settles on my legs and I run both my hands through his soft fur, which is warm under my touch like he just left his spot in front of a toasty fire. I didn't realize how chilled I was until my legs started to thaw under his hefty weight, the warmth seeping through my jeans.

"You're the goodest boy, making me all toasty. Thank you, purr boy." At that, the cat looks up at me with what I swear is a judgmental stare, and stops purring.

"Not a fan of the baby talk or the nickname?" I ask the cat in a more neutral tone this time. His answering blink is all I get, so I reword the question while my hands keep up their petting.

"Purr-purr?" I try. Still, I get nothing from him.

"Sir Purr?" At this, a weak vibration starts up under my hands and I decide to try one more.

"Sir Purrington?"

Ladies and gentlemen, we have liftoff.

Sir Purrington preens under this name and a solid purr works through his body and vibrates into my limbs. He curls up in my lap and a sense of rightness settles in me.

Since Alberad Island, I have felt somewhat unmoored. I'm not someone who likes to complain out loud, nor do I enjoy drawing attention to myself. I usually go with the flow and remain in the background, letting others take center stage and make the big decisions.

But, right here, under a lonely oak tree with Sir Purrington curled up on my lap, it feels like I can finally take a deep breath and like something has clicked into place.

I close my eyes and breathe deeply while my fingers stroke Sir Purrington's soft fur, and an easy smile settles on my lips, basking in this peaceful moment before reality is bound to come crashing in again.

10

Adelbert

I hurry down the corridor and push open the hidden door that only a few staff members are aware of, and the library welcomes me like an old friend.

A sense of peace descends on me as I breathe in the scent of paper, ink, and glue—the holy trinity for a bibliophile like myself—and I savor the absolute quiet and complete solitude in my favorite place.

Vastly different from the rest of the stone castle, the large library's wooden interior is warm and rich, and invites you to get lost between its shelves for hours on end.

An intricately designed wooden barrel ceiling running down the center of the cavernous main room divides the library into two sections: Elvish tomes on the right, other languages on the left. Numerous ladders lean against the tall oak shelves, amplifying their height. Their wood grain is familiar to my hand even from this distance.

Elvish culture reveres intellect, and from a young age we learn to distance ourselves from emotions and focus on facts. Any opinions one might have that are not based on facts, are frowned upon.

And being raised on the grounds of Alberad, this has led

me to spend most of my available time in this library, searching for answers to any questions I might have and finding companionship with the books. Sometimes I'd be drawn to the windows, watching other species playing outside, then have to shake myself out of the desire to join them.

Elves do not play. We study. We lead.

I don't allow myself to linger too long, choosing to heed the call of the clock ticking against me and head toward the Elvish section on the fates, taking care to keep my steps light as I march across the polished wooden floor.

The urgency to dissolve this mystifying bond so that all of us can return to our lives as usual, is hot against the back of my neck, compelling me to work swiftly. A few theories have entered my mind as to what could have caused the markings and the bonds. However, checking for any precedent cases is imperative before I will permit myself to share any of the theories with my friends and their bonded partners.

My most compelling lead is based on the boat that the women chartered that took them to the Alberad Caribbean Estate. It was named *Amarto*, which is the Elvish for "the fates."

"This is early. Even for you."

My father's voice startles me and my feet instantly come to a halt, icy nails scraping down my back. Thoughts that he has discovered our predicament rush to the fore, and an image of him calling all my friends and their bonded partners to be examined and interrogated flashes through my brain. I need to protect them.

Thus, like I have done since I was old enough to master my emotions, I take great care to regulate my breathing and not to let a fraction of my concerns show on my face.

I lift my brows and incline my head in greeting. "*Vater.*"

With his trademark Alberad icy-blonde hair, I can't believe I didn't see him lurking between the shelves. Nithard Alberad wipes at the nonexistent dust on the spine of a book and prowls from the shadows.

"You have returned ahead of schedule," he says in his customary flat voice.

"Yes," I acknowledge but don't give him any extra ammunition.

"Eager to finish your research? I must say, I am very much looking forward to your presentation this fall."

"Yes, I am well prepared."

My father's jaw tightens. "I shall hope you do not embarrass me by postponing for another year. It has already brought so much shame to the Alberad name."

"Yes, *Vater*. My apologies."

His upper lip curls back. "I do not need your apologies. I need your excellence."

"Yes, *Vater*." I incline my head again.

He narrows his eyes at me. "I expect everything went smoothly at our Caribbean estate?"

I take a surreptitious breath and follow my age-old method of dealing with my father: keep responses short and deflect as soon as possible.

"Everyone had a great time. Is there any way I can be of assistance to you this morning?"

My father picks some invisible lint off the lapel of his jacket.

"Nothing I cannot manage. Though, I did detect a peculiarity in the ward this morning on your side. Must have been you crossing over earlier than anticipated."

My Adam's apple bobs on a hard swallow at the thought of not being thorough enough when we crossed the wards. I resist the temptation to curl my hands into fists at the mere possibility of my father discovering Florence sitting alone on the bench outside.

Knowing I need to conclude this conversation before he gets more suspicious, I say, "It most likely was. I better be off now. There is one specific case I would like to revisit before finalizing my presentation."

My father raises his chin and looks down his nose at me,

despite my taller height.

"I have high expectations of this... 'research' of yours that has taken so long. I still do not understand why you have not consulted me. My expertise has been sought by many who have come before you."

I bow my head in submission, or perhaps to hide the frustration that is surely evident on my face by now.

"I wish to keep my theory private until the day of presentation."

My father's mouth turns down, disapproval radiating from him like I have just dog-eared his favorite book.

"So you have said. Best be off." He makes a shooing motion and walks in the opposite direction.

When the main door shuts behind him, I finally allow myself to release the breath I had been holding.

I glance at the windows and note how much lighter it has gotten in the short time I spent talking to my father. An unpleasant sensation stirs in my chest thinking about Florence sitting unguarded and alone behind the stone wall, and a sense of urgency nips at my heels as I hasten to the section dedicated to the fates.

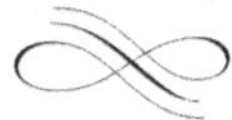

Canting my head to see around the stack of Elvish tomes in my arms, I adjust my grip, taking care to hold the books steady against my body. I may be in a rush to return to Florence, though, not at the risk of facing the librarian's wrath over a damaged book.

Luckily, I make it through the back corridor without encountering anyone else, and I exit into the morning light.

My feet carry me to Florence, and I ignore the brief, weak sensation in my knees when she spots me and a wide grin blooms across her face.

That smile will plague me for months once she has left.

If seeing my father today proved anything, it is that I

should get her out of Germany and away from me sooner rather than later.

Perched on Florence's lap is our resident library cat—the laziest, most inept of creatures. It showed up at Alberad one day, made itself at home, and no one has been able to get it to leave.

"You're back," Florence whispers brightly. Her eyes are on me, but her attention remains on the cat as she keeps stroking it.

"What are you doing with the cat? It is not a pet."

"What? He's lovely and so sweet," Florence says with her lips forming a pout.

"It is meant to be working. In the library. Chasing mice away."

"Oh." The word comes out on a breath of disappointment. It seems I cannot manage to do anything else than displease people this morning.

"Let's go," I say and incline my head in the direction of my home.

Florence tilts the cat's head up by scratching under its chin, and the cat starts up a preposterous purr.

"I'm sorry, Sir Purrington. I hope we meet again. Thank you for keeping me warm," she coos at the cat.

My jaw goes slack. "Sir what?"

"Oops, I should've asked. What's his name?" Florence asks expectantly.

"It does not, in fact, have a name. As I have said, it is not a pet. We just call it 'cat.'"

"He seemed to like it when I called him Sir Purrington," she explains with a defiant little tilt of her chin.

"How does a cat— Never mind."

Florence gently picks the cat up and sets it on the ground. The cat then proceeds to weave itself between her legs, rubbing itself against her like she's its favorite possession.

It stirs an oddly uncomfortable feeling in me, causing my scowl to deepen.

How could one woman affect me so formidably when I have only known her for days?

"It has never acted like that in front of me or anyone else I've seen," I state, astounded by the strange behavior of the cat. I know it hasn't caught a mouse in years and usually sneaks into the kitchens to steal food, but it is meant to have minimal contact with people in order for it to perform the duties we expect it to.

Florence straightens her shoulders and a smirk pulls at the left corner of her mouth.

"That just means I'm special."

"Hmph," is all I can manage, choosing not to address that statement directly.

"Can I help you carry some of those?" Florence asks, gesturing to the eight tomes in my arms.

I nod. "I would appreciate it. Let me set them on the bench first. It would be easiest to avoid touch this way."

I move toward the bench and Florence scoots out of the way, giving me enough space to avoid accidentally brushing against her skin. The cat follows her movement, and Florence crouches down to whisper to it while both her hands keep running along its fur.

On the island, I was painfully aware that Florence and her sister are very tactile people. Sadie was practically attached to Everett from the moment they met, both of them having a hand on the other almost constantly.

I cannot imagine what that must be like. Elves do not touch. Or hug. We have no need for that. I have had lovers over the years and they have served a mutually beneficial purpose. It has never developed into anything that could be construed as... feelings. I do not have space nor time for that in my life.

My responsibilities come first.

My research.

My legacy.

It has been difficult to keep my research confidential,

but once I have perfected it, all the secrecy will have been worth it. I have taken great care not to reveal my studies to anyone else, despite my father's best attempts.

When I present my findings, it will alter the way magic is viewed.

Hefting the largest six of the ancient Elvish tomes into my arms, I straighten up and point to the two left on the bench.

"Can you manage these two without tripping?"

For fuck's sake, she didn't trip on purpose. Why did you have to say that?

"I think I can manage."

For the first time, Florence's smile seems pasted on, the light in her blue eyes dimmed, and it reinforces my resolve to get her away from me before that becomes a regular occurrence.

Why does my heart prick at the thought of saying goodbye?

Without another word, I turn and stride in the direction of my home, knowing she'll follow and unwilling to see whatever emotion she's trying to mask.

11

Florence

I manage to make it back to Adelbert's house without tripping and without more than a couple of necessary words exchanged between us.

"Please follow me to my study."

Oh look, he speaks in full sentences.

He wasn't very talkative before, but he was especially sullen—even by his own standards—on the walk. Where before, I thought his steps were light, on the way back it almost seemed like he was restraining himself from full-on stomping through the forest.

Once through the door, I keep a few paces behind Adelbert, waiting for him to set down his stack of books. The two books in my arms are digging into my skin, and I shift as I wait for him to move aside so I can set mine on the ornate desk. The ancient books are written in a beautifully elegant script I could only wish to read, and I assume it must be Elvish.

Tracing a finger along the title, I shore myself up and ask, "Is everything alright?"

Adelbert scoffs. "Of course not. If everything was 'alright' then you wouldn't be here, would you?"

Ouch.

My head rears back and I suck in an audible breath, my eyes blinking furiously. I'm struck speechless.

Shaking his head, he lets out an exasperated sigh and runs a hand through his hair, slightly tugging on it at the end.

"My apologies. That was harsher than I intended. I'm just under a lot of pressure right now. But it's no excuse for speaking to you like that."

"I understand. I'll… um…" I swallow and blink against the burning sensation in my eyes. "I'll let you get to your work. Would it be alright if I sit in the garden?" I squeak out.

"Florence." My name holds more emotion than I've heard from Adelbert since we met.

I tuck my hair behind my ear and will a smile to my face.

"I don't want to disturb you. Maybe we can measure the limit around the house, and then I can wait outside without bothering you any further."

Adelbert's lips press into a flat line and a muscle jumps in his jaw.

"I shall remain in this room all day. We can measure the distance from here, but it should be all the way to the tree line. Come."

Adelbert pops open a drawer on an antique bureau in the corner and pockets some type of fabric before marching toward the front door.

Once again, I find myself trailing behind him as we make our way through the house I have yet to explore.

The house is an old three-story manor and looks like someone else had decorated it, unless Adelbert has an interest in what Dede would call "old-money chic." Wooden floors, high ceilings, and with antique paintings lining the walls, I think it's okay to say that he's most likely inherited it and hasn't bothered to change much from the previous owner.

Not like I'm going to be asking him such personal questions anytime soon.

We exit into the now-bright morning and I breathe in the fresh forest air, already feeling better after our little exchange.

Adelbert comes to a stop in front of his study window on the side of the house.

"Our bond is not as strong as Everett and Sadie's. If you go beyond the hundred-yard limit it should not have such severe effects as the sensations she experienced on the island. I would still like to take precautions and minimize any discomfort either of us could experience."

I nod. "That makes sense."

"Please wait here. I'll test the boundary and mark out a perimeter for you."

Without waiting for a response from me, his long legs eat up the distance to the edge of the forest, his hands flexing at his sides.

My eyes track him as he slows down and nears the tree line. I bring my hair over my shoulder to braid the length, the movement familiar and soothing to me, and I start humming a song in the hopes that it will lift my mood.

I'm trying to give Adelbert some grace, but how he spoke to me earlier was incredibly hurtful. It's not like I *chose* to be here. It's fate, or "the fates" as he calls it, playing tricks on us and binding us to each other.

Confrontation makes me extremely uncomfortable and I try to avoid it at all costs, but the comebacks I have for him are lying on the tip of my tongue. I really wanted to give him a piece of my mind but that's not going to help anyone. It will probably just aggravate his feelings toward me. Best to just stay out of each other's way for the time being and wait for this all to blow over.

Dede has always been the one to speak her mind and enjoys having all the attention trained on her. I don't like being in the limelight, and just the thought of it sends a shiver racing down my spine and cuts off my humming.

"I am approximately ninety yards from my study now."

Adelbert projects his voice over the clearing around his house and I stand a little straighter. "I shall proceed slowly from here. Please call out if you experience any discomfort."

I raise one hand and give him a thumbs-up I'm sure he'll see, knowing my voice does not have the same strength as his.

Unsure of why it surprises me, but Adelbert turns his body, gaze concentrated on me as he cautiously walks backward into the tree line.

My arms drop to my sides and my brow furrows at this move. Is he being... considerate? Caring?

A couple of paces later, a gentle pressure pushes against me from behind, and I arch my back as the sensation grows stronger. It must be the bond guiding me toward Adelbert, and I lift both my hands to indicate that he should stop.

"Did you feel that?" I try to ask across the long distance.

"Somewhat. Please remain there."

Adelbert turns to the tree and ties some kind of material around a long limb. He proceeds to walk in a wide radius around the clearing and every so often stops to tie another ribbon to a tree, marking out the distance within the boundary from the house.

I follow him with my eyes throughout the whole process, and never experience that pressure from the bond again.

Dede was practically pulled out of her seat and across the room when Everett exceeded the hundred-yard distance limit, which only serves to reinforce Adelbert's stance that he and I should never have physical contact, or we'd suffer similar consequences.

I almost want to agree. Watching my sister look so scared with everyone hovering around her, not knowing what's happening, was awful. But the moment Everett stepped up and tilted her chin toward him, I could see so much tenderness between them, and I knew my sister was in safe hands. If Dede had to be bonded to anyone, I'm happy that it's Everett.

I swallow against the slight stab of envy at having someone so instantly dedicated to ensuring your comfort and happiness.

Instead, I focus on the lovely trees surrounding the house.

"All done. Please stay within the demarcated area while I remain in my study. It will be most unpleasant for either or both of us should you venture beyond those marked trees."

"I'll be careful," I promise. Trying to lighten the mood, I add, "And I love the pretty ribbons. I didn't know you were a ribbon kind of guy."

If looks could kill...

"They were my grandmother's."

"Do I want to know why you have your grandmother's ribbons?"

Adelbert cocks his neck to the side, making his joints crackle and pop, and he rolls his lips between his teeth before he finally speaks.

"The house belonged to my *late* grandmother. Some of her things have remained since I have become the sole resident on the estate."

"Oh no. I'm so sorry for your loss." I reach a hand forward to comfort him and Adelbert jumps out of the way.

Eyes wide and breathing hard, Adelbert hisses, "Could you be more careful?"

"I—"

"I think this is enough for today. Please help yourself to coffee and food in the kitchen. I'll be in my study."

Like a popped balloon, hurt pricks any of the optimism I had stored up for the day, and my good vibes slowly leak out. My shoulders deflate and I bite my tongue, disappointed in myself. Disappointed in Adelbert.

Surely he knew it was a mistake with good intentions behind it?

With a final nod, Adelbert whips around on his heel and heads inside while I mentally berate myself.

I'm usually more careful with my actions, but with Adelbert, the urge to comfort or touch him is so strong that I become clumsy and seem to do or say the wrong things, inadvertently making him more annoyed with me than he would be if I just stayed invisible.

I nod as I resolve to become just that, vowing to myself not to bother him anymore.

I'll give him all the space he needs while he figures out a way for me to go home. I'll do my own thing and stay out of his way. I'm already encroaching on his space. No need to make myself a burden to him on top of it.

13

Florence

I feel awful for just spewing all of that out and making Adelbert feel bad, but I'm also a little proud of myself for channeling my inner Sadie and verbalizing my discomfort.

I am a little hungry, starving actually, but I felt like I couldn't bother him while he's doing such important work.

And perhaps the thought of enjoying a meal together is what also held me off from going through a stranger's kitchen cupboards by myself. I'm a guest after all, not a resident.

I spent most of the day outside just basking in the beauty of the forest, taking in all the sights and smells and sounds, memorizing it for when I'll be able to paint it with thread. But I did keep an eye on the house in case Adelbert took a break. My plan was to join him for lunch.

But he never came out of his study.

We enter the kitchen and I hang back in the doorway as I take in my new favorite room in the house.

The kitchen is cozy with a strong character that's both old and new at the same time. It has solid wood furniture that looks hand carved but modern appliances are scattered throughout. Rough, exposed beams hold up the low ceiling, making it feel almost medieval, and to one side is a large oak table with live edges I want to trace with my fingers.

"Sit." Adelbert points at a chair at the dining table before moving to the fridge. He pauses, head drooping and shoulders rising with a deep inhale before he slowly turns back to me again. "I mean, please have a seat while I prepare something for us to eat."

A grin tugs on my lips—my frustration with him all but forgotten—but I bite it back, trying not to ruin the moment by expressing how endearing that self-correction was.

"Thank you. Is there anything I can help you with?" I ask as I carefully pull back the heavy wooden chair and lower myself onto it.

Adelbert angles his head. "What do you like?"

"Oh, anything is fine."

"Any allergies?"

"Nope."

"Any dislikes?"

"Not really."

"Tell me."

"Oh, um, don't worry about it."

"Tell me."

"I don't like peanut butter," I blurt out.

"That's fine. Anything else?"

"Not that I can think of while you're interrogating me."

Adelbert scrubs a hand down his face, and his shoulders slump. "Interrogation is not my intent. I am merely trying to establish what you can and cannot eat, or what you do and do not like. You seem to be hesitant about expressing your needs, therefore, I am trying to help narrow down your preferences through various questions."

"Oh." I grimace as the truth and logical manner of his thinking hits me, and a blush creeps across my cheeks and burns my ears. "I don't mean to be a burden to you. I'm only here for a little while and I'm trying to make things as easy as possible for you."

"It would be easier if you would just tell me what you would like to eat," Adelbert sighs out.

"What are you having?" I attempt to dodge the question, not prepared to be as bold as I was in front of my room earlier.

"I was thinking about making some *Kartoffelpuffer*. They are German potato pancakes."

"That sounds wonderful. But please let me help you."

"I am afraid this part of the kitchen does not have enough space, and the possibility of accidentally making contact is too high. However, I appreciate your offer of assistance." Adelbert inclines his head in that gentlemanly bow he likes to make, an apology hiding beneath his frown.

My smile is a little wobbly but I let it curve my lips to show him that I understand. I'm not quite sure what to do with myself because the silence stretching between us does not feel as companionable as it was previously, so I just follow his movements with my eyes as I fiddle with the hem of my shirt.

Adelbert moves around the kitchen like he's familiar with every square inch of the space. He returns from the pantry with a few potatoes and meticulously peels them on the central counter.

Thankfully, he's first to speak as he proceeds to roughly grate the potatoes.

"Was it your sister you were talking to earlier?"

I instantly perk up. I love talking about Dede, and I'm so happy things are going well with her and Everett. I just hope she will give things between them a real chance before she self-sabotages their relationship with her own fears.

"Yeah. Sadie seems to like Vegas a lot."

"Everett called me this afternoon. I am not fully certain what transpired between them, but what he shared with me helped my understanding of the situation, and I was able to confirm a theory."

"That's great news, right?" I'm not sure how much I want to disclose about what she told me either, but it seems like a good thing if what Everett told him matches up with what Adelbert has found in his readings.

Adelbert nods as he strains the liquid out of the grated potatoes through a kitchen towel and sets the bowl aside.

"It is definitely encouraging to know that I am moving in the right direction of figuring things out."

I find myself sitting up straighter in my seat so I can follow his movements, curious about how he's making these potato pancakes. He comes back from the pantry with flour, an onion, and an egg.

Feeling like he's the most comfortable he's been around me yet—maybe due to the distance between us, or maybe because of the kitchen he seems so at home in—I try to push my luck and ask some personal questions.

"Do you like cooking?"

Adelbert's movements halt, and he looks up at me. Angling his head, a lock of his silvery hair flops onto his forehead, and my hands itch to run through the silky-looking strands that he usually keeps so perfectly styled. But right here, in this moment, he looks so at ease, like the weight of all the stress he's been carrying around is not as significant, and it makes my heart ache in a very funny way.

The lightest of grins, if one could even call it that, tugs at a corner of his mouth.

"My grandmother taught me how to cook. We spent a lot of time in this kitchen. She taught me everything I know about cooking."

"You look very comfortable there and like you know what you're doing." I grin back at him.

Adelbert picks up the onion and starts grating it too.

"This is a comfort food we made often. We may not have 'hugged out our feelings' but she liked to cook them out."

"That sounds lovely." I don't know what he's doing with the onion, not being able to do this level of cooking myself, so I lift slightly from my seat and crane my neck to see better.

Adelbert mixes the ingredients in a bowl and squints his eyes as a memory seemingly plays through his mind.

"It was, in its own way. Don't misunderstand, she would boss me around and there was no space for emotions in her kitchen, nevertheless, one would say it was a bonding experience to cook together."

"Wow. I'm envious of that. I can only throw together the basics and call it a meal. Despite my mom trying to teach me, I've never had a real knack for it. Even Sadie is better than me and she's not especially good either." Dede and I sometimes tried our hand at cooking fancier meals, but they mostly ended up burned, so we gave up trying too many new things and stuck to salads and sandwiches.

"That is a pity. Cooking allows one to feel more connected to their food." Adelbert looks genuinely disappointed, though I'm not sure if he's pitying my lacking skills or if it's me he's disappointed in.

I want to ask him so many more questions about his grandmother, this house, how he grew up, but I don't want to push this tenuous peace that's currently between us. I shift the conversation back to Everett and Dede.

"Please don't feel obligated to tell me anything, but if you feel comfortable with it, I'd really like to know more about the theories you have about the bond."

Adelbert pauses again and looks at me from across the room. His eyes narrow for a fraction of a second, and then he nods to himself.

"I think it best that you know since this affects you too."

Adelbert puts down whatever he was mixing and plants both hands on the counter in front of him. He fixes me with an intent gaze, his eyes blazing quicksilver.

My heartbeat picks up a new rhythm and my palms become clammy at the ominous charge in the air, but I quickly stretch my lips into a smile and nod at him to continue, hoping he can't pick up on my rare spike of anxiety.

"You're safe with me. I wish you no harm," he reassures me in a tone I suspect he thinks sounds soothing.

"Okay." My voice comes out as something between a whisper and squeak, betraying the mask I tried to slip on.

Adelbert's lips thin before he continues.

"To put it bluntly, around the bonded person, we monsters seem to be reverting to our more baser beings. We have been conditioned to control ourselves and have learned to suppress our monstrous natures to a certain extent, in order for us to blend into a mostly human society. But based on what I read today, and Everett's phone call earlier, those suppressed 'urges'—for lack of a better word—are coming to the fore. I have a hunch for why this is, but I need definitive proof before I will explain more."

I bring my hair over one shoulder and drag my fingers through the waves as I process his words.

"I hope this isn't a rude question to ask, but can I ask what this means for you specifically and how this will affect me?"

Adelbert nods like he was expecting that question.

"You need not worry. I never intend to come near you or touch you or influence you in any manner."

My eyebrows lift at that statement, now even more curious.

"Okayyy," I drag the word out. "But what does that mean?"

Adelbert clears his throat and takes a step back to lean against the counter behind him, crossing his arms over his chest.

"So you are already aware that I can create wards." He doesn't phrase it as a question, but he still waits for me to answer him, so I nod back. "That's one aspect of my magic. I can also read emotions fairly well and I have the ability to exert some influence to alter emotions."

"So you can make me happy or make me sad? Is that what you're saying?"

"Yes and no. I personally do not wish to alter anything about you. I believe in complete autonomy. However, should you feel fear or any extreme emotion, it grates against me and the need to bestow calm or to 'fix' it becomes almost unbearable. I spend most of my time alone, thus it has certainly been quite trying to have you in my home."

A quick pang moves through my chest and my brows draw down. "I am so sorry this is happening to you. I didn't think my being here would affect you this much. I'm usually pretty happy and easy-going. How can I help you be more comfortable?"

"Honestly?" Adelbert tilts his head and looks at me like I'm a puzzle he's trying to figure out.

I nod, really wanting to ease his stress and discomfort. "This is all just temporary, right? I want you to be comfortable in your own home. So, how can I help?"

"My one request is that in order to not be disturbed by outside emotions, I remain rather isolated and can focus on my work without disruptions. I have not yet found a means to dissolve the bond, therefore, I am not certain how long you will have to remain here."

My eyes widen and a strange noise escapes from my throat. Adelbert uncrosses his arms and grabs the edge of the counter on either side of him.

"And now I have distressed you. My apologies."

"No, no. It's better to be direct and honest about such important matters."

"I agree. I told you what I need, now how about you tell me what you require? It sounds fair, does it not?"

"Sure."

I take a deep breath and square my shoulders, gathering my courage to ask for what I want, convincing myself that I'm not a burden for making requests when he's already so busy.

"I don't suppose you get delivery services here, do you?"

"Human ones, no. But I can make a request with the pixies that run Pixie Parcels. I've granted them access to pass through my wards to deliver necessities. Anything you need, they're able to get it."

"Pixies are real?" A broad smile blooms on my face and my feet bounce on the floor, my mood suddenly lifted with this new piece of information. "Are they cute and small like in the myths? What kind of magic do they have?"

Adelbert's face softens and a corner of his lips start to tug up but he blinks the expression away.

"Maybe you can meet one when they do the delivery. But let's not get distracted now. What do you need?"

"Well, it's not a *need* exactly."

"Florence." The way my name rolls across his lips is like a seductive caress that almost makes a whimper escape from me.

This is not the time to catch feelings, Florence. Even the horny ones, I chide myself.

"Embroidery supplies." The words just burst past my lips and I quickly bring both hands up to stifle anything else that wants to come through.

Adelbert inclines his head, and that strange quirk to his lips that can't quite be defined as a smile plays along the edges of his mouth.

"You will have to excuse me. I do not know what all entails 'embroidery supplies.' Could you perhaps specify or show me examples?"

I keep my hands over my mouth and nod, grateful he's not dismissing the request or laughing me off as some people seem to do when they hear I do embroidery. Most people think it's only a hobby for older people but I adore thread painting.

"What else?"

"Nothing." The word comes out muffled from behind my fingers and I shake my head.

Adelbert merely stares at me with an alarming amount of patience until I drop my hands and place them on my lap.

Seemingly satisfied with this, he asks, "How do you take your coffee?"

"Oh, anything is fine."

Adelbert raises his brows.

"I prefer tea," I admit in a voice barely above a whisper, my shoulders somewhere around my ears.

Adelbert keeps staring at me with quiet determination and raises his brows a fraction higher.

"Oolong tea." My whole face heats with my confession.

Adelbert's mouth turns up a fraction of an inch. "Good girl. Now that wasn't so hard, was it?"

Did he just make a joke? Adelbert. It was a joke, wasn't it? Should I say something or would that make him uncomfortable?

Before I can make up my mind on how to respond, he moves toward the counter in front of him again and resumes making dinner. There's almost a fluidity to his movements. His actions are smooth and well practiced, and I only stare on in quiet fascination. Not drooling.

He's been so formal and distant with me until we entered this kitchen. But maybe there's something about this environment that relaxes him. Even his speech started losing that formal edge after a while, and he opened up about his grandmother.

I wonder what it will take to see more of that side of him.

Movements never ceasing, Adelbert flicks his eyes up to me. "If you need anything else, please let me know. I'll give you a couple of minutes to think about it while I finish cooking."

Should I ask for a vibrator? I might need one tonight to counter all this tension.

CHAT LOG

Florence: Adelbert is a really good cook. Couldn't get a photo of the food, but here's a link to a random blog of the same thing we ate.

Florence: *photo*

Florence: Look at all those steps! He didn't even read a recipe.

Sadie: Holy shit! That looks amazing! I'm seriously impressed!

Florence: It tasted even better! What you guys doing today?

Sadie: I got flowers this morning. Look!

Sadie: *photo*

Florence: Oh my goodness. Is this real life?!

Sadie: Right?! They're so beautiful!

Florence: I'm sure you thanked Everett "properly" *winking face emoji*

Sadie: On the way to his house now *face blowing a kiss emoji* Excited to see it *star-struck emoji*!

Florence: I'm sure you are. *fire emoji* *laughing emoji*

Florence: Send pics later!

14

Adelbert

Last night, Florence and I ate dinner in a rather companionable manner. She was able to explain what she needed for her embroidery and I immediately put in an order with Pixie Parcels. Florence also told me more about her business and showed me a few of her sold pieces, per my request, and I find her to be an exceptionally talented artist.

I have never bought my own art, but I like the idea of one of her designs gracing the walls of my house.

I am also curious to see how she'll portray the Black Forest. I wonder if she will be able to capture its true character. If anyone could do it, though, it would be Florence.

After dinner, we went off to our separate wings and I allowed myself some rest. My eyes felt too heavy to properly concentrate on the detailed texts I still need to comb through.

When I tried to relax for a split second, my hand drifted to my cock, visions of Florence in all kinds of positions flashing beneath my tired eyelids. Florence spread out on my bed, pushed up against a wall, laid out on the kitchen table, on her knees in my study... I just about ran to the shower to wash away my filthy thoughts under a stream of icy water.

I know the fated bond is pushing us together, and most

of these thoughts probably stem from that, but the emotions the bond evokes in me are leaving me unsettled.

My whole life I've prided myself on my elvish nature and being able to control myself. However, with this woman forced to be in close proximity to me, I find myself facing new kinds of challenges.

Today, I woke at dawn as per usual, and retrieved the delivery left by the front door. I've warded my home so the pixies can enter the grounds, but not the house itself. I am very careful with who I allow access to my home. The possibility of my father showing up here whenever it suited him makes my skin tighten.

I enter the kitchen with the packages and place them on the table. Then, I set the kettle to boil for Florence's tea while I unpack the contents of the delivery, all while my mind races through theories and connecting dots.

I collect Florence's fabric, a selection of thread, an embroidery hoop, small sewing scissors, and an array of embroidery needles and place them on a tray on the kitchen table. The fact that she can take these separate items and create such elaborate pieces that mimic nature so closely absolutely fascinates me. I also prepared a small basket for her to carry everything should she want to spend time outside again.

The teapot I ordered is unbearably dainty with cornflowers painted on it. I spent an inordinate amount of time scrolling through options before settling on this one. It reminded me of Florence and I thought she might like it.

I rinse the pot out, place an oolong tea bag inside, then fill it with boiled water, letting the tea steep while I brew some coffee for myself. After my coffee is done, I remove the tea bag from the teapot and place it on the enchanted cup warmer I also ordered, unsure of the time Florence will wake and wanting the tea to remain warm for her.

Opening the box that the *Hefezopf* is in, I am hit by the aroma of the fresh yeasty bread. I breathe in the scent, and memories of baking in this kitchen with my grandmother flicker through my mind, bringing an easy smile to my face.

I mentally thank the pixies, and their knowledge of where to get the best baked goods and keep them fresh throughout the delivery period, as I cut a couple of slices of the braided bread.

I butter Florence's slices, and prepare two small jars of jam for her to choose from—apricot and fig, not strawberry. Then, I grab a cup and saucer, and place everything in front of her seat on the table.

I give the arrangement a final glance and contemplate leaving a note, but ultimately decide against it. The collection is pretty self-explanatory.

Feeling pleased with myself that Florence would be delighted with this presentation, I grab my mug of coffee and head to my office and close the door behind me, ready for today to be the day I find answers.

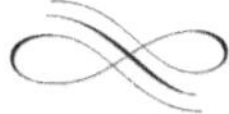

I make a concerted effort not to stare out the window or look up too much, having noticed Florence glide across the clearing a time or two.

Today she is wearing a long yellow dress and it pains me to admit to myself that I recognize she must have embroidered flowers along its hem. They are too similar to the flowers on her jeans yesterday to be a coincidence.

Does she do that to all her clothes?

Stretching my neck, I lean back in my chair and finally let my gaze linger on the sight outside my window. The clouds hang low across the valley today, threatening with a thunderstorm in spots. I cannot see Florence but I can sense her on the western side of the clearing.

It is odd to have someone in my vicinity at all times. For years, I have lived alone–days filled with studying, experimenting, practicing. Now, my thoughts are divided, oscillating between my work and Florence.

I have not given this much thought before now, for I do not spend much time outdoors, but Florence's skin seems rather delicate under the power of a summer sun. On the off chance that she has not taken proper precautions, I gather my power and cast an extra layer to the wards around the house. It will not be able to withstand the sun's rays fully, but it could lessen the effects of sunburn on Florence's exposed shoulders.

Tonight, I will put in a new order for the strongest sunscreen I can find on Pixie Parcels.

Frustrated that I have not done enough to ensure her physical comfort, I get up with a humph and stomp through the quiet house. The sound of my shoes clomping along the wooden floors annoys me even more. She has only been here two days but her constant humming has somehow altered the once-comforting silence of my house.

"Florence!" I call once I'm outside.

"Over here!" Florence raises an arm high above her head and waves at me from where she's sitting against one of the marked trees on the boundary line, embroidery piece in her other hand. A wide grin spreads across her face and her eyes light up when she sees me. Something tightens and loosens within me at all once, confirming one more theory I had.

"It is not healthy to be outside this much. I hope you have taken some precautions to guard against the strong effects of the sun," I say once I'm close enough, crossing my arms.

Her big smile wanes.

"It's okay. I've got sunscreen on." Her tone is friendly, though it has lost that brilliance it had mere moments ago, and I mentally curse myself for fucking up again.

You could have been a bit nicer about it, couldn't you? Insensitive twat.

"That is good," I acknowledge. "I have also reinforced the

wards. It should lessen some of the harshness from the sun. But do take care of yourself. I expect a summer shower or two to be heading this way today."

"Thank you. That is very thoughtful of you. I am just trying to get an outline done of the valley. If it starts to rain I'll head inside."

I nod and feel strangely unsure of what to do next. The feeling is rather unwelcome and makes my skin itch.

"Have you eaten?" I blurt out ineloquently.

For fuck's sake, what's wrong with you?

"Yes. Thank you for the pastry and the tea. The teapot is so quaint! It kept the tea at a perfect temperature. And all the embroidery supplies. I wanted to thank you the moment I found them but didn't want to disturb you in your study. Can you tell me the total? I'll be sure to transfer the money to you as soon as I'm inside with my phone," Florence asks with utter sincerity, her blue eyes wide as an innocent doe as she looks up at me.

"I do not require your money. You are my guest. It is a gift," I state gruffly. My lips turn down in distaste. The thought of taking her money grates at me.

Florence opens her mouth to reply just as I glance at my watch.

"Did you have lunch?" I ask before she can protest the gift, realizing breakfast was a very long time ago and she probably has not had anything since.

"I—not yet." This time, Florence's smile falls flat, and I do my utmost to reinforce my mental walls so that I do not read her emotions.

It is such an invasion of privacy and I despise it when other elves try to do it to me. Learning to mask emotions from a young age has been the only way to cope around them, especially my father.

I remember when I was at school and one of the professors tried to catch my friends out for something they did—which they definitely did do, though I was not going to let them take the fall for having a little fun. He asked them a series of questions and not only listened to their answers but read their physical cues and emotions, too. I knew whatever he found would get back to my father and I would be berated for it, no matter if it was my fault or not, so I intervened and manipulated their emotions until the professor was thrown off.

After that, I secretly coached my closest friends on how to put up mental barriers to guard themselves from future interrogations. It gave them the perfect excuse to get up to more trouble—something Jasper, Jamie, and Everett took full advantage of, to the rest of the group's delight.

Perhaps I have become so adept at concealing my emotions over the years that I have started concealing them from myself as well.

"Are you hungry?" I ask Florence.

"I can help myself," she says with weak confidence in the statement and her eyes not quite making contact with mine.

"Would you, though?" I raise a brow at her.

Florence bites her lip, and the desire to reach forward and free her lip from its abuse is almost visceral.

Maybe I could ease the sting by sucking it into my mouth, and...

Without a word, Florence leans forward and packs all her supplies into her basket. My fingers reach forward to help but I catch myself in time, shoving my hands in my pockets instead.

Satisfied that she's almost done, I stride toward the house, leaving all my uncouth thoughts behind and surreptitiously adjusting my hardening length. I come up short when I see the new arrival sitting in front of the door. Florence recognizes it before I do and speeds past me.

"Sir Purrington! What are you doing here? Did you walk all the way?" She crouches down and speaks to the cat as if it is possible for it to answer her questions.

I glare at the creature, completely dumbfounded as to its presence at my home.

"What is it doing here?" I ask no one in particular.

"Maybe he missed me and was ready for a new adventure. Weren't you, Sir Purrington?" Florence answers me but keeps her focus on the cat, stroking over his fur as it rubs against her legs. "Yes, you were. Are you hungry?"

The cat perks up like it somehow understood *that* question and walks itself over to the door. When I don't hasten to open it, the cat stares at me with its strangely alert eyes until I maneuver myself around Florence and turn the knob.

Florence heads inside with the cat on her heels, its tail high in the air as it swaggers past me while I hold the door open, still unsure of what just happened.

This day could not possibly get any stranger.

15

Florence

Sir Purrington keeps up with me as I head directly for the kitchen. There's a definite bounce to my step as I hum a happy tune, excited about having a cuddly companion in the quiet house.

Adelbert follows a couple of paces behind us—his steps not as jaunty as mine. I place my embroidery basket on the kitchen table just as he enters the kitchen and comes to a stop by the central counter.

His usual scowl is currently competing for the title of fiercest yet. His brows draw deep over his light eyes as he runs first one hand and then the other through his hair, slicking back the soft-looking strands in a particularly attractive manner I should not be thinking too much about.

But try as I might, I can't help lusting after my temporary roommate.

"Is it okay if I give Sir Purrington some food?" I ask Adelbert as Sir Purrington rubs against my legs, moving in a figure eight between my feet for maximum effect.

"I'd prefer it if you don't. It lives in the library and should be chasing mice for meals. Not become some pampered prince living off human food."

"But he came all this way." I pout. "It's okay if you don't want to give him any special food. I can just feed him bits and pieces of what I was going to eat."

"I will not allow you to take your own food and give it to a cat," Adelbert says sternly, fingers flexing next to his hips.

Finding the backbone I so often seem to lack, I place both hands on my hips and fix Adelbert with a look. "Excuse me?"

He takes a breath and sighs it out loudly. "That came out wrong."

"I hope so." Externally, I am giving such strong Sadie vibes that he must be convinced of my confidence. Internally, however, I am cringing and flinching at using that tone and I really hope he can't read that emotion.

"Let me attempt this again. How about you have your meal, and I'll prepare something separate for the cat?" Adelbert asks me and then addresses Sir Purrington directly, "Then you can go back to Alberad library and do your duty. Good?"

Sir Purrington lets out a displeased-sounding meow, clearly stating his opposition to that idea.

My lips threaten to turn up into a smile. "Do you think perhaps the cat doesn't have the exact same level of obligation you feel to the school?" I hedge.

"I do not think many people do," he says so softly I don't think I was meant to hear it.

Adelbert catches my eyes briefly, and I can almost swear I see a bit of sadness lining his. But just as quickly, he covers it again with a familiar guise of indifference.

I can't help but wonder how complicated his life must be. He seems so dedicated to making choices that benefit everyone else that he might be neglecting his own desires. I'm curious if Alberad is even where he wants to work, but I know this level of questioning will not be welcomed. Not now, possibly not ever.

So many people are currently counting on Adelbert, and he doesn't need to be distracted by me. After seeing him so comfortable in the kitchen last night, I vowed to myself that I will try not to add to his burdens. And if it means staying out of his way, then I'll do just that.

"Do you maybe have a can of tuna?" I ask Adelbert in an attempt to bring the conversation back to neutral ground.

"In the pantry. I will get it. You wait with the cat."

I sit down at the table and Sir Purrington jumps into my lap. I lavish him with affection while Adelbert begrudgingly prepares his meal.

Adelbert places a dish on the floor with a saucer of water and Sir Purrington jumps down and immediately starts eating.

I lean forward to let my hair curtain around my face to hide my smile. He just looked so cute and domesticated.

Adelbert, not the cat.

"When you are done with your amusement, would you like some *Königsberger Klopse*? With *Salzkartoffeln*?"

I peek out from behind my hair and stare blankly at the handsome elf.

"Come again?"

"German meatballs and salted potatoes?"

I nod and bite back my grin.

"That would be lovely."

This time, I don't offer to help, knowing he's in his happy place—though I know not to mention it out loud.

Adelbert has been so focused on making sure that I am eating after our little misunderstanding yesterday, and he was super sweet by preparing my embroidery supplies and breakfast. I wish there was something more I could do to help him.

After he told me that he prefers I give him space so he won't be disturbed by my emotions, I decided to spend the day outside. It's where I enjoy being the most, anyway. But maybe, just maybe, if we can have more meals together like this, I can make it my personal mission to get him to relax—perhaps even smile—and he can just be himself and not worry about everything else that is weighing on him.

This morning, I took all my supplies and went to sit close to the boundary Adelbert marked, right under the pretty ribbon he tied to a tree. Even though it's summer here, there's definitely a little nip in the air that I felt on my bare arms, but I wanted to be as far away from the house as possible.

My spot had the most beautiful view of the valley. Hills rise and fall for miles and miles with a symphony of different shades of dark green dappling their slopes as far as the eye can see.

I must have lost track of time as I outlined the valley with a forest-green thread, getting lost in the motion and comforting sound of needle and thread passing through the stretched material of the hoop. The *whoosh* and *pop* of my stitches helped get my mind in that blissful state of blankness, free from the worries and stress of the past few days, as my focus was solely on recreating the scene in front of me.

When he came charging across the clearing, I was honestly happy to see him. But getting scolded for not realizing how long I had been in the sun really popped that bubble of joy.

I don't blame him, though.

I sometimes think Adelbert has good intentions but his delivery definitely needs some work.

The sizzles from the stove and the swooshes and thunks of Adelbert's knife on the wooden cutting board hypnotize me as I witness the meal come together. He adds a bunch of ingredients to the skillet and the delicious aroma wafts over to me, making my stomach rumble in anticipation.

Adelbert grabs two plates and dishes a couple of meatballs onto each, dribbling the gravy he cooked them in on top. He adds the potatoes next, and I have to swallow the excess saliva down before I drool on the table. Keeping his head bowed as he deftly adds some garnish—*garnish*—he flicks his gaze up and looks at me.

"Any allergies besides your strong dislike for peanut butter?"

"Nope. All good. Want me to tell you a secret?" I ask,

hoping that maybe I can bring us back to that sense of camaraderie we had last night.

"Sure," Adelbert answers hesitantly.

"I hate peanut butter so much that I sometimes tell people I have an allergy just so they take it seriously."

Adelbert's brows furrow. He looks like he can't decide if he should be impressed or disappointed in me.

"That's... that's... not very nice, Ms. Everly. But also incredibly clever."

"Was that just a backhanded compliment you gave me, Mr. Alberad?"

"I believe it was."

A huff escapes from him and one might almost call it a laugh.

I call it a win.

Adelbert brings our late lunch over and carefully places mine in front of me. I hold my hands completely still on my lap so he knows I won't make any sudden movements that could cause accidental contact.

An unexpected, and not at all unwelcome, feeling of giddiness bubbles in my chest as he takes the seat opposite me, and a blush blooms across my cheeks.

For someone who doesn't want me in his space, Adelbert's being very accommodating and kind, even if he won't blatantly admit it.

I pinch my leg to ground myself, a reminder that this is not a date—just two people sitting down to eat a home-cooked meal. But it's been so long since I've been on a real date that maybe I've forgotten what they're actually like.

"Want to know my secret?" Adelbert asks, and I can't help but sit up straight in my chair, eager for another glimpse of the male behind the frown.

"Hit me," I say and place my elbows on the table, my chin cradled in between my hands.

"I tell people I am allergic to strawberries."

"Are you?"

"Not even a little. I just don't like the idea of the seeds being on the outside. It's like an inside-out fruit." Adelbert's mouth turns down in disgust and a shudder runs down his body.

I burst out laughing, doubling over in my seat and clutching my stomach. When I look up, Adelbert's eyes sparkle with a joy I have not witnessed in him before and a warm, fuzzy sensation takes root deep inside me.

THE BRETHREN CHAT

Sawyer: Is it true that women need chocolate to survive?

Jamie: Who told you that?

Sawyer: Louisa says she can't function without chocolate. I don't have any at my cabin.

Harvey: It is not required sustenance, but it will make your life a hell of a lot easier if you get her some.

Erik: How long until the bond is gone?

Daehan: Don't know. Bertie?

Adelbert: Still unclear. Better to get the chocolate. Make her feel comfortable.

Sawyer: Is there a special kind?

Edmond: Ask her. She'll tell you. But if in doubt, buy the expensive option. You'll thank me later.

16

Adelbert

I drag my feet through the dark, quiet hallways leading toward the kitchen the next morning, in desperate need of caffeine.

Florence and I continued to chat about trivial matters over lunch, our conversation so engaging that I stayed in the kitchen much longer than I intended. I have never gotten so lost in a moment with another person as I did yesterday, it has only ever happened with my work. I even forgot to take my phone with me when I left the study, which resulted in a couple of missed calls from Jamie, Jasper, and Edmond.

After returning to my study, I was hit by a wave of arousal that I am fairly certain was Florence pleasuring herself in her room. Try as I might, my mental barriers could not withstand the strength of her emotions as they built and built, until I finally unzipped my pants.

I pictured Florence laid out on my desk, legs propped on either side of my chair as I fed my cock into her silky pussy. The image was so vivid that I didn't even have time to grab a tissue, spilling into my hand as Florence's orgasm pulsed through the house.

Before my guilt could get the best of me, I pretended I was rubbing my warm, sticky cum all over her skin, painting her with the essence of my basest being.

Then, I wiped away all the evidence and zipped up my pants like nothing had happened. I didn't allow my brain to linger on what I just did as I got back to work and returned the calls I had missed.

What my friends divulged was the final element I had been missing and I confirmed all my theories around an hour before dawn, just before falling asleep at my desk for a couple of minutes.

I stumble into the kitchen with one hand against the wall. An interesting emotion presses against my psyche, causing my head to snap up.

"Good morning," Florence says brightly from her spot at the kitchen table. The cat is curled up on her lap and a cup of tea is steaming in front of her.

I blink a couple of times in hopes that it will wake me up faster.

Is it mirth I sense from her?

"The coffee just finished brewing. Can I pour you a cup?" she asks sweetly.

I frown back.

"Why are you awake so early?"

"I wanted to get out of your hair early so you could work in peace without all my emotions disturbing you," she says guilelessly. "Unfortunately, it's pouring rain this morning so I'll have to find a new spot to sit and work."

I look out the window and verify her statement. It's a typical summer rainy day.

I can't believe how out of sorts I feel this morning that I missed her presence in the kitchen as well as the weather outside. My head feels like it's stuffed with cotton wool after digesting last night's findings and processing how it will affect me.

I stifle a yawn and explain as I fill a large mug with coffee, "It's no problem. I have finally found the answers. We'll have a group call tonight and I'll tell everyone about it."

My eyes dart around the room, trying to get my head in the moment but I think I am still too shocked to properly process it all. I plod over to the table and drop into the chair across from Florence.

"Good morning. Excuse my manners. It has been a long night."

Florence sits up straight in her chair, looking rested and content. Her cornflower-blue eyes twinkle with a light when she says, "Guess what?"

I wrap my hands around my mug and bring it to my lips. "I don't think I'm ready for guessing games yet. Why don't you just tell me?"

"I met a pixie this morning!" Florence squeals excitedly and does this odd little dance in her seat.

An unexpected warmth blooms in my chest and my mouth tips up in one corner. I lower my cup again, wanting to give Florence my full attention. "Yeah? Who made this morning's delivery?"

"Lindsey. She is so beautiful! And she glows!" Florence gushes, her whole demeanor animated. "She's only a foot tall but she's so strong. She carried all of the deliveries and they were practically bigger than her."

"Pixie dust," I explain. Though pixies are stronger than they look, the dust helps with levitating objects.

Florence presses her hands to her chest. "And her wings! The finest, most delicate green gossamer wings with an exquisite iridescent glow." She closes her eyes and shakes her head. "I'm sorry. I got carried away and blabbered all over what you were going to say. You said you found the answers?"

"It's okay. I'm glad you got to meet a pixie." *You might be seeing her again.* "Do you want me to tell you what I found, or would you prefer to hear it with the others tonight? I'm waiting for everyone to see my message across the different time zones, but I spoke to a few last night."

"I'd rather hear it now. That is, if you don't mind explaining it twice?"

I can't quite decide which I would prefer. But it might be better to tell her now in private so she can come to terms with the enormity of the situation.

"Have you ever heard of 'fated mates'?"

Florence sits back in her chair and gathers her long hair to bring it over her left shoulder. Her eyes flit around the room before settling on mine, studying my face with open curiosity.

"I can't say I have. I mean, I can kind of deduce what it means, but the short answer is no. Is that what's happening to us?"

"Not exactly. But it could be. With other couplings of course," I quickly rectify before she gets the wrong impression.

I take a large gulp of coffee and groan as the flavor makes its way across my tongue and down my throat, closing my eyes to savor the first taste.

"Is the coffee *that* good?" Florence teases. Good-natured humor laces the question and I strangely find that I am not annoyed by the jesting.

"What did you put in this? It tastes different from when I make it."

"Would you believe me if I said magic?" She arches her brows and I huff at her silly joke.

"Talking about magic... For the sake of this conversation, I will mostly be referring to you and me, and how my findings will affect us."

Florence nods and starts stroking the cat on her lap. Its rumbling purr reverberates through the room, adding to the gentle patter of rain, and creates a calming atmosphere. A sentimental person would perhaps call it "soothing."

I choose to ignore all of that and continue with my explanation, looking Florence directly in the eyes, her rapt attention fixed on me.

"We have established that the fates designed our meeting under a particular star alignment. This fated event also caused the proximity bond to keep us close. I found a case of this happening once before—a very long time ago—but the reasons for it remain unknown. It does not occur often, so we should handle this with a degree of reverence."

I pause to check if Florence is still following and she nods for me to continue.

"This bond is called a fated bond. The good news is that it is not permanent."

Florence's eyes widen and her hand stills on the cat. It lets out a feeble meow and Florence starts stroking down its back again.

"It's not permanent? That's good news, right?" She tilts her head and the soft light makes her look almost... angelic.

I place one hand on my lap and flex my fingers, forcing my magic to retreat so I can focus on explaining the challenging situation we are in.

"Yes. I believe so. However, I cannot establish any kind of timeline for when it will dissolve."

"It'll just naturally go away?"

"For us, I believe so. Yes."

"Why for us? Not for the others?"

I take another large sip of my coffee, savoring the taste while I contemplate my wording.

"As I was saying, this is called a fated bond. The critical aspect to this bond is that it gives you choice. If one chooses not to pursue a romantic relationship, the bond will dissolve after an undetermined amount of time, the distance limit will be erased, and we can return to our lives as if nothing happened. I believe the marking will also fade at that time."

"Not that you'd ever want to pursue anything romantic with me, I know that, but what would it mean if you did?" Florence asks neutrally. I don't know how I feel about that. *Did I expect her to sound disappointed?*

Florence's direct question catches me off guard since she is usually more reserved about expressing herself. However, it reflects the thought I almost dared to entertain for a fraction of a second last night before refocusing on dissolving it. I run a finger along the edge of my shirt collar and shove away the heavy weight in my chest.

"I believe that if we were to *choose* to pursue a relationship, grow genuine feelings for each other, and make a conscious *choice* to be together, then the fated bond will become a mate bond."

"And a mate bond is..."

"Permanent. Stronger than marriage. It will connect our souls together. For different species it would manifest in different ways."

"How would it manifest for you?"

Why does she ask such interesting questions? Why does she not merely focus on herself and how to get home?

"I believe my magic could be amplified, but I could also be wrong. I do not plan on finding out."

Florence swallows hard. "And for Sadie and Everett?"

Again, she chooses to think of others and not herself.

When does she put her own needs first?

"I believe his vampiric traits have surfaced. Each species returns a little more to their basest beings. Their inherent proclivities come to the fore. Some of the phone calls I have received through the night have confirmed this."

"Are there others also experiencing what Everett and Sadie are?"

My shoulders slump and I let out a long sigh.

"Yes. And it is even more complex. In two other cases, partners have been added to the bond. But I can say their bonds were amplified because of physical contact. Be it purposeful or accidental."

"I have so many questions right now. Bear with me, please."

I nod for her to continue.

"So, the physical contact thing is serious? That exacerbates the bond?"

"Yes. Physical contact will make the bond grow stronger. It

is my belief, based on what was reported to me and from what I read, that the urge to be close to your partner becomes intense and perhaps even uncomfortable."

"Does that mean someone else could enter our bond?"

I shake my head vehemently. The thought of anyone else claiming Florence causes a strange sensation in my chest that I do not wish to name. Yet, I do not desire to claim her for myself either.

"It is my understanding that Jasper had a preexisting... situation... with another male. Jasper had to travel to this male's location for work purposes. Natalie, consensually, went along with him. More consensual activities occurred between the three of them and it was discovered that the other male had a twin marking on his thigh the following morning."

"And he wasn't on the island?"

"No. He rarely travels away from his region."

Florence narrows her eyes at me.

"You're saying that as if it's a top secret location."

"It is," I state. Even though Cole and I are only acquainted, I cannot hazard to reveal more about his location. It could jeopardize Christmas across the world.

"Okay," Florence says slowly, a look of puzzlement on her face but she does not push for more. "Are there other bonds that have added more members too?"

"Yes. Do you remember Rollo, the wolf shifter? It seems his brothers also have a fated bond with Diana."

"Brothers? Like how many?" Florence blurts out.

"I believe two."

"So Diana has three males bonded to her?" Florence's eyes are so wide it looks like they are in danger of falling out of the sockets.

"It is not strange at all. It's quite common in some shifter cultures to have a polyamorous relationship."

"I can't decide if I'm nervous for her or jealous." Florence laughs lightly.

An odd discomfort rises in my stomach and an unbidden growling sound claws itself up my chest and escapes from my mouth.

"Diana will be fine," I grit out and loosen my fingers around the mug, afraid I might crush it. "They have sworn an oath to protect her, just as I have sworn one to you."

Florence's face sobers, the humor in her eyes dying down at my tone. Though, as always, she chooses not to remark on my rudeness and redirects the conversation seamlessly.

"Yes. So, where does that leave us and when do I get to go home?"

My eyebrows draw together and I internally wince at her question. Being the person solely responsible for finding a means to resolve these bonds, and failing to do so, is a clear indication of my inadequacy. I shudder to think what my father will say if he discovers what I have been hiding. His expectations and standards have felt like a noose around my neck my whole life, a constant reminder of the legacy I need to fulfill as the sole heir of Alberad.

I take a sip of my coffee and make a conscious effort to place it gently on the table. Sitting back in my chair, I set my hands on my lap and alternate flexing each finger. Then, I look Florence in the eye to deliver the news.

"I cannot give you an answer at this stage. We are at the mercy of the fates, it seems. The information I combed through was inconclusive when it came to dissolving the bond. If I have any spare moments, I endeavor to continue searching."

Florence nods and taps a finger against her rosy lips that I will never taste. For some reason she is very calm and I do not understand this response. I was expecting ire or resentment.

"Okay," she says with a pleasant grin, not a hint of sarcasm in her face, her tone, or her emotions. "If there's nothing we can do about it, then I'll just make the most of my time here." Her shoulders lift in a good-natured shrug. "What's next?"

Is Florence going to be this accepting of everything? She's not going to fight me or be angry?

I speak slowly and clearly in case the information that she will be staying with me for an indefinite period of time has not yet sunk in.

"We will have our video conference this evening and then I think it best that you make yourself comfortable in your wing of the house for however long you have to remain here."

Florence's nose wrinkles as she scrunches it in thought, causing me to shift my gaze away from her and to the downpour outside the window.

Our warm summer weather in this region is interspersed with cooler overcast days. It is common to have either a couple of morning showers that clear in the afternoon, or late-afternoon thunderstorms on other days. I find petrichor to be a rather pleasant aroma that blends well with the smell of the tomes I use in my studies, and it almost makes me look forward to locking myself away with my books for the rest of the day.

"Do you think it will be days, weeks, or months?" Florence asks me without a trace of derision.

"Again, it pains me to say that I am unsure of the duration of this bond. But it will be best for you to prepare for a lengthy stay," I explain carefully.

"Is there anything I can help you with?"

"No, thank you." *Why would she ask that?* "I have been working on my research for years, and this fall, I will present my findings to the top scholars in the supernatural community. I am very much behind schedule as I had put my preparations aside while dealing with the bonds. From tomorrow, I will return to my studies."

"Oh! That sounds really important. What's your project about?"

"I prefer not to say." *Especially since you are having an effect on it and could possibly alter my findings,* but I will never admit that to anyone.

"I understand. You have a right to your privacy." Florence

smiles, though the sincerity of her expression is undermined by the flash of what could either be disappointment or perhaps hurt in her eyes. I am very well acquainted with a look of disappointment, however, I am not so familiar with hurt. I will grant Florence her privacy, just as she respects mine, and not read her emotions.

The cat stands on her lap and rearranges its body to plop down heavily again, causing Florence to gasp.

"If the cat is bothering you then just put it on the floor, or let it outside so it can go back to Alberad."

Florence's hands shoot out to the cat and cover him like a protective blanket.

"Oh no. I like him very much. He's like my personal heated blanket."

"Are you cold?"

"Um... not all the time, but there is a little bite in the air today."

"Why are you not wearing something warmer, then? Put on a sweater or something," I reason, noting for the first time the goose bumps running up her arms. I do not understand why she would choose to sit in a dainty T-shirt when she is clearly cold.

"When I packed for my trip, I was planning on summer vacation in the Caribbean. In July, I did not account for cooler weather in the middle of a forest in Germany. So forgive me for being slightly unprepared."

The moment Florence realizes that she said all of that out loud, and with such an intriguing attitude, she folds in on herself and closes her eyes as if to hide from me. She covers her face with both hands for extra effect.

Speaking from behind her hands, her voice is muffled as she says, "I'm sorry. That was so rude of me. Please pretend you didn't just hear me say that."

I tamp down my amusement and don't let a single thread of it show on my face and give her an affirmative grunt. That was incredibly endearing but she does not need to hear that.

"I will see to it that you have something warm to wear from now on. We can order you more clothing or we can send for some from your house in Kentucky. Whatever you prefer. I will cover the cost since you are my guest and I am already disrupting your life."

Florence lowers her hands and bands her left arm across her chest to rub her right biceps. Her free hand goes back to the cat and strokes his ginger fur soothingly.

I wonder what it feels like to have so much physical contact with another being. Surely, it must be taxing.

"Please don't worry about that. I do have a job and I can take care of myself."

"Except when it comes to staying warm. Or feeding yourself," I point out.

Why am I such an asshole? Did I have to be so brusque? Do I want her to hate me? Her inability to take proper care of herself bothers me for reasons that I do not have the time to examine.

Florence's hand stills and she looks at me with a reserved smile.

"I plan to be better about it now that Sir Purrington will be staying with us. I thought it's only right that I make myself comfortable in the kitchen, like this morning, so that I can take care of him as well as myself without bothering you anymore than strictly necessary. I will also not presume to think you would need *my* help."

"I—"

"But if you do—with anything, at all—please know that you can ask me." The warmth in Florence's voice and the earnestness shining through her eyes take me aback.

"Thank you. I do not deserve your kindness," I admit, knowing I have not done enough for her, have not been good enough to her. Never will be.

"I wouldn't go as far as to say you don't deserve it, but you're getting it anyway."

Then, she winks at me.

My heart does this very strange thing where it feels as if somebody kicked it and it flew off a ledge, only to come back and start beating uncomfortably hard and fast.

Before I have the opportunity to gather my wits about myself, Florence gently places the cat on the floor and gets up from her seat. She moves to the counter where she had placed the fresh box of pastries. I frown as I try to puzzle out what is happening.

No one has ever been kind to me for the sake of being kind. There is usually some caveat. Even with my grandmother. She was not a warmhearted elf, though, she tried to show me traces of affection by teaching me to cook so I could become self-sufficient.

Does Florence have an angle she is playing? I doubt it.

I guess only time will tell.

Florence

The next morning when I arrive in the kitchen, I find a similar layout to yesterday waiting for me on the counter. There's a fresh pastry on a plate and the delicate cornflower teapot is sitting on its magical warmer. But next to it is something new.

A sweater.

A soft, wooly, ivory men's sweater that I instantly hug to my body then slip on over the sundress I'm wearing. The fit is long and loose on me, and I fold the sleeves over my wrists, feeling more from Adelbert in this moment than he's ever said to me. A contented feeling spreads from the center of my chest and travels to the tips of my fingers and toes, warming me up from the inside out on another cool morning.

Adelbert really is the noble male I thought he was, staying true to his word to get me something warm and taking care of my needs in his own way. He may not be very expressive, and given what he's explained to me about how emotionally closed-off elves are, it makes sense, but his chivalry runs deep.

I finish my tea and breakfast and move to the living room where Sir Purrington is already stretched out in front of the window, basking in a thin ray of sunshine penetrating through the morning cloud cover.

"Good morning, Sir P. You were the bestest cuddler last night. Thank you for keeping me company," I say to the relaxed cat as I crouch down next to him to smooth down some of his orange fur. True to his name, he starts up a satisfied purr at my touch and something settles in my heart.

I grab my embroidery supplies and hum my favorite song as I curl up on the couch to continue working on the valley piece. I have so many scenes of the Black Forest that I want to thread paint that I think this will turn into a series dedicated to my time here.

The morning passes quickly and quietly as my attention stays riveted on the scene unfolding on my hoop. The colors layer over each other and the depth of the scene pulls me right in, making me feel like I'm outside. I'm brought back to the present a time or two when I adjust my position and catch traces of what must be Adelbert's aftershave on his sweater. I may even lift the collar to my nose and burrow into the sweater, but I'd never admit it to anyone.

Last night we had a video call with everyone from the island, plus the new members that have been bonded, to give them the news that Adelbert shared with me yesterday morning. Adelbert laid out all the information very succinctly and gave the opportunity for others—who were willing—to share their experiences so far. He didn't press anyone to disclose personal information that they weren't ready to tell.

Dede and Everett shared that they have accepted their bond and she has decided to stay in Las Vegas with Everett and move in together. I'm so happy for my sister. Every time we talk on the phone, or even just when we message, I can tell how much she likes him and how happy he makes her. The male is practically obsessed with her and it's exactly what she deserves.

I have a feeling they're going to be relationship goals for everyone.

It took all day yesterday to process everything related to fated bonds and mate bonds. Then, with the extra information that was added during the video call, I almost spiraled when I thought about how drastically my life is changing and that I'm stuck in the Black Forest until the bond dissolves.

When I got in bed, Adelbert's face flashed in front of my mind and the tightness in my chest loosened a fraction when I realized all of this is clearly out of our control and I'll be safe with him.

The idea of a mate bond, though, of the fates intervening to match you up with the one person they have chosen for you, that they think you are compatible with, is the most romantic thing I've heard of. But since there is no chance of anything happening between Adelbert and myself—despite my glaringly obvious attraction to him—I made the conscious decision to treat it as an extended vacation in a lovely rental home with a reclusive roommate.

Knowing Adelbert hardly ate or slept while searching for answers to the bonds, and he still has his big presentation coming up, I want to do my best to help him any way I can.

The only ways I can think of to help him are to stay out of his way and not let my emotions get close to him while he's concentrating, and also to perhaps prepare some lunch for him when he gets caught up in his study.

With that thought in mind, I get up from the couch, take my sweater off now that the weather has warmed up, and head to the kitchen.

I'm not a great cook, but I can throw together a mean sandwich or salad, maybe even a basic pasta on a good day. Today is a sandwich day.

I'm a little excited about being the one doing the cooking for a change, and my humming soon turns to singing and dancing as I prepare the food.

There's just something about this kitchen that feels warm and welcoming. The solid wood counters and the exposed beams on the ceiling give it an inviting charm that's not present in the rest of the house. It's not that the house is unwelcoming, but there is an emptiness and a coldness to it that's remarkably absent in the kitchen.

When I'm satisfied that what I've put together is edible, I grab a pen and piece of paper to add a note. I mentally debate between options of what I should write, then finally settle on something that might cause an amused lip twitch.

What did Sushi A say to Sushi B?
What's up, B?
(wasabi, get it?)

I tiptoe toward Adelbert's study. I don't want to linger outside his door because I know my presence might disturb him, but as I put his plate on the console table across from the door to the study, I can't seem to move my feet.

There are some strange mutterings and then an object crashes to the floor. I let out a yelp of surprise and the door flies open a second later, causing me to stumble into the console table behind me.

"What's wrong?" Adelbert stands in the doorway and his gaze flicks up and down my body. His hands ball into fists and the veins on his forearms stand out sharply against his pale skin.

Try not to salivate, Florence.

"I'm sorry." I clutch a hand to my chest, my heart fluttering like a hummingbird's wings.

"What happened?" he barks, looking at my hand, then searching my face.

"Nothing's wrong. I just brought you some lunch. I thought you might have forgotten to eat," I explain and angle my body so he can see the plate behind me.

Adelbert's scowl softens and he rocks back on his heels.

"Oh. Thank you." He glances at the intricately carved cuckoo clock in the hallway, the movement granting me a glimpse into his study.

Unlike the rest of the house, it's a very masculine room with a desk made of a thick slab of wood in front of a large window overlooking my favorite spot in the garden. Against one wall, the live edges of natural floating shelves add a rustic feel to the otherwise traditional furnishings. I can just make out an antique globe lying on a rug in the center of the room. That must have been what I heard fall.

"Is it lunch time already?" Adelbert asks me.

"Yes," I say slowly and start to cautiously move backward little by little away from him. "I'll leave you to it."

"Fuck," Adelbert lets out on a heavy exhale and runs a hand through his hair.

Before he can say anything more, I turn around and speed walk back toward the kitchen.

As I walk away, something occurs to me. The door flew open but Adelbert's hands were nowhere near the handle.

I must have missed something when I stumbled back.

Adelbert prepares dinner for us again later that night and we talk about anything except what happened over lunchtime.

The pattern seems to repeat itself every day.

On rainy days, I sit inside on the same couch in the living room, and on sunny days I move to the garden. I make light lunches, leaving a plate—and a joke—for Adelbert on the console table in front of the closed door to his study, and enjoy mine in the kitchen with Sir Purrington as my constant companion.

Every evening, Adelbert and I return to the kitchen around the same time, an unspoken agreement between us to enjoy one meal together. I sit at the table, head propped on the palm of my hand as I stare at him while he cooks something different each night.

Adelbert is a talented cook and makes a variety of dishes,

most German, but some are inspired by friends from other countries. On one of the cooler nights he even makes us *doenjang-jjigae*, a Korean soybean paste stew that Daehan taught him how to make. It's so good and the meal warms me right up, sparking a new-found desire to travel to Korea and taste more of their food.

Not being a great cook myself, I kind of wish Adelbert would teach me. But, I respect his boundaries and always remain seated at the table and far away from the possibility of having any physical contact with him.

While Adelbert cooks, Sir Purrington usually cuddles up in my lap right until Adelbert sits down with me. Sir Purrington then has his dinner and disappears to a warm corner in the house, and Adelbert and I end up talking, sometimes even for hours, while we enjoy dinner and wine.

Slowly, we get to know each other over these nightly chats. Even though I always seem to crave a little bit more from him, I'm happy with the easy rapport between us. I only indulge my attraction to Adelbert when my door is firmly closed behind me and I can muffle my screams as I come around my own fingers, pretending they're his.

Adelbert thaws around me and his formalities wane with each day that ticks by. He tells me more about his grandmother. Despite being in love with an orc, she was forced to break up with him when her parents presented her with her chosen elf partner. Just like everyone in his lineage for hundreds of years, she had to agree to an arranged marriage, or face shaming her whole family. She moved off campus and into this house the moment she was able to, days after his grandfather died and his father took over as head of Alberad.

I can't help but think that this is also a major factor in Adelbert's reason not to entertain thoughts of anything more happening between us. I'm sure his father has already got prospective mates lined up for Adelbert to marry the moment he deems Adelbert worthy, but we never speak about it.

My wish for Adelbert is that he can have some kind of say in who is chosen for him. I hope it's someone who will love him the way he deserves to be loved, because the male I've gotten to know is so much more than the Alberad name.

Adelbert also tells me of his upbringing, his mother—who is the head of another school, more elite than Alberad and whom he hasn't seen since he was young—and many stories of his friends and the shenanigans they used to get up to and how he'd ultimately bail them out of trouble.

Adelbert asks about my embroidery, my mother, and her husband. We touch on the death of my father many years ago, and I talk at length about Dede and my love for her.

Tonight, a few weeks after my arrival, the conversation turns more serious.

"So, you're going to be the head of Alberad eventually, right? Is that something you've always wanted?" I ask Adelbert, now feeling slightly emboldened to ask more personal questions after we've both revealed little truths about ourselves over our meals in the kitchen.

Adelbert traces a deep groove in the grain that runs along the thick wood of the table. The oak table top is made from one piece of solid wood and has cracks and knots visible that give it that natural and homey feel—a little bit of the forest from outside brought into the home.

Adelbert doesn't look up at me as he answers.

"Choice is not a familiar concept in my life." His throat bobs on a swallow and I sit completely still, giving him the time to find his words.

Sir Purrington trots into the kitchen at that exact moment and jumps onto my lap. He curls into a ball and purrs deeply as I start petting him.

Adelbert takes a deep breath before he continues talking, his gaze on his hand as he draws a circle around one of the knots in front of him.

"I live a life of privilege. I can acknowledge that. I have my own house, have no concerns about money, and I have a promising future ahead at Alberad. However, I have never been given a choice in my life. Not in my family. Not where I live. Not in my career. And now... not even in my mate."

Adelbert looks up at me, his lips pressed into a thin line and an apology in his eyes. Something squeezes in my chest and an uncomfortable lump forms in my throat.

With a tone that is flat but earnest, Adelbert says, "You have the ability to make choices for your future. To live whatever kind of life you want to. Wherever you want to. You only have to wait for the bond to break. You can walk away from me with only a memory of the time spent in this house. But I will remain here. In the same house. With the future that was planned for me before I was even conceived."

Imploring me to understand, Adelbert's brows draw together and his shoulders slump.

"That's why I want to give you a choice. I do not wish for you to be limited to this life. To this place. To me."

Suddenly, it all makes sense.

I give Adelbert a small smile and try to tamp down any of the hurt I feel. My heart mostly hurts for *him*, at living a life that is so burdened by his sense of duty. His choices have been taken away from him, and being given a fated mate, is just one more thing he'll never get to choose for himself.

He deserves to find his own love, in his own time.

Maybe in another life things could be different for us. But not this life. Not now.

I wonder if anyone has ever put Adelbert first. Made him a priority. Just taken care of him without expecting anything in return.

I'd like to do that for him. As his friend.

My eyes take in his sharp jaw, the breadth of his shoulders, his long elegant fingers, and I silently bid farewell to any traces of romantic notions I might have had.

My mouth opens and closes as I try to find the right words before finally settling on what makes the most sense.

"I understand. The moment the bond breaks, I'll be out of your hair."

Adelbert nods in acceptance and we only last a couple of minutes in the stilted silence before calling it a night and disappearing to our separate wings.

I enter my room and lock the door behind me, thankful for the first time that Sir Purrington didn't follow me. I promise myself that this is the last time I'll get myself off to thoughts of Adelbert. I need to let him go.

But tonight, I'll make it count.

Grabbing the collar of Adelbert's sweater, I bring it to my nose and unashamedly breathe in the light scent of him that still clings to it. This is the closest I will ever get to him.

I tear the sweater off my body and flop onto the bed. My dress follows next and I chuck it onto the floor, then quickly slip my underwear off too. I wriggle until I find a comfortable spot and spread my legs as wide as they can go, pretending Adelbert is watching me offer my pussy to him.

I drag the sweater across my body, letting the soft wool caress my skin, as one hand slips between my legs. My breasts grow heavy and my nipples harden to points as I imagine Adelbert's hands gliding across my body—stroking, kneading, fondling.

I grab one breast and tug on the nipple, a whimper falling across my lips. I bite down on the sleeve of the sweater in the hopes that it'll keep any sounds from leaking out of the room, just as I drag one finger through my drenched core.

Fuck, I wish I asked for that vibrator now.

I add a second finger and slowly circle my clit, then pump them in and out of my slick pussy. I repeat the action until I'm squirming on the bed.

"Oh, Adelbert," I mewl around my makeshift gag as a

shudder rolls through my body.

I redouble my effort, closing my eyes as one hand alternates between my breasts and the other furiously flicks my swollen clit.

Behind my eyelids, Adelbert leans down and swallows my cries as I break into a million pieces, coming on his fingers. My legs tremble and my back arches off the bed, pleasure coursing through my veins and shutting out the world. My arousal drips down between my legs in clear evidence of what I wish the male could really do to me.

This is the last time, I promise myself as my heart rate slows and I crawl beneath the covers. Alone.

CHAT LOG

Florence: Look how cute Sir Purrington looks here.

Florence: *photo*

Sadie: THE CUTEST!

Sadie: Look at my new shoes.

Sadie: *photo*

Florence: Love that for you! Glad your mate is spoiling you!

Sadie: I miss you.

Florence: I miss you too. So much.

Sadie: Do you think you can come to my store opening?

Florence: Don't think so. Adelbert is preparing for a huge pre-sentation. He can't really get away.

Sadie: Should I ask Ev to ask him?

Florence: No, don't. It'll put too much pressure on him.

Florence: Send pics of your store progress!

Sadie: Only if you send pics of your Black Forest series.

Florence: *photo*

Sadie: GORGEOUS!!!!!!! These deserve to be in a gallery!

Sadie: *photo*

Florence: Love the aesthetics of the place. It's soooo you! Can't wait to see it in IRL one day.

Florence

On yet another rainy day, I'm bundled up on the couch and staring at the dove-gray sky outside. Rain falls in a delicate pitter-patter against the window, the droplets' rhythmic beat drowning out the continued grunts and muttered curses coming from Adelbert's study.

I never ask what he's doing in there and I never knock on his door. I vowed to myself not to ask him. I want him to trust me enough to tell me, *if* he wants to.

With my hands wrapped around my tea cup, my eyes track the racing drops on the window, following their silvery streaks, guessing who'll make it to the bottom first. When two drops finish at the same time, I can't keep a smile from quirking my lips and reflecting on my own loneliness.

In the evenings, Adelbert and I continue to have our joint dinners and we make polite conversation, keeping everything casual and not asking any more personal questions, subconsciously waiting for the bond to peter out. After his confession in the kitchen that night, I've been striving to give him even more space.

In contrast, Sir Purrington has been a steadfast companion and the affection he requires from me sates a little bit of the longing I have for physical touch. If it wasn't for the cuddly cat, I might have cracked and attacked Adelbert with a hug by now.

Thunder rumbles in the distance and I burrow deeper into my sweater, today's being the same color as the dreary sky outside. Despite my strongest effort, I can't help but bring the collar to my nose and inhale deeply.

Adelbert shows his caring side to me as he cycles through various sweaters, always leaving a clean one next to my breakfast setup—which he still prepares *daily*—when the previously worn sweater is in the wash. I'd like to imagine him cuddling and sniffing those sweaters the way I do, but I'll never know.

I wait with bated breath for our dinners together. Even though my days are filled with doing what I love, I'm starving for company. I enjoy the nature surrounding Adelbert's house, but I feel constricted by the limit placed around the clearing. I'd love to explore other parts of the forest or maybe even go in search of a pretty meadow for more inspiration.

I have finished five large embroidery pieces since I've been here. Each piece tracks a different feature of the Black Forest as summer slowly ebbs away. I need to list them for sale soon, but something is keeping me from doing it. It's almost like the ones I'm making are missing a major piece in the series.

I also miss my sister. Dede is getting ready to open her store soon and I wish I can go for the opening, but I won't ask Adelbert about traveling there as his presentation date looms closer. No way will I be adding to his stress.

Outside, the trees around the clearing are veiled by the fine curtain of rain surrounding the house. My feet tap against the wooden floorboards and I mentally groan with the boredom of being stuck in the same routine. I finally allow my curiosity that has been gnawing at me to come to the fore, my desire to set off and explore a wing of the house I've never entered too much on a day like this.

So far, I've kept my movements to the living room, my bedroom, and the kitchen, occasionally venturing down the hallway past Adelbert's study to look at my favorite painting there.

But today, I can't sit still any longer. I unfold my legs from the couch and sit up. Sir Purrington perks up from his cushioned bed I've made him.

"Want to go on an adventure?" I ask my furry friend.

Sir Purrington extends his legs in front of his body and stretches lazily before trotting off toward the dimly lit corridor.

It's as if my feet have a mind of their own as they follow Sir Purrington and take me to Adelbert's wing.

I keep my footsteps light as I pad down dark hallways, skimming my fingers along the wall as I make my way farther into the house than I've been before. A tingling sensation works its way through my body and my heart starts pounding harder with each step. I try to slow down next to some landscape paintings that line the walls but nothing catches my attention enough to come to a complete stop.

A light tugging deep in my stomach pulls me toward a particular spot and my feet almost start skipping of their own accord, the excitement bubbling up through them as a sense of urgency intensifies.

Until I see it.

I come to a halt in front of a beautiful portrait of a male who looks to be a great ancestor of Adelbert. My eyes track over each detail, not quite understanding what I'm seeing.

In the center of the frame is a serene male with a secretive curve to his lips that brightens the entire image. He has the unmistakable Alberad platinum-blond hair, but where I expect to find silver eyes, his are a warm shade of hazel brown. The brushstrokes are painstakingly small, so fine you can hardly see them. And, as if to keep the male the sole object of your attention, the entire background has been painted in a solid dark brown.

"I see you have found the painting of an Alberad forefather."

I shriek at the sudden sound of Adelbert's voice and take a step back. I glance around the gloomy hallway, trying to find Sir

Purrington as if he should've warned me of Adelbert's arrival.

The traitor is nowhere to be seen.

"When did you get here? Don't you know not to sneak up on people?" I chastise Adelbert as my cheeks flush with embarrassment at being caught, my heart ready to jump out of my chest.

"I was hardly trying to be quiet. You were just unaware of anything outside your realm of vision. What are you staring at?"

Do I detect amusement in his voice? This is the first time in weeks he's attempted levity with me.

I clear my throat and tuck some hair behind my ear. "I'm sorry. I don't know if I'm allowed to be here, but my feet—and Sir Purrington—just kind of brought me to this painting."

Adelbert tilts his head and studies me, then the painting. His brows contract into their more familiar frown.

"Interesting."

"Why do you say that?"

Adelbert crosses his arms and looks at the painting as he speaks. "This is a four-hundred-year-old painting and the only kind of it in the house. I pass it on a daily basis since my bedroom is right over there." Adelbert points with his chin at a door on the left and continues with curiosity lacing his words, "I have not looked at this painting in years. However, related concepts to it have been on my mind lately."

"Could these concepts maybe be about why this male has branches coming out of his head?" I ask and take a step closer to the painting without crossing into Adelbert's comfort bubble.

"He is a woodland elf. My grandmother used to tell me old stories about them. Legend states that my lineage descended from these elves. What you are seeing are actually horns resembling branches."

"That's so cool. Could your ancestors talk to trees?" My excitement spills over to my words as I imagine being able to be one with nature and having conversations with the tall trees surrounding this property.

Adelbert pauses a moment as he thinks and runs a hand along his sharp jaw.

"If I recall correctly, there is a book of fairy tales in my grandmother's study about the different types of elves. We do not differentiate between our kind today, so I would have to read up on it again. Though, to answer your question, it is said that we could commune with nature once upon a time. It is believed that we were the protectors of the forest."

"Why do you think elves don't have the ability anymore?" I ask, saddened that they have lost such a unique ability I'd give anything to have.

"I believe our magic has lessened over time for an unknown reason." Adelbert pauses for a moment and narrows his eyes as a thought seemingly occurs to him. "It could even be similar to our bond. If the magic isn't encouraged and nurtured, then perhaps it could lead to diminishing in strength."

My lips turn down at the corners.

"That's so sad. Do you wish you still had that much magic?" I know I would give my front tooth to become friends with nature.

"I cannot see a benefit to it in my daily life, but I would not mind expanding my abilities."

Adelbert is such a pragmatist. If he would allow it, I would love to force him out into nature to just sit and take in the beauty around him. He's missing out on so much by being stuck in his study all day.

"Wouldn't it be so cool if you could talk to trees, though?" I ask him, hoping it's just this angle of questioning he needs to think about the possibilities of being able to communicate with the plants around his house. "Some of the trees in the forest must be hundreds of years old. I can't even imagine what they've seen or heard over the course of their lives."

Adelbert's top lip curls back and he looks at me with confusion.

"I cannot imagine what one would like to say to trees."

"What about what they would want to say to you?"

Eyebrows raised, Adelbert just blinks at me and nods.

"Hm. Interesting observation," he says with something akin to approval in his eyes. "I have to get back to work now. You're free to move about the house. Wherever you want. I apologize if I have not stated that more clearly earlier."

"Thank you. I wasn't sure if I could, so it's good to know." I beam at him.

Adelbert stares at me for a moment longer than usual, then gives his head a small shake.

"I will see you at dinner. I am making schnitzel tonight."

"Sounds delicious. I'll stay here a bit longer to study the painting. I might recreate it with thread. There's something about the way the branches twist that fascinates me."

"Horns?"

"Horn branches." I wink at Adelbert and I swear that there's a smile threatening to tug his lips up.

I turn back to gaze at the painting and give Adelbert a moment to process his emotions. He remains next to me for a few more seconds before quietly returning to his study.

I'm not sure if I imagined it, but it felt like Adelbert's eyes were studying me instead of the painting.

19

Adelbert

After I meet Florence in front of the painting of my ancestor, led there by that insufferable cat who is always in her presence, I return to my study.

Florence raised some very interesting observations earlier. My research and what occurred to me about our bond could give me a final connection that ties everything together. If my assumptions are correct, it could mean that the future of elves and our magic will be directly affected.

Sitting down at my desk, I try to jot down some of my thoughts, only to be stopped when my phone vibrates with an incoming call.

I inhale deeply and twist my neck until the joints pop.

"*Vater*," I answer and silently brace myself for whatever is coming.

"Adelbert, have you reinforced your wards lately?" my father asks. I internally pat myself on the shoulder for the forethought of strengthening the wards when Florence arrived, and reinforcing them daily. For my own peace of mind, I need to keep her safe from everyone, especially Nithard Alberad.

"Yes, I have," I acknowledge, keeping my back straight in case he can hear my poor posture through the phone and can berate me for that too.

"I have not detected you crossing back into my wards around Alberad. Upon inspection, I found the wards placed around your home would not allow me access."

I fight my hardest to keep a grin off my face nor to let this small victory become apparent in my voice.

"Is there something you needed from me, *Vater?*"

"There is one month left until your presentation. It would be beneficial to you to share it with me before the others. I would not want you to humiliate the Alberad name with any lacking skills, be it content or presentation based," my father needlessly reminds me yet again.

"I—"

"Do not interrupt me, boy. I have another meeting to attend today, therefore, I shall return tomorrow to hear your presentation," Nithard Alberad states succinctly, his tone inviting no argument.

Reaching deep within the well of patience I always need when dealing with my father, I say, "I thank you for the offer. However, there is no need for that, Vater. I would prefer to keep my research private until the day of the presentation."

"I do not understand you," he hisses.

"Apologies, *Vater.* I do not mean to offend you," I say as calmly as I can manage.

"Well, you did. Now, do not embarrass me. I will see you next month."

My father hangs up and I slump back in my chair.

Not needing to dwell on that conversation, I get up and pace the length of my study. The litter of discarded items scattered across the floor mock me in my failure to control them. But I ignore them, stepping around them as I redirect my thoughts to Florence.

As I stood with Florence in that hallway, I was completely entranced by her as she shared her thoughts with me. The way she views the world, the way she chooses to see the positive in situations—even in me—befuddles my mind.

When Florence first arrived at my home, I allowed myself to enjoy her company, her humor and light, before I realized how temporary her presence here would be and that it would benefit neither of us to form any kinds of attachments when they will only be dispelled as soon as the bond is gone.

The last couple of weeks have been strained between us. Over dinner one night, I explained to Florence why I am against the concept of fated mates and that I think it is unfair to have our choices in something so personal taken from us. Since then, she has given me a wider berth than usual. She has remained polite but our conversations remain depthless, so unlike her initial weeks in my home.

Have we really been living together for almost two months?

I stop pacing and gaze out the window toward the spot that Florence favors. The rain seems to have finally stopped and a ray of sunshine pierces through the low clouds, illuminating a bright patch of grass across the clearing. I pick up the fallen globe from the floor and spin the world on its axis as I evaluate the odd sensation in my chest.

I find that I am missing the easiness of the companionship Florence and I shared until my confession brought an end to it. I have attempted to restore some semblance of it through our nightly dinners, but Florence seems set on remaining polite but distant, not quite her usual effervescent self.

I place the globe back on the shelf and rub at my temples. The fated bond is chafing against my consciousness, wanting me to make her comfortable and, I could even venture to say, "happy" here. Never before have I had such a need for another person's happiness as I do hers.

Surely it is the fated bond forcing these thoughts. Right?

My eyebrows draw down to a point of discomfort when it occurs to me that Florence has stopped her incessant humming.

Am I the cause of that?

This is unacceptable. I pride myself on how well I read

others, even without accessing their emotions. How could I have been so blind to Florence's deteriorating emotional state?

I rub at the discomfort in my chest, and a plan comes together, determined to get Florence to her initial level of vivacity again.

Tonight, when I prepare *Jägerschnitzel* for us, I'll pair it with wine and *Spätzle*. Maybe change the setting too. That might aid in bringing back some of her spirit.

After a few more failed attempts to concentrate on my work—too preoccupied with planning dinner—I close the study door behind me and start hunting for supplies for what I have planned.

I sense Florence out in the garden, quite possibly taking advantage of the clear sky after this morning's downpour, and head to the seldomly used dining room to gather everything I need. I finish setting up outside before entering the kitchen to start preparing the meal.

Usually, Florence is here when I start cooking. Her company is a more or less pleasant balm that quiets some of the constant worries and stresses that occupy my thoughts. However, tonight I start cooking earlier than usual and don't expect her to be in the kitchen.

I prepare the egg noodles, side dishes, a mushroom sauce, and a bottle of white wine.

"Something smells amazing," Florence says as she enters the kitchen, a wide grin adorning her face and the cat following close on her heels.

Florence walks to the table where we always enjoy dinner together and pulls out her chair.

"Don't sit!" The words fly out of my mouth far harsher than I intended them to be and Florence's shock is so acute that it penetrates my shields I have up against her emotions. Her shock soon morphs to hurt and her smile becomes brittle.

"Of course. I'm sorry. I can just get Sir Purrington's dinner and then I'll be out of your way."

The cat ceases rubbing himself against Florence's legs and stands completely still in front of her. His gaze is fixed on me and his tail flicks with agitation, and what I assume to be judgment too.

I put down the bowl I'm holding and scrub a hand over my face.

"Please don't leave." This time my voice has an edge of desperation clinging to the exasperation I feel toward myself. I don't manage to look up at Florence, letting my head hang forward as I await her disappointment to hit me next.

It never comes, though.

A hint of curiosity pokes at me and I lift my head to find Florence staring at me with a puzzled expression. She gathers her hair and brings it over one shoulder, toying with the ends in a familiar habit.

"I have to say, I'm a little confused about what I should and shouldn't do at this moment," Florence finally says after an awkward stretch of silence.

I take a deep breath in and release it, along with my tension, on a slow breath out.

"I prepared a dinner setting for us on the *Terrasse*—the back patio."

Florence's relief and excitement hit me. Somehow my shields had stayed down when her shock slammed into me, and I quickly put them back in place in order for me to respect her privacy. I do not want to inadvertently take advantage of emotions she has not readily shared with me.

"That sounds absolutely lovely. How can I help?" Florence asks me as a radiant smile beams from her, our misunderstanding already a thing of the past.

I admire that particular quality in Florence so much. Her ability to take a negative and discard it so easily. To assume the best of a person, even when he has proven he is selfish and self-absorbed. She is so resilient and thus far I have not appreciated her sacrifice for living with me for such an extended period.

"Please. If you could perhaps grab the wine and the glasses, then I'll take care of the rest."

Florence steps forward and collects her items before silently returning to her position, waiting for me to provide further instructions.

I gather everything onto a tray and lead the way to the *Terrasse*, an odd sensation of butterflies rioting in my stomach. Florence follows a couple of paces behind me and I turn just in time to see her jaw go slack as she takes in the table setting with the sunset in the background.

The golden light limns her in the most perfect way, highlighting her delicate features.

Florence looks positively radiant. *Stunning*.

I have not allowed myself to truly appreciate her beauty in a long time, afraid it could lead to unwelcome emotions, but I do not think I can manage remaining impartial much longer.

20

Florence

My mouth hangs open as I take in Adelbert's setup. The white table linen, the plates, the candle sticks, all of it framed by the most exquisite sunset.

This is not a date. This is not a date. This is not a date.

From the vantage point of the house's altitude, the rolling hills fade from bright green to darker avocado shades the farther the eye can see. The sky is painted in a gradient of celeste blue right above us, fading to dusty rose, apricot, and light topaz as the sun dips toward the horizon. The view reminds me of my first morning in Adelbert's house when we were on our way to Alberad library and I was almost overcome by the beauty before me.

I place the wine and empty glasses on the table and take a moment to drink in the sights, smells, and sounds of the forest surrounding me. My time here hasn't been exactly what I would've planned for myself, but I am extremely grateful for each moment, and this right here, affirms that again.

"Would you like to take a seat?" Adelbert asks me as he pulls out one of the chairs and inclines his head toward it. He's never done something like this before and I am a little curious about what's going on.

This is not a date.

"Thank you," I say slowly and inch my toward him, giving him enough time to move away so we don't accidentally brush against each other.

Adelbert rounds the table to his own seat and we sit down at the same time.

The atmosphere is a bit awkward and I am suddenly not quite sure what to do with my limbs. I settle for folding my hands on my lap and subtly look at Adelbert for any cues.

The uneasy silence lengthens as we stare at anything but each other, the chirping of some friendly birds the only sound. I'd love to ease the tension, but I seem to say the wrong things lately, so I sit up straight in my chair and wait for him as he gathers his thoughts.

Adelbert clears his throat. "How is your embroidery faring?"

"It's going well, thank you," I answer warily.

"Do you need more thread? Or hoops? How about fabric?" Each question has Adelbert's eyebrows climbing a little higher up his forehead.

"I'm still good since the last restock you ordered. And I saw Lindsey the other morning. She gave me some colors that weren't listed on Pixie Parcels," I explain. Lindsey found this perfect gold thread that looks just like sunshine and said she had to give it to me.

A line forms between Adelbert's drawn brows. "The pixie helped you? How does she know what you need?"

"Some mornings we chat when I'm up and she's doing a delivery. Did I do something wrong?" Though our meetings are brief, I try to meet Lindsey for a quick chat when she's scheduled to make a delivery. Besides Adelbert and Sir Purrington, Lindsey is the only other being I can talk to in person.

"Not at all. I was not aware that you have become... friendly with her." Surely, that's not a bit of jealousy I detect in his tone.

I smile sadly at Adelbert. "She's so lovely. I'll miss her when I'm gone."

Adelbert shifts in his seat and scratches the back of his neck. He leans back and then sits forward again, leaning his forearms on the table.

"Can I see some of the art you have created? The new ones, I mean." Adelbert meets my eyes before looking away again. There's a glimmer of vulnerability there, but that can't be right.

"Is there something you don't want me to feature? Everything is focused on the forest. I won't do anything to reveal the actual location of Alberad or your home," I promise.

"I'm not worried about that. I'm just... curious," Adelbert mutters with the subtle pout.

I have no idea what's going on with Adelbert today and why he's acting so out of character from his usual, distant self.

I nod and play with the stem of my empty wine glass. "Uh, sure. I'll show you after dinner."

Adelbert sits up straighter. "Thank you. What is your ultimate goal with your embroidery? What would you like to do?"

I pause my movements and arch my brows. "Um... is there a reason for this interrogation?"

Adelbert groans and throws his head back against his seat. He presses his hands over his eyes before dragging them down his face.

"I must apologize," he says with one hand on his chest. "I am only trying to get to know you better. I know embroidery is such a big part of your life, I was merely trying to learn more about you."

Is he nervous? Is that why he's acting so strange?

"Oh." I bite down on my lips to keep my smile from spreading and hook my feet around the chair legs. "My ultimate goal is to have my pieces exhibited in galleries. But embroidery is not a very common form of art, and I do need to make a living. Selling my art is my bread and butter."

Adelbert leans forward again and rests his palms on the table. "If you had a choice, would you want to keep them?"

I take a moment to think it through, considering each piece I've created. "Maybe not all of them, but the sentimental ones, yeah," I say slowly, weighing the words carefully. "There is one specific piece that I have not been able to part with yet. I've also not uploaded any of my new Black Forest pieces. I'm too attached to them."

"I loved the art you showed me before. I know if there's anyone who would capture this forest in all its due glory, it would be you."

A warm feeling clamps around my heart and melts through my veins, lighting me up from the inside out. "That's a really nice thing to say. Thank you."

"Would you like some wine?" I almost get whiplash from the sudden topic change.

"Yes, please."

Adelbert reaches for the bottle before my answer is fully out of my mouth. I keep my eyes on his movements as he expertly goes about opening the bottle and pouring us each a glass.

"Should we make a toast?" Adelbert asks me.

Where is he going with this?

"Sure," I say hesitantly and raise my glass.

Adelbert raises his glass too and then sets it on the table again as his shoulders slump.

"Why don't you hum anymore?" The question is just above a whisper, the words thick and without accusation.

I blink in confusion. "What do you mean?"

"You were always humming. You used to sound like you were filled with joy wherever you were. But you haven't hummed lately. Am I the cause of that?" The words are pulled from Adelbert like a pained confession, as if I'm drawing them out of him instead of him offering up his own observations.

"I wasn't aware that you were keeping track of my humming," I say cautiously.

"It's not... I'm not..." Adelbert sighs deeply and leans

forward, bracing his hands on the table. "I do not wish to be the reason for your unhappiness." Pure earnestness etches into his face, the silver of his eyes bright with concern.

"Oh." I'm not quite sure how to respond to that, so I just bring my hair over my shoulder and braid it to give my hands something to do.

"How do I—" Adelbert looks up at the sky and flexes his fingers before looking back at me. "I mean, what will it take to get you humming again? Happy again?"

"It's not that I'm *un*happy," I start, uncertain about how much I'm willing to reveal to him.

Adelbert raises his eyebrows and motions for me to continue. I take a sip of my wine to buy time so that I can choose my words carefully.

"I didn't make a conscious decision to stop humming. I honestly wasn't even aware I was doing it that often. I guess..." Despite my best efforts, my eyes get watery and I try to blink the emotions away. Sir Purrington appears out of nowhere and rubs himself against my legs, providing a little bit of the comfort I crave. I reach down to pet him and offer an apologetic smile to Adelbert before Sir Purrington saunters off again.

"Please take your time and continue when you are comfortable," Adelbert says with more compassion than I have ever heard from him.

"I guess... I just miss people? Especially my sister."

"Would you like to go visit her?"

"In a perfect world, yes. But I know that's not possible with the bond and everything you have going on."

"I have heard that she is opening her store soon. Perhaps we could travel there for the opening?"

"You'd do that?" I ask in utter disbelief. "Don't you have that presentation coming up soon?"

"I do. But your melancholy is bothering me too much to concentrate," Adelbert says with a completely straight face.

My head rears back.

"I am sorry my loneliness is hard for you," I say with a bit of a bite in my words.

Adelbert leans back in his chair and one side of his mouth tugs up.

"You've got some fire in you. It's better than that cloud of sadness you've been carrying around."

"If anyone has a cloud of something, it's totally you," I say and point a playfully accusatory finger at him.

"Oh, most definitely. I'm the cloud and you're the sunshine," Adelbert states with a solemn nod, like it's an actual fact the world should be aware of.

I pause and quirk my head at him, my brow furrowing as I ask, "You think I'm sunshine?"

Adelbert's mouth turns down.

"You used to be," he says sadly. "How can I fix it? What will it take to get you back to your perpetual state of happiness?"

I want to puzzle out this male, this sudden concern of his. Instead, I answer truthfully, vulnerably.

"If you were anyone else, I'd say a hug would be really nice right now. I think I'm a little touch starved."

"I do recall that you and your sister seem to be of a more tactile nature."

"You mean we're very 'touchy-feely'?" I laugh.

"In your words, yes. I do not understand the need to be constantly touching another person. I have never been someone who has craved any form of physical affection."

"Don't knock it until you've tried it." I give him a lopsided grin. Empathy for not knowing what it is like to have that connection with someone, even if just platonic or familial—never mind romantic—burns deep in my chest. "You're missing out, you know? You have no idea how good it is to have that physical comfort provided by someone you love. The touch of a hand, the caress of hair, the comfort of a warm embrace. It settles something in me."

Adelbert's stoic mask slips for a second and I could swear there's a flicker of longing on his face, but he quickly recovers and dons his ever-present serious veneer. He picks up his fork and knife and gestures for me to do the same.

I let go of the serious topic and follow suit. The most delicious flavor combination bursts on my tongue as I take the first bite. I close my eyes and a happy "Mmm" sighs out of me.

At the same time, the wind caresses my cheek and I relish the moment as I lean into the phantom touch. Invisible fingers briefly card into my hair and my smile stretches as the sensation grows stronger, almost becoming tangible. My eyes pop open and travel around the clearing, trying to find more traces of the wind in the leaves, but everything is absolutely still.

Adelbert's gaze focuses on me in the most intense way and his chest moves up and down like he's just sprinted across a field.

"Are you okay?" I ask him and brush some hair behind my ear.

Adelbert stares at the motion for another second and nods.

"Let me see what I can organize and if it would be possible to fly to Las Vegas for a day or two. It would have to be a very short trip, but I would like to make it work for you. Now, please, enjoy your meal before it gets cold."

I smile and rub at my chest, feeling so grateful for this male. He may be rough around the edges and he may not always know how to deal with me, but I think he has a sweet center hiding beneath that tough scowl and brusque manners.

21

Adelbert

After dinner, I return to my study and grab my phone, set on giving Florence what she craves.

"Bertie. This is a pleasant surprise," comes from the familiar voice.

"Everett." Despite trying for my usual neutral tone, a note of optimism manages to creep in.

"Everything okay over there? How are things with you and Florence?"

"Fine," I answer automatically, and then take a moment to reevaluate. I lower myself into my seat and contemplate how I want to word things. I have trusted Everett since we were roommates at Alberad, but I also do not want to reveal too much about my situation at this moment.

"Florence misses Sadie," I state blandly and factually.

"I can imagine. Sadie misses her too. We'd love to see you and Cece soon. We'd visit, but things are a tad busy right now with the preparations for the opening."

It takes me a second to process what he says before I settle on something that bothers me.

"You call her Cece?"

"Yeah," Everett answers hesitantly. "Sadie and Cece talk

almost daily and include me in many of their chats. Cece says as I'm basically her brother-in-law so I get to call her by her nickname. What do you call her?"

"Florence. That's her name." I sound slightly disgruntled but I take pride in the fact that my voice is without a hint of jealousy. Because I'm not jealous. At all. I quickly change the topic before my perceptive friend calls me out on more than I'm willing to acknowledge.

"Talking about the store opening coming up, I'm thinking it would be a good idea to fly in a day early before the others arrive. It will give time for the sisters to reconnect without being distracted by the rest of the crowd."

"That's a really great idea. What about your presentation? Isn't that coming up soon after?"

I tip my head back and lean it against the back of the chair as I study the ceiling.

"I still have a while to prepare. It's either going to be revolutionary for elves, or I'll be an even bigger disappointment for my father."

"Is he still the wonderful monster he was when we were at school?" Everett asks, sarcasm dripping thickly from his words.

I answer truthfully. "I think he's getting worse with age. Disappointment in me is quite possibly fueling his moods."

I get up and start pacing through the messy study, stopping when I ask Everett, "Do you remember my father's face when he caught you and Jasper streaking through the grounds in our senior year?"

Everett barks out a chuckle.

"That was so much fun. I still tried covering my junk with my hands, but Jasper just let it all hang loose with fists raised in victory when he passed the rose bushes."

I recall the night in question. Everett and Jasper were wild and reckless as they ran naked around the perimeter of the school buildings. The rest of the males from our wing watched them from our secret vantage point where we used to play truth or dare.

"Could you blame him?" I empathize. "He needed to celebrate completing the course. A worthy accomplishment making it through without detection or injury. A knot the size of his would hardly be fun getting snagged on thorns."

Everett chuckles again. "Knowing him, he might actually be into it."

That has me letting my own huff of laughter. My humor sobers as I say, "And yet, somehow, I still got blamed for your streaking. I wouldn't have minded if I perhaps could have joined in with a special cock of my own. Might have made it worth it."

"It always felt like you were on the cusp of having fun, but old Nithard would always find opportunities to ruin the moment right before you'd commit."

I mimic my father's staunch tone. "'The future of Alberad is weighing on your shoulders. Do not disappoint me or your forebearers.'"

Everett's wistful smile is evident in his voice when he says, "I wish you could start over somewhere without him dictating your whole life."

"Honestly, that thought has not even had the privilege of entering my mind."

"But if you could, would you?"

I take a moment to consider that. "Yeah, I think so. I do feel like I have a future in academics, but the thought of seeing other schools and not being limited to Alberad sounds too good to be true."

"Never say never," Everett advises.

"Not as long as Nithard Alberad is alive is a better saying perhaps."

"True."

There's a comfortable silence between us, years of friendship lending quiet support and understanding to each other before Everett says brightly, "So, Vegas. When can we expect you two?"

We handle the logistics of the trip and call it a night soon after.

For the first time in weeks, the near-constant pressure sitting on my chest has eased a fraction and I look forward to the morning and telling Florence the good news.

22

Florence

The next morning I wake with an extra pep in my step. Something about last night made me hopeful and I'm once again looking forward to my days in the Black Forest. It's not even fully about the plan to visit Dede, and perhaps get some of my own warm clothes so I'm not constantly wearing Adelbert's, but it's like something between Adelbert and myself has shifted.

I enter the kitchen with Sir Purrington like every other morning before. But where I expect to find my daily tea, pastry, and sweater, there's a rather attractive elf standing with a light of his own twinkling in his eyes—despite the serious expression on his face.

"Good morning. To what do I owe this surprise?" I ask Adelbert cheerfully, coming to a stop just inside the entryway to the kitchen. I haven't seen him this early in the morning since my first week here and my heart shuffles its rhythm at the thought of having company for breakfast.

Adelbert leans against the counter behind him, bracing his hands on either side, and says matter-of-factly, "I am certain you have grown tired of your daily pastries, so I am cooking you breakfast. How do you take your omelet?"

For some reason, my eyes snag on his grip on the

countertop and travel from his very toned arms up to his shoulders.

Were his shoulders always this broad?

I blink the thought away, only for Adelbert's gaze to lock on mine. Something passes between us and it almost seems as if there's a smirk playing around his mouth, but that can't be right.

This is Adelbert, after all.

"Maybe just a bit of cheese?" I answer him, but it comes out as more of a question.

"And?"

"Tomato, if you have some. But it's no bother if you don't. Honest!" I quickly add, not wanting to put him out more than necessary.

"And?"

I'm unsure what else Adelbert wants me to say, so I just add, "Please?"

My heart rate picks up with all the sudden questions so early in the morning. I'm not ready to filter my responses yet or gauge my honesty levels when I'm caught off guard, but I set my mind to being polite and kind since Adelbert is going out of his way to be nice to me. Again.

"Onion?" Adelbert asks.

"Um, sure?" I try but fail to hide my grimace.

"Okay. No onion."

"Are you reading my emotions?" I ask Adelbert and almost move my hands to cover my body, like that could somehow help me from being so transparent.

"I do not need to read your emotions when they're written so blatantly on your face," he states flatly but not unkindly.

A flush creeps across my cheeks as I realize how obvious I am being and cringe in embarrassment.

"I'm sorry. I'm not particularly fond of onion in the morning. It's great, but I prefer it with dinner, lunch even."

"Florence, you do not need to justify yourself to me."

My shoulders sag in relief and I let out a slow breath.

"I'm sorry. I don't know why I'm feeling nervous this

morning."

"What have I told you about apologizing?"

I open my mouth, almost ready to do it again, but catch myself in time. With a small shake of my head, I square my shoulders and move to the kitchen table, plopping down on my chair.

"So, care to tell me why we're eating breakfast together today?" I ask brightly and not at all suspicious—which I'm incredibly proud of myself for.

Adelbert's head quirks to the side.

"Would you believe me if I said it was to enjoy your company?"

I roll my eyes good-naturedly.

"Not in a million years," I answer honestly. There's no way Adelbert would willingly choose to spend more time with me than with his books or whatever he gets up to in his study.

Adelbert's lips pinch together and he runs a hand through his hair. I do not notice how his biceps flex with the movement, and I bend down to pet Sir Purrington who trots off after a couple of scratches.

By the time Adelbert joins me at the table with identical omelets plated, the tense mood from before is all but forgotten.

"I talked to Everett last night," he starts. "About possibly visiting Las Vegas. If you still desire to travel there, that is."

My hands pause their movement and I sit up straighter in my seat.

"Is that a trick question?" I ask Adelbert and narrow my eyes at him. Distrust is rife in my voice for dangling the trip in front of me with that kind of condition. I would never say no to visiting my sister and supporting the opening of the store of her dreams.

There's a brief tug on one side of Adelbert's mouth and his eyes glow with, dare I say, mischief?

"I am merely ascertaining if you are still in favor of what we discussed last night," he says haughtily.

"Bullshit, Adelbert Alberad." I point a menacing finger at

him then think again and cross my arms over my chest.

Adelbert's lips stretch into a magnificent grin, two rows of perfect, white teeth on display. The sight makes my breath catch in my throat and my eyes widen in wonder.

"You have dimples!" I whisper shout in amazement, perhaps even a little bit of accusation creeping into my tone. "Where have you been hiding those bad boys?"

Adelbert's smile grows in its brilliance and he shakes his head.

"Suffice it to say, it only took you calling me out on my bullshit to activate them."

Then, he does the unthinkable.

He laughs.

The sound is a little more than a couple of audible huffs but they're beautiful. My answering smile matches his and giddiness spreads throughout my body, tingling across my skin down to my tippy toes that are tapping on the ground.

"I think I am going to make it my personal mission to make you smile and laugh every day."

Adelbert's smile falls.

"Please don't. I am hardly worth the effort."

"I think you are absolutely worth the effort," I counter.

"I beg to differ."

"Then differ we shall," I say smugly and raise an eyebrow at him.

Adelbert lets out another huff and shakes his head, but a faint smile remains on his face as he starts eating. We fall into easy conversation and I even manage to make him laugh twice more before our meal is finished.

"So, back to your study for the rest of the day?"

Adelbert tilts his head from side to side, keeping his gaze locked on me.

"I am toying with the idea of trying something different today. My concentration has been... lacking lately, and it could benefit me to have a change of scenery.”

“Want to do some embroidery with me?” I raise my eyebrows in invitation, not expecting him to take me up on my offer but suggesting it anyway.

“Maybe not embroidery but I would not mind seeing how you spend your day.”

“Oh yay! Let’s do it. Let me quickly get the dishes, and you change into some comfortable clothes. We’ll be spending the day outside. Some sunshine might do you well.” I smile at him as I gather our plates and move to the sink.

“These clothes are comfortable.” Adelbert stands and motions at his business-casual attire.

I take a moment to assess his formal, tan dress pants and cream button-down.

“If you say so, but we’ll be sitting on the grass. Don’t come crying when you get stains on them,” I joke.

Adelbert frowns and asks blandly, “Why do you not use a picnic blanket?”

I blink at the elf, confused how someone so intelligent can be so oblivious at times.

“And where would I find one of those?” I ask.

“In the linen closet.”

I hit my forehead in mock obviousness.

“Now why didn’t I check the linen closet that was shown to me during my personalized house tour? Oh, right, because I wasn’t given a tour and because I don’t like snooping around.”

Adelbert eyebrows climb high up his forehead.

“Sassy under that sweet layer, I see.” There’s no derision in his tone, only the hint of a smile.

Instead of cringing in on myself and uttering the apology that is sitting on the tip of my tongue, I flick a strand of my hair.

“There’s a lot you don’t know about me.”

“Of that, I am certain. Now, follow me so I can show you the linen closet and we can prepare for a picnic.”

Adelbert

fter gathering all the supplies, Florence and I head out for our day outside. I have had such difficulty with my concentration over the past couple of days that a small break in my daily routine might be what I need to recalibrate.

Thoughts of Florence have also been bothering me without cease, diverting large portions of my focus from important matters. I am finding it increasingly difficult to tell what is the bond and what is essentially *me* genuinely enjoying her company.

"I usually like sitting over there," Florence says and points to the spot I know she frequents.

"I am aware. Though, today I thought I would show you a different spot since you can venture farther from the house now that I am with you. If you would prefer that, of course."

"I would absolutely *love* seeing other parts of the forest. The bit I've seen is so beautiful but I feel like there's much more to be discovered," she says, beaming a brilliant smile at me.

I acknowledge Florence's excitement with a nod and lead the way to an area I used to like to play in when I was a child and did not want my father discovering me enjoying such frivolous activities.

Much like our first venture through the forest, Florence

follows quietly behind me. This time, my steps are slower and I am less tense, therefore less likely to snap at her for being distracted by the surrounding sights.

Last time, the stress of entering Alberad with a human and the pressure to find a resolution to the bond were riding me hard, and I may have come across ruder than I intended. On top of that, meeting my father so unexpectedly threw me off.

With that in mind, I slow down until I walk beside Florence. She moves over slightly, always taking care not to accidentally touch me.

I card a hand through my hair and glance sideways at Florence as I say, "I must apologize for the last time we walked through the forest. I may have been a bit short with you."

"Oh, that's okay. I understand." Florence waves a dismissive hand in the air. "You were under a lot of pressure and you had a stranger thrust upon you and invading your private space."

"Yet, you had to move to a new country with a very rude stranger after just learning that monsters are real," I counter.

"But you're kind of a nice monster."

I scoff. "Nice is not something that is usually used when referring to me."

"Well, you've been nice to me," Florence says with a tilt to her chin.

"I could be nicer," I admit.

"Don't be so hard on yourself." Florence's eyes fill with empathy and her hand lifts as if she wants to reach out to me, but she catches herself in time and lowers it again. She laces her fingers together and quickly changes the topic when she notices my expression.

"Knock knock," Florence starts and the whole mood instantly shifts.

Seeing the mirth dancing in her eyes, I decide to play along.

"Who's there?"

"Yoda. Lady," Florence says carefully, enunciating slowly.

"Yoda lady who?" The moment the words fly out of my mouth, I hear exactly what they sound like.

"I didn't know you could yodel like that," Florence says through giggles. She has to stop walking as she doubles over with laughter. Finding it impossible to withstand her cheerfulness, my own chuckles bubble up in my throat and join hers.

Being with Florence feels like a warm blanket on a cold night, causing an unnamed emotion to coil tightly in my chest.

Once our laughter subsides and we can resume walking, Florence says, "So, tell me more about where we're going."

I have this strange urge to hold her hand, but I quickly shake the thought away and point straight down the path at the bright light seeping through the gap ahead.

"We're heading to a meadow I really like. It's still within my warded area so we're safe from being detected."

"Is there anyone specific we should be happy about not being detected by?"

I think about my father, the other professors, and decide to be truthful.

"My father is my biggest concern. Especially at such a sensitive time. But we are safe here." I give her a reassuring look before I continue, "This meadow is where I played as a young boy, and it is where I come to clear my head when needed."

Florence pauses and my own feet halt. She places a hand on her chest and looks at me with the most sincere expression I have ever seen on someone's face and my heart loses its rhythm for a second.

"Thank you for sharing such a personal place with me. It means more to me than I can express."

We stay like that for a moment, eyes locked on each other, and I search her face. The desire to do something irresponsible—like threading my fingers into her hair and taking sweet, sipping kisses from her luscious lips, tasting her until she melts into my arms—rushes to the forefront of my brain. I swallow hard instead and form my lips into something that resembles a smile.

"You are most welcome."

A contented silence settles between us as we resume walking, and I shove my free hand in my pocket to keep the flexing less noticeable, the other firmly grasping the picnic basket. Florence remains in my peripheral view at all times. I want—no, need—to see her reaction once we make it to the clearing.

She does not disappoint.

Florence's hands fly to her mouth and her eyes fill with tears. A single drop makes its way down her cheek and the visceral need to wipe it away makes me stumble back a step.

The movement catches Florence's eye and she turns to me with so many emotions blatantly apparent in her face. There's awe, thankfulness, joy, and I lower my shields a sliver to read the final one. Curiosity.

Florence bites her lip, then takes a shaky breath.

"How did you...? Is this...? I mean, wow! It's even more beautiful than my dream."

I tilt my head, not quite following what she's getting at.

"Come again?"

"This meadow. I had a dream about it months ago, but it was in fall and the colors were spectacular. I did an embroidery piece on it. But it was definitely this particular spot."

"You had a dream about my meadow?" I ask incredulously.

Florence crosses her arms across her chest and pink stains her cheeks.

"Well, right until now I kind of thought of it as *my* meadow." She tucks her hair behind her ear and stares somewhere behind me as she speaks. "But yeah, I completed the piece well before the trip to the Caribbean. I have pictures of it on my phone back home. I mean your home. Not that your home is my home. I know it's temporary. I just mean I left my phone in the bedroom that I am using while I am a guest in your house for a yet-to-be-specified period of time," Florence rushes out with hands flying all over the place to emphasize her point. The pink on her cheeks intensifies to a darker shade of red, the color spreading to her ears and down her neck, blooming across her chest.

I avert my gaze the moment it travels to her perky breasts—pretending I never imagined coming all over those tits—and I look at the field with scattered cornflowers, surrounded by tall trees on all sides and a stately oak tree toward its center.

"You are welcome in my home however long you want. I would like it if you treated it as your own. Go through all the cupboards, study all the paintings, explore all the rooms. It is my fault for not making you feel more comfortable. I aim to rectify my behavior and show you each room personally." I flinch as I replay my words in my head. "Okay, maybe not *each* room, but I vow to try my best."

"You're so sweet. Thank you for offering."

"I am not sweet."

"You're ooey-gooey delicious caramelly goodness under that grouchy shell, Mr. Alberad. If I was allowed to touch you I'd totally tackle you into a tickle fight right now." Florence lifts her hands in front of her body and flutters her fingers in a tickling motion.

"Oh, fates, no. A tickle fight?" I shudder at the thought and automatically stride toward the oak tree.

Laughter tinkles through the air behind me and the next thing I know, Florence is skipping—*skipping*—past me, her purple dress fanning out behind her as one hand gathers some of the material around her thighs to ease the motion.

I straighten my back and lengthen my strides, not wanting to be outdone by Florence. Too late, I realize how comical the two of us must look in this peculiar race and a smile creeps onto my face—completely unbidden, of course.

Right at that moment, Florence turns to look back from a couple of yards ahead of me and a radiant smile bursts across her face when she spots my grin.

"Last one to the tree is a rotten egg," Florence calls out with laughter ringing in the air.

My pace quickens even more to reach her, but Florence's foot suddenly catches on something. Her eyes widen as momentum propels her toward the ground and my heart catapults in my chest. I cannot allow her to be hurt because of me.

Summoning all the power I can gather in a split second, I reach out and hope for the best.

It works.

I catch her.

Not physically, but with my magic.

My magic I have not revealed to a single soul in this world.

Until now.

24
Florence

One moment I'm careening toward the ground, and then I'm caught by some invisible force. I'm eased into a standing position again and my heart gallops in my chest. I turn to Adelbert as I try to make sense of what just happened, but judging by his pallor, he's just as shocked as I am.

"I can explain," he says with arms raised in surrender.

"Okaaay." I bring my hair over my shoulder and start playing with the ends in a soothing manner, since I don't know what else to do with my hands as I wait for Adelbert to stop pacing and find the words he needs to explain what just happened.

"Let's sit," Adelbert says then quickly adds, "if that's okay with you of course."

"Sure." I nod slowly, frozen in place as I wait for him to make the next move. A tense silence stretches and after a couple of seconds of no direction, I gently suggest, "How about by that majestic oak tree with the long limbs? He looks friendly."

Adelbert's nose scrunches up in the cutest way before he strides over to the tree.

"I don't know about 'friendly' but you do have a point," he says as he glances over his shoulder to me.

Adelbert sets the basket down on the lush grass and

together, we lay out the soft buttery-cream blanket, each of us sitting down on opposite sides. If it were anyone else, I would consider this a really romantic date. In terms of setting and view, it is most definitely the best I've ever had. Though, there is no way I would reveal that to him just in case it will make him even more stressed than he already is.

"So, about what happened..." Adelbert rubs the back of his neck then pulls his collar from his throat. He brings his hands in front of his body, turning them over a couple of times before looking at me.

His nerves are clear and the weight of whatever he wants to tell me pushes down on me like a suffocating cloud of smoke. How much worse must it be for him.

Outwardly, I try to look as encouraging and supportive as possible, so I smile at him, trying to project comfort and confidence, but internally my stomach feels like a hole has opened and all my organs are slowly being sucked into an abyss.

"Take your time. You don't have to tell me anything, but if you want to, I'm here for you," I say, keeping my voice hushed to match the heaviness of the mood.

Adelbert clears his throat and his expression turns to focused determination.

"I want to tell you. And, I want to show you. I am only hesitant since absolutely no one else in the entire world knows about what I will reveal. This is what my research is based on. What I will present next month."

My lips part and I bring a hand to my mouth, stunned that this very private male wants to share something so significant with me.

"Whatever you say or do, it is completely safe with me. I promise not to tell a soul. Not even Sadie. Cross my heart," I vow solemnly and draw a little cross over my heart to emphasize my point.

Adelbert's face softens at that and his shoulders lose a bit of their stiffness.

"Not even Sadie?" He quirks a half smile. "Then I know you are very serious about this matter. Thank you."

Adelbert's chest rises on a deep breath before he dives into his explanation.

"You remember how I said that in the past, elves had different kinds of gifts and that I believe our magic has lessened over time?"

"Yes, like the portrait and the male with the branches?"

"Horns. But yes," Adelbert corrects. "My research is into the magic we possessed before. A very long time ago, we were more powerful and were not only empaths but commanded another form of magic."

"Okay, that sounds really cool." I recall our conversation in front of the portrait and ask, "Like the 'speaking to trees' magic?"

"Unfortunately, I have not been able to confirm that theory yet, though it is possible. The magic I am able to confirm is called a mage hand."

I lean forward, my eyebrows raised as curiosity and excitement mingle. "Mage hand? How does that work?"

Adelbert's tone remains neutral and controlled as he continues, "I have been conducting numerous experiments to gauge the range of my power, but since you arrived, my power has actually strengthened."

"Could it be because of the fated bond?" I ask.

"That is my assumption as well. I do not possess complete control of the magic. However, what I have seen is that I am able to manipulate and move larger objects and make more intricate movements from a certain distance," Adelbert explains in such a logical manner it's as if he's explaining weather patterns to me.

I grin broadly and squeal, "That's amazing. Is that how you caught me when I almost fell?"

Adelbert gives me a single nod, then says the best thing, "I could demonstrate it for you, if you would like of course?"

"Oh! Yes, please! I'd love to see that." I clap my hands and wiggle my butt in excitement, ready to see real magic up close. Repositioning myself, I sit crossed-legged so that I am facing Adelbert directly. He, in contrast, does not share the same level of excitement but shifts so he's facing me too.

Adelbert places a red apple in the center of the blanket and sits back again. With furrowed brows he concentrates on the fruit, hands resting on his lap and fingers twitching.

My eyes grow wide as the apple slowly lifts into the air. Adelbert lets it levitate at eye level for a couple of seconds and my mouth goes dry at how extraordinary this feat is. The apple hovers closer to me and my heart rate picks up to a strong staccato rhythm. I hold out my hand and the apple is placed gently onto it.

I duck my head to look at it more closely, inspecting it this way and that, marveling at how incredible Adelbert is as he sits completely still on his side of the blanket, seemingly awaiting my judgment.

"That was seriously impressive. You say no other elf can do this? Why keep it a secret?"

"I am hoping that by keeping this a secret until the formal presentation that it will give me some leverage with my father. I keep practicing and extending my skills so that other scholars would have the desire to learn mage hand magic too. Perhaps I could convince my father to allow me to teach special classes dedicated to it, instead of relegating me to a desk, doing administrative work, as required for my future role as head of Alberad."

"You're exceptional, Adelbert," I praise him, completely in awe of this skill and the fact that he had to teach himself and keep it a secret the entire time. I swear his chest puffs out a little at the compliment. "If your father can't appreciate this level of skill, then he's an idiot."

Keeping his eyes fixed on mine with an intensity I have not yet encountered, Adelbert says, "I think I can do more than that. My magic is wriggling against my skin, wanting me to push it further than usual."

I sit up a bit straighter, place the apple in the center of the blanket again, and rest my hands on either knee, ready to see more.

"Great! What do you want to try?" I ask giddily.

Adelbert rolls his shoulder back and asks in a voice so gentle, I almost can't believe it's his, "Is it okay if I touch you? Not physically, but with my magic?"

I cant my head to the side, curious about this new side of Adelbert that is gentle and nervous and so cute that I just want to squeeze him. I had told myself no more lusting after him, to give him space. Unfortunately, my heart doesn't understand what my brain wants it to do.

Offering him a small smile, I swallow against the tightness in my throat and choose my words carefully.

"I want to help you in any way I can. You have my consent to touch me however you want. I trust you."

Adelbert inhales a sharp breath and licks his lips.

"I don't deserve you. But I will do my utmost to never lose that trust."

25

Adelbert

lorence is most certainly a dream. I am sure of this. I have never met anyone as cooperative, kind, understanding, and gentle as her. I need to protect her at all costs, even from myself.

Yet, when I sit in front of her like this, I can't help but be drawn to her. She's extraordinarily beautiful. The way the light catches her entrances me as it peppers her skin with little spots of sunshine filtered through the leaves above us. But more so, she seems to be illuminated from within, casting a glow on not only herself but those around her too.

Florence will make a great partner for someone someday, once she is free of me. My life is plain, simple, limited. Some might even say "boring." It is not what I would want to burden her with, no matter how much the fated bond presses at me to touch, to take, to claim, to… love.

However, I can make her stay with me more enjoyable than it has been. I can reveal parts of myself to her that I haven't revealed to others, because Florence is a safe space. That I am sure of.

"Tell me if anything feels uncomfortable or if you want me to stop," I tell Florence as I ready myself, gathering my magic into me with each purposeful breath.

Florence narrows her eyes in thought, then tilts her lips

into a playful smirk as she says, "You know what? Lower those privacy barriers of yours so you can read my emotions. I give you full consent so you can see if anything makes me uneasy."

"Are you sure?"

"Don't doubt me, Adelbert. I wouldn't have offered if I wasn't," she says a bit sternly then leans back on both hands, inadvertently offering her very pretty breasts to my hungry gaze.

I swallow hard and think of my studies, my presentation, my ancestors until my thoughts become neutral again.

"I'm going to start now," I announce.

I reach out with my mage hand toward Florence's right forearm and gently stroke the skin. Even through the magic, I can feel the softness of her skin, the sensation jarring me at how vivid it is, like I'm physically touching her skin to skin. The magic is much stronger right now than when I'm moving objects around in my study.

I monitor Florence's emotions and I register her surprise in both what she's exuding and the widening of her eyes as she looks down at her arm and sees nothing there.

"Wow. I can feel that," Florence says with sweet wonder coating her words.

"How about this?" I ask and increase pressure, wrapping my hand around her forearm and applying a little pressure.

Florence's eyes close and a smile spreads across her face.

"It's like an arm hug! Thank you," she says dreamily and sighs in contentment.

My lips purse and I give my head a small shake at how fucking kind this woman is, thanking me for something as simple as squeezing her forearm.

I want to give her more.

I move the mage hand up to her elbow. I'm able to move the thumb in a soothing circular motion in the bend of her arm, right on the sensitive skin.

"Mmm," Florence hums in satisfaction, causing my cock to

twitch. With my eyes, I trace the goose bumps racing down her arms, and my own satisfaction blooms in my chest.

Encouraged to continue, I trace the flowery pattern around the sleeve of her dress and move up to the exposed skin of her neck and shoulders.

I drag a single finger across her delicate collarbone to the base of her throat and pause there for a breath as I readjust my hardening cock.

"More," Florence demands breathily, eyes still closed as she tilts her head to the side, inviting me to touch the other side.

I skim my touch from the outside of her left shoulder and work it closer to the center, gently cupping her neck.

Florence leans forward into the touch and lets out a long, needy moan.

It is the sexiest sound I have ever heard and my cock hardens to an uncomfortable degree.

For the first time in my life, I want to say "fuck it" and throw everything I've worked so hard for away. I want to dive across this silly blanket and cover Florence with my body, give her my full weight, and fuck her into oblivion. To hell with the consequences.

Sense wins out, though.

Lazy eyes open languidly, and Florence stares at me with fully dilated pupils, a hunger in her eyes that matches my own.

"Give me more," Florence breathes and licks her lips.

I reposition myself so I'm kneeling, and Florence's eyes move to the evidence of my arousal outlined against my leg. I should have listened to her and worn more comfortable pants because this cannot be good for blood flow. It won't deter me though.

Doing something I have longed to do since I met her, I trace the cupid's bow of her upper lip with the index finger of my mage hand.

Voice husky with desire, I say, "These lips." I am unable to form a more complex sentence as all my brain power has been redirected to my cock.

Florence's lips part and she moves her head slowly, sultry gaze fixed on mine while I keep the mage hand absolutely still, letting her trace her own lips with my magic.

I am really enjoying this side of Florence—a bolder side, freer to act and take what she wants. I wish she would demand more from me, both now and in our everyday lives.

Emboldened by Florence's easy reception of my touch, I skim a single digit down from her lips, over her chin, down her elegant neck, her chest, and pause when I reach the material of her dress, right above her cleavage.

My breathing is labored and fire licks at my skin with the crackling tension between us.

With a voice full of heat, Florence demands, "Don't stop now." Then she quickly adds in a more sober tone, "Unless you want to, of course."

My heartbeat picks up, pounding a steady rhythm, spurring me on.

"I don't want to stop. May I remove your dress, Florence?" I rasp out.

"I think it's safe to say my answer is yes to anything you want to do right now," Florence says as she arches her back toward me.

Unable to resist any longer, I hook a phantom finger over her dress and pull it down until a breast pops free.

I groan at the sight, my mouth watering with a desire to taste her.

My gaze flicks up to Florence's, and I swallow down all the filthy things I want to say. There's something so fragile in this heated moment between us and I don't want to break it. Keeping my focus on her eyes, I drag my mage finger around the underside of her exposed breast and move across to her other one to lower the material there so both are free to the elements.

"Pure perfection," I whisper in reverence as I stare at her laid out before me. Her breasts are small and pert, with rosy nipples jutting forward, begging to be played with, tugged on, sucked.

If I were an artist, out of all the sights in the world, this would be the one I want to capture, immortalizing it for my viewing pleasure whenever I please.

Florence leans back on her arms, her long golden hair hanging free behind her, head thrown back but eyes trained on me. With her back bowed like this, her body looks like a delicious feast offered especially for me. I want to sink my teeth into every inch of her, taste her, devour her.

The purple of Florence's dress, the white of the blanket, the green of the grass, and the first hints of yellow in some of the trees form the most exquisite palette that will be imprinted on my brain for the rest of time. I wonder if I could ask her to make me a piece of art so I won't forget any of this.

"Touch me, Adelbert." There's a light demand in Florence's tone, though her need and arousal press against me, commanding me to keep going. I have no intention of fighting my desire today.

"Like this?" I ask and cup one of Florence's breasts, gently kneading the flesh with my magic. I marvel at how much I can feel and do with her. My power is so much stronger in this moment than I have felt in my life.

Feeling confident that I can do more, I move my thumb and forefinger and pluck a nipple.

Florence whimpers and I do it again. I roll her nipple between my fingers and tug on it, testing her reactions to see how much pressure she prefers. With my barriers down, I feel free to explore her body, knowing how much she is enjoying each touch.

With one particular pinch on her other nipple, Florence makes the most luscious mewling sound, causing precum to leak out of my cock, quite possibly leaving a wet spot on my pants. Though, in no way am I removing my gaze from the magnificent woman in front of me to check on something so inconsequential.

I bite down on my lip to keep myself present and in control so I don't do something irresponsible like reach for Florence with my physical hands. I have such a strong desire to learn every inch of her body, to bring her pleasure, but I don't want to overstep.

Are these thoughts because of the bond, because I want to explore my magic, or because of Florence?

This is hardly the time to get hung up on such thoughts, so I leave the option open for her to choose.

My voice comes out gravelly when I ask, "Do you want to stop here or keep going?"

"One thing you need to know about me, Adelbert, is that I don't like edging. So if you are not planning on making me come right now, then you better be okay with me doing it myself."

I rise to my knees, my body automatically gravitating toward her. However, I catch myself and fall back on my heels again, shaking my head at how quickly I almost lost control of myself there.

"Have you ever climaxed from nipple play alone?" I ask Florence, curious if she'd like me to continue just as we've been doing and nervous to push her too far.

Florence moves her head from side to side then slowly uncrosses her legs, widening them before placing her feet down flat on the blanket.

"Think your magic can manage other areas too?" Florence's voice exudes confidence, and so does her body, but a breath of nervousness seeps into the air around her. It is extremely endearing to know she is battling her nerves the same way I am and she is only putting up a front to keep me present in the moment. I don't call attention to it, though.

Matching her confidence instead, I say, "I guess we will have to find out."

Florence's grin grows and I can sense her appreciation that I am playing along.

I reach toward the picnic basket with my right hand and move it behind me, not wanting my view obstructed by anything.

When I look back at Florence, her chest is moving up and down more rapidly than before. Anticipation thickens the air between us and my heartbeat picks up its rhythm.

I stretch out my fingers in front of me, flexing them as if I'm readying my mage hand for what I am about to attempt.

"Adelbert," Florence says in a gentle whisper, "you don't have to do anything you are not comfortable with."

I huff out a laugh and shake my head.

"Florence, I only wish you could read my emotions right now. There is nothing I would like more at this particular moment in time than to touch your pretty pussy and watch you explode in ecstasy."

A warm blush steals across Florence's cheeks, traveling down her pale chest, tinging the skin there with the same reddish color. She throws her head back and shakes out her hair. When her gaze lowers to meet mine again, there's a fire burning in them.

"Then what are you waiting for?"

26

Florence

Throwing that challenge down was the final push Adelbert needed. Today has taken such a very unexpected, yet very welcome, turn. If you had told me I'd be laid out on a picnic blanket about to get finger fucked by the most handsome male in existence, there's no way I would have believed it.

But here I am. In my meadow. Adelbert's meadow. *Our* meadow? The meadow of my dreams. I am sure the fates planted the image in my head way before Sadie and I even thought of the Caribbean trip. I can't even remember whose idea it was anyway. The season might not be exactly the same as what I dreamed about, but in another month or so, it might be.

I wonder if the bond—and I—will be gone by then...

Pushing out any negative thoughts, I fix my eyes on Adelbert's, reveling in the pure hunger he isn't even trying to mask. I let my knees fall a bit more to the side and suck in a sharp breath when his magic hand wraps around one ankle.

"Your skin is so soft and smooth," Adelbert says as he strokes what I assume is his thumb against the inside of my ankle.

It has been hard not having had a hug or a reassuring touch since I've come to Germany. Yes, Sir Purrington soothes a little of the ache, but it doesn't fully replace that human-to-human, skin-to-skin sensation I crave.

Even though I know it's not his physical hand, this sensation right here on my body still feels like it could be Adelbert. The fingers are long and elegant, just like his, and the touch grows more confident with each pass across my skin.

Adelbert doesn't toy with me for too long. He grabs my skirt, gently shoving it up my thighs, revealing more skin to his wolfish gaze with each inch he uncovers. I make no move to help him, just keeping my back arched and my legs open, as if I'm some wanton queen in another realm. If today is all I get with Adelbert, I will make the most of every second.

With my dress settled around my waist, my breasts free to the open air, and only a thin piece of material covering my soaked core, I feel more powerful than I have with any previous lovers.

All because of the way Adelbert is looking at me.

Like I'm some kind of Christmas present he has just unwrapped. I choose to believe that I am the reason for his awestruck expression, and not that he is marveling at how strong his magic is.

"Would you like me to take my panties off?" I ask Adelbert as his eyes remain riveted on what I'm sure must be a wet spot in the center of my underwear. His magic hand is wrapped around my knee, thumb rubbing absentmindedly at the sensitive skin on the inside.

Wordlessly, Adelbert nods and his Adam's apple bobs on a hard swallow.

I shift around to grab the sides of my panties and slip them off, tossing them in the corner of the blanket. While I'm busy removing them, the thought that it might be good to also get rid of my dress, strikes me. So I do just that, and lift it over my head to place it in the corner too.

Adelbert falls back on his butt and his breath comes in shallow pants as he takes in my naked body.

"You're... you're...." Adelbert stammers, silver eyes roaming over every part of my body.

"Naked?" I suggest.

"The most exquisite thing I have seen in my entire life." Adelbert's voice is full of sincerity and my eyes threaten to tear up.

Not wanting to derail from possibly getting an orgasm out of this situation, I save that comment in a mental file to be examined at a later—hopefully postclimax—stage and say, "Your turn. Take it off, baby."

The endearment slips out and my eyes bulge as I realize what I just said. My heart starts racing, preparing for Adelbert's rejection, but he either didn't register what I said or is choosing to ignore it.

Wordlessly, he untucks his shirt and starts unbuttoning it, a playful smirk lifting his lips as he catches me sitting up straighter to get a better look. Adelbert shrugs his shirt off and my eyes catch on his fated tattoo, which matches mine in placement.

Adelbert notices where my eyes have drifted to and angles his body so I can get a better look at the overlaid sun, moon, and star on the left side of his ribs. I twist my own body to match his and we study each other silently for a moment.

"I am glad it was you," Adelbert whispers.

"I am glad it was you, too," I whisper back.

Adelbert then pops open the button on his pants. The sound of the zipper lowering drowns out the birdsong around us and my focus is on him only. He drags off his pants and underwear in one swift motion to reveal his cock.

Even his cock is elegant. Long and smooth and curved just right, I know he'll hit that perfect spot inside me. But that's not a thought for today.

We both take a moment to drink the other in and, not able to hold back any longer, I lean back and widen my legs further than before.

Adelbert's mage hand moves swiftly up one leg and rests in the crease between my inner thigh and pussy. I dare not move in case it spooks him. Butterflies swirl in my stomach and my heart pounds in anticipation.

A single digit strokes lightly against my pussy lips before entering me slowly.

"Florence." My name sounds like a prayer from Adelbert. "You're so wet, so warm, so tight." The final word comes out on a growl and his finger retreats to be joined by a second.

A loud moan escapes me at the sensation of being filled and Adelbert angles his magic fingers and rubs at my G-spot.

"So good, baby. Touch yourself for me, too. Show me how you like your cock stroked," I tell Adelbert as I start riding his invisible hand.

"Yes, Liebling. Watch me. Watch what you do to me."

I whimper as Adelbert removes his fingers from my pussy, but my fascination grows as his phantom fingers glisten with my essence, and he coats his cock with my arousal. It's the most erotic thing I've seen in my life.

Now lubed up with *me*, Adelbert runs his right hand over his wet cock and grins in satisfaction. His mage hand returns to my pussy and I moan loudly as he smoothly thrusts two fingers back in.

Impressing me further, Adelbert multitasks like a pro. He rubs my clit and fucks me with his phantom fingers as he pumps his hand up and down his cock on the other side of the blanket.

Whimpers turn to panting as I chase my climax, moving my hips in time with Adelbert's strokes. His harsh breaths match my rhythm, and masculine grunts fall from his lips.

Adelbert adds a third finger, stretching me so good as he strums my clit. My moans become louder and Adelbert's sexy sounds propel me closer to the edge.

"Yes, baby. Just like that. Keep going," I tell Adelbert, loving how he reads all my cues.

"Are you going to come for me, Liebling? Let me feel you squeeze around my fingers before I spill for you," he says through clenched teeth, eyes locked on where his fingers are entering me.

"Yes, yes, yeeees." My screams ring out across the meadow and a flock of birds take flight. My eyes close and my back arches as my orgasm slams through me, momentarily stealing my breath. My pussy contracts around Adelbert's fingers as tingles race across my skin.

I open my eyes just in time to see Adelbert explode into his hand, his load so much that it shoots onto the blanket, almost reaching me. Yet, he never looks at it. His blissed-out, half-lidded gaze is only fixed on my face, his jaw slack, blinks slow.

Peaceful.

Beautiful.

Not mine, I remind myself.

Adelbert

No one has ever given me a pet name before. The closest thing to a term of endearment I have had is "Bertie" which some of my friends from school call me.

When Florence called me "baby," it felt so natural and so right that I didn't want to draw attention to it. Calling her "Liebling" also just slipped out. It's a fitting nickname for her and one I hope she never asks me about.

After the most erotic, intimate—magical—experience of my life, we put on our clothes and slipped into a familiar quiet that I wished my friends would have understood I craved regularly. Somehow, Florence is able to read these needs of mine—something about the tranquility of her nature soothing some tightness in my innermost being.

While Florence does some embroidery, interpreting the meadow onto her hoop, I lie back on the blanket, contemplating how *alive* my magic feels out here, and even manage some shut-eye in the shade of the old oak tree—another first for me.

When I wake, the sun is much higher in the sky and partially obscured by some threatening clouds.

"We best be on our way to the house before the heavens open up," I tell Florence, breaking the long, comfortable silence with my strangely formal words. I don't understand why I am like this, but this is new territory for us, and I'm not sure how to navigate it.

Being her usual, sunny-side-up self, Florence smiles affably and nods, already starting to gather her supplies. My magic itches under my skin, and the desire to help her takes over. With my mage hand, I reach for her supplies, gently taking them from her hands and placing them in the basket I brought, while I scratch at my scalp.

Florence stills and watches on, her lips slightly parted as the various items float through the air and settle in the basket.

"You're amazing, you know that?" Florence breathes.

Unable to help myself, my mage hand reaches out and dusts along her jaw, moving up to her temple and rake my hand into her hair. Florence follows the movement and tilts her head, nuzzling into my hand for a second before I run it all the way through her silky hair down to the ends around her lithe waist.

Florence's eyes pop open, and she rights her head.

"It was you, wasn't it?" she says accusingly. Or maybe it's just me reading the accusation in her tone.

I instantly recall my mage hand and lift all three hands up in surrender, ready to apologize for whatever I've done to offend her.

"The other night. On the patio. I thought it was the wind, but it was your magic that touched me, wasn't it?"

My shoulders slump and I stare at her dainty feet while I gather the courage to admit what I did.

I clear my throat and say, "Please accept my most humble apology. I should not have touched you without your consent."

Florence ducks her head to catch my eye. "It's okay. I'm not angry, just surprised is all. I thought it was the wind and it felt so nice to have that touch. But if I'm being completely honest, I kind of wish you would have told me then."

"You do?"

"Well, yeah. It's a pretty big deal, but I understand if you didn't trust me with such a big secret." The sting of my betrayal becomes apparent and I realize I misread the accusation earlier. It was hurt in her voice.

Before I can come up with an adequate excuse, Florence continues, "But that's all water under the bridge now. Onwards and upwards, right?" She beams at me and, in that second, my whole world stands still.

What I thought was the bond driving me to her might actually be my own feelings. Florence sees me and doesn't judge me. Just accepts me with all the numerous flaws in my character. She *understands* me.

There is still no way things could work between us. While she can provide what I need, I am unable to give her what she needs. My whole future is planned. Arranged. Expected. I have responsibilities.

For her own sake as much as mine, I need to keep my distance. I need to protect her from me.

For a short time, I allowed myself to imagine life with her—laughing, playing, loving. But it is unfair to lead her on when I can't give her what she deserves. I need to step back. Today was as far as it can go.

Resolute in my decision, I wordlessly gather everything and trudge toward the forest. Florence's light footsteps remain a few steps behind me until we're almost at the house.

Stopping in front of the front door, I turn and look at her. I take the opportunity to study Florence's graceful features—the pink on the apples of her cheeks, the glimmer of light in her kind eyes. I memorize the tiny details of her body—like how the hollow at the base of her throat lines up perfectly with the Cupid's bow on her rosy lips, the light smattering of freckles dusting her shoulders that I want to kiss one by one.

The urge to wrap my arms around Florence and not to push her away has my chest cracking open and my heart ripping in two.

Try as I might, I can't shield all the emotions she has awoken in me.

I make sure to look directly into her bright eyes when I say, "Thank you for sharing today with me. It was... amazing. *You* are amazing." My voice cracks at the end and I have difficulty swallowing around the odd pain in the back of my throat, but I forge on. "Of course, we cannot allow this to happen again. Because the bond might intensify," I add hastily.

Florence sees right through my excuse and her smile turns sad, understanding. She crosses one arm over her torso and holds her elbow.

"It's okay. It was fun. For today only. A good memory."

The sadness in the air is so acute that I don't know if it's her emotions I'm feeling, or my own. Time seems to slow down as Florence's eyes brim with tears and a single one escapes and tracks down her cheek. Unable to resist, I cup her face with my mage hand and wipe the warm drop away.

"You are more exquisite than I could have imagined, Florence Everly. Perfect. Beautiful. So deserving of everything I cannot give you: love, affection, attention, the world. You deserve to have it all, and more."

With a quivering voice, Florence says, "You are a good male, Adelbert. I wish you could see yourself the way I see you. You're going to make someone very happy one day."

Then she goes into the house, leaving me outside.

I allow myself a couple of shaky breaths before I steel my spine and head to my study, hating myself more with each step I take.

The door shuts behind me with a snick, and I lean against it before sinking to the floor. Resting my head against the door, I stare up at the ceiling and let all my thoughts run through my mind so I can properly process what happened today.

I can't allow myself to form any kind of attachment to Florence. I need to remain firm on this. Despite how perfect she was this afternoon, it can't happen again. If my desire for her increases only marginally or if the bond strengthens, she could get stuck here.

What would that mean for the future of Alberad? What would that mean for me?

I'll make sure Florence is comfortable, taken care of. I'll be kind and considerate, as much as is expected from a host to a guest.

We'll travel to the opening of her sister's store and maybe the bond will have broken before Florence even has to return. It will simplify everything.

I take a fortifying breath and stand up, bracing myself to run through all the exercises I want to demonstrate at my presentation. For some unknown reason, my magic feels weaker tonight. It could be because I exerted too much energy with Florence, but I didn't feel tired then. My magic didn't even feel strained.

I will keep practicing and practicing until I have perfected everything and prove that what was thought to be dormant magic in elves, has once again been awakened.

28

Florence

Cece!" My sister shouts and flings herself into my arms. I hug her back so hard, I'm afraid I might bruise her ribs. Dede knows how much I need this touch so she doubles down and squeezes harder.

No matter how hard I try, it's impossible to stop the tears from coming. I let them run freely down my face, unwilling to let go of my sister.

Everett sent his plane for us the day after the meadow incident. Adelbert and I were polite to each other as we took seats on opposite sides and I pretended to instantly fall asleep. Lindsey offered to feed Sir Purrington while we're gone and to send updates, but we'll only be here for a night before we have to go back again.

"I missed you," I say into Dede's neck, wetting her hair with my tears. Lowering my voice, I add, "You guys totally just fucked before we got here, didn't you?"

"Shh. You can't call a girl out like that right when you arrive," Sadie says in mock outrage, tears still thick in her voice. "At least give me some conversation foreplay first."

I hold her shoulders and lean back so I can look at her face. "Sorry I ruined your makeup." I try to fix it by wiping some of the mascara under her eyes.

Dede shrugs. "It might have been ruined before you got here," she says with a devilish smirk and a quick glance to Everett. "Either way, worth it." Dede winks at me and I laugh as she wipes my tears away. It feels good to laugh and to be reunited with my sister.

"Hi, Cece," Everett says and holds out his arms for me.

"Hi, Ev." I easily step into my brother-in-law's friendly embrace and hug him back. It's the first time I have physically touched a male in over two months. Despite the kindness of the gesture, I can't help but wish it were Adelbert's arms instead.

From the corner of my eye, I notice the muscle jumping in Adelbert's jaw and the way he crosses his arms over his chest as he pretends not to watch us.

I know Adelbert is attracted to me, and I acknowledge that he won't let it go anywhere, but I don't want to hurt him either.

I step back from Everett's platonic embrace and turn to Dede. "Tour?"

"Yes!" Over my shoulder, Dede says to the males, "It's sister time now. You boys play nice on that side of the store. Try not to listen in so we can gossip freely, please. Thank you," she singsongs the last word and blows a kiss to Everett, then takes my hand and practically skips in her stilettos to the far side of the store.

The store's opening party is tomorrow and everyone from the island will be traveling to celebrate with Dede and Everett. We arrived a day early so we could hang out with them alone. In a rare moment of vulnerability, Adelbert explained that he's not in a good headspace to see all of his friends and their bonded partners, but he wants to make the trip for me.

I'm just happy to be here and get whatever time I can get with my sister.

Dede leads me by the hand toward a giant display of glittery shoes arranged in a rainbow. It's so pretty and the most Sadie-thing I've ever seen. She talks me through the arrangement, the store's layout, and shows me the luxurious dressing rooms—with one conspicuously closed curtain. We settle on a velvet bench on the far side of the store and look out at Sadie's Sweethearts.

"Your dream came true," I say wistfully, my eyes misting again with happiness for my sister. I take Dede's hands in mine and squeeze them. "I'm so proud of you."

Dede gives me a watery smile. "Everett helped. A lot."

"I know how much he did, especially financially and I don't want to take away from that. But, don't let his involvement diminish your accomplishments. This is your dream. *Your* talent. *Your* vision. Your mate just… facilitated it," I say, gently determined to make her acknowledge how much she has achieved in such a short amount of time.

"That's putting it mildly, but I get what you're saying. He's been so supportive. We make a really good team," Dede sighs out dreamily with a goofy grin on her face.

"I know. The fates really got it right with you two. Perfect match." I really mean it. There is not one person who has ever understood my sister the way Everett does, who indulges all of her whims.

"Talking about the fates and matches…" Dede gives me a pointed look and inclines her head toward the door where the males are deep in conversation. "What's the latest with you and Adelbert? You two are giving me major Beauty and the Beast vibes."

"What do you mean?"

"Tale as old as time," Dede sings. "You two… up there in the house… secluded in the middle of the forest… You're sweet Beauty, and Adelbert—obviously—is the Beast," she explains like I should have connected the dots easily.

I shake my head and laugh at the notion. "Only difference is there's nothing beastly about him, unless you're counting his grouchiness."

"Well, I thought Everett looked human enough, but let me tell you, there's *nothing* human about my mate."

I pretend to cover my ears. "Too much information." Lowering my hands, I sigh and continue more somberly, "There's not much to report about me and Adelbert."

Dede raises her eyebrows and asks slowly, "Do you want there to be something to report?"

"I don't know, Dede," I admit with a sad grimace and slump back against the seat.

Dede shifts and twists her body toward me, tucking a leg under her to give me her undivided attention.

Studying my face, she says more than asks, "You like him, don't you?"

My heart aches at the question and my mouth turns down. I lift my hands to cover my face, mumbling out my admission from behind my fingers, "How could I not?"

Dede reaches for my hands and lowers them. I expect to find sadness in her eyes, compassion even. Instead, my sister arches one brow and smirks at me.

"Ever thought about just jumping him one day? Or waiting for him in the kitchen with nothing but an apron on? Some women might have used their wily ways to convince him about how right the fates are."

I choke out a laugh and bat a hand at her. "Ha! That might work for you and Ev, but it's not like that for us."

Dede turns serious and rubs a soothing thumb on top of my hand.

"What's it like?" Her voice is soft and earnest, her eyes filled with empathy.

I don't want her to be unnecessarily hard on Adelbert, so I explain to her the best I can why he won't take me as a mate.

"Do you know what Adelbert's job is?" I ask.

"I know he's an academic, and one day he'll take over at Alberad," Dede answers.

I nod. "And where's his house?"

"In the Black Forest, next to Alberad." This time her statement sounds more like a question.

"Which of those things did he choose for himself?"

Dede narrows her eyes as she considers the question. "I'm assuming neither. But, isn't he happy?"

"I don't think he's brave enough to answer that question," I say sadly. "The point is, he's never made a decision for his own life. His lineage dictates his future. And now, I'm just another thing that the fates have dictated for him too."

Dede's eyes widen and a breath whooshes out of her. "Oh. That's complicated." She scrunches up her nose and adds haughtily, "I still think he's dumb for not worshiping at your feet already. But I get where you're coming from."

I sigh deeply. A tiny part deep within me agrees with her, but I'd never do something against Adelbert's wishes.

My eyes drift to the males on the opposite side of the store, valiantly pretending we're not here with them.

Taking in Adelbert's tall frame, the way he crosses his arms across his chest and tilts his head to concentrate diligently on whatever Everett is telling him, I tell my sister, "There's so much more to him than what he shows the world. So much depth. Warmth. Kindness. Strength. He notices things about me that others don't. He leaves me sweaters to wear every morning. He makes me tea. He appreciates my art. He cooks dinner for me. Every night. I can always count on him."

Dede whispers the question I have not allowed myself to consider, "What if he chooses you?"

I turn to look at my sister. Hope brims in her eyes but I squash it when I answer, "I can't allow myself to dream, Dede. We're checking if the bond might dissipate with this trip. If it's gone by tomorrow then I'll go back to Kentucky. Otherwise, I'll be back in Germany again tomorrow evening."

"Do you want the bond to break?"

My smile is wan. "Show me a dress I should get."

Dede narrows her eyes and points a playful finger at me. "I see what you did there, but I'm going to let it slide. Come on, I've already picked one out for you."

I try not to pay any attention to Adelbert, but a strange tether keeps me aware of his position in the building at all times as Everett shows him around.

After a day spent touring the store and for the sisters to catch up, we all head to Everett's house. The women sit out on the balcony to watch the sunset and the Strip light up—apparently one of Sadie's favorite sights—while Everett and I are in the kitchen downstairs, preparing bibimbap for dinner.

"So, have you made a move on Florence yet?" Everett asks abruptly, trying to catch me off guard.

"That is none of your business," I grumble as I julienne the carrots.

"So, that's a yes?" Everett tilts his head and places his head in my field of vision.

I move the carrots aside and start on the zucchini, frustrated by how weak my magic feels here. Not like I would use my mage hand in front of Everett and Sadie, but it feels like a missing limb.

"We have not physically touched. At all," I finally answer.

In front of me, Everett leans an elbow on the island and props his chin in his hand. "I feel like you're avoiding the question, but I'll allow it. Does Florence know how much you like her?"

I scoff, "What? How could you possibly deduce that?" I keep my movements smooth and unaffected, but I know Everett can hear my racing heart.

His trademark smirk appears on his face and he leans back, crossing his arms over his chest in a very arrogant manner. "You have not stopped staring at her since you arrived. Every time she laughs, your head snaps up. Even when you pretend you're listening to what I'm saying, your eyes always glance back to wherever she is in the room."

My eyes almost flick up to the stairs where I can sense Florence is, but I refocus my effort on chopping the zucchini into fine strips. The pull to her has become stronger with each hour that has passed since our dinner on the *Terrasse*. I inhale deeply and put the knife down to brace my hands against the counter, hanging my head forward.

Everett's brows furrow and he turns pensive. "I'm pretty sure Florence likes you too. Why don't you guys give it a shot and see if there's something there?"

"I can't." The answer is ripped from my throat. "She deserves to be happy somewhere with a nice human man who can give her everything I cannot."

Everett straightens his stance and his hands ball into fists. Shaking his hands as if he is struggling not to shake me, he hisses, "Stop being so fucking self-sacrificing. Don't you think the fates know what they're doing? You two were put together for a reason." Everett slaps a hand to his chest, passion fueling his words. "Look at me and Sadie. Perfect fit. No one else gets me on so many levels. And I'm sure it's the same with Florence. But that woman will never make the first move because—" he points his index finger at me to emphasize his next words "—she. Gets. You."

Not waiting for a response from me, Everett charges ahead. "Do you know how hard it was for Florence to come to Vegas? She misses Sadie so much, but she never asked you to fly her out here, because she knows the pressure you put on yourself. That your father puts on you. And she doesn't want to add to that pressure. Because... she understands *you*."

His words hit me like a sledgehammer to the heart, and my stomach somersaults. My body slumps and my chin dips to my chest.

Everett rounds the island between us and places a comforting hand on my shoulder.

"You deserve happiness, Bertie. I literally hear your heart beat faster when she smiles. Your head might tell you one thing, but, just this once, let your heart lead. Allow yourself to feel love."

Whispering, I confess, "That first moment I saw her on the island, it felt like my breath was snatched right out of my chest. She dazzled me with her beauty, but it's her soul that has enchanted me."

"So do something the fuck about it," Everett says with a friendly slap to my shoulder.

Imploring him to understand, I ask, "How can I? How can I limit her to a life in the forest? Being tied to me means she's stuck there. I don't have anything to offer her."

Everett takes a step back and his brows draw down over his eyes. "You really don't see what a catch you are, do you?"

I scoff and reach for the zucchini, ready to get back to chopping vegetables. Shaking my head, I put it down again.

"What do you mean? I'm a grumpy elf without a sense of humor whose future has already been determined."

Everett comes to stand next to me and leans a hip against the island.

"Has it?"

I turn to look at him. "You know it has."

Tapping his fingers on the tabletop, he scrunches up his face then relaxes it as he shakes his head. "The fates just intervened and gave you a mate. Chosen from among billions of people across the world. One special person. And you're choosing to turn your back on her for some kind of altruistic reason? Have you ever considered asking Florence what she thinks about being chosen? That by not choosing her you've essentially taken her choice away from her too? Think on that."

Without another word, Everett leaves the kitchen while I'm frozen in place. My whole world just turned upside down.

I thought I had it all figured out.

Maybe I don't.

30

Adelbert

A day later I'm back in my study at home after our whirlwind trip to Las Vegas, feeling more conflicted than ever.

I plop down onto the carpet with my back against the bookcase. Resting my forearms on my propped-up knees, I hang my head forward between my shoulders, recounting each interaction I've had with Florence since I've met her.

Watching Florence interact with her sister in Vegas—constantly hugging, touching, holding hands... smiling and laughing—made me feel even more inadequate for not being able to do any of that for her. She looked positively radiant.

Sadie had packed up all of Florence's belongings in Kentucky and what she did not return to Germany with, has been put in storage.

Now that she has a suitcase full of her own warmer clothes, she hardly has need for my sweaters. Knowing I won't be seeing her with the rolled-up sleeves sends a pang of discomfort through me. Soon, she won't have any need for me at all.

The entire trip, from the moment we boarded Everett's plane that he sent for us, at the store, their home, and on the way back, Florence did a terrific job at acting as if everything was fine between us. Not that Everett or Sadie bought the ruse, but they didn't call us out in front of each other. Everett did a good job of that on his own.

I took part in every conversation, keeping my replies polite but curt, as every waking thought centered on Florence.

I let out a deep sigh and look up just as the cat waltzes into the room and sits down directly in front of me, staring at me with the most judgmental eyes.

"Yeah, yeah, cat. I know. Judge all you want. I'm judging myself, too," I tell the lazy creature who has now basically become a resident in my home.

The cat tilts his head and his tail flicks behind him, his agitation clear.

I let my head thud back against the hard shelves as I replay the scene in the meadow and the pivotal moment when I pushed Florence away.

When that tear raced down her cheek, it stabbed at a part so deep in my chest, I thought it couldn't be touched.

In front of me, an oddly disturbing growl comes from the cat and I sit up straighter.

"What's wrong?"

The cat's ears flick forward and backward and his tail picks up speed as it lashes against the floor.

"I find your behavior alarming. I do not know what to do with you. Go find Florence," I say and wave at it, trying to shoo it out the door so I can wallow in peace.

The cat yowls again, stretching the sound to a frightening degree and stalks off to the window, pacing up and down in front of it while a beastly sound rumbles from him.

For the first time, I notice how dark the afternoon has gotten. The rain starts to batter against the window panes and lightning flashes in the distance.

How did I not notice this earlier?

With an icy hand squeezing around my heart, I turn back to the cat.

My pulse races and my eyes threaten to bulge out of their sockets as I shake my head, already refusing to acknowledge the truth.

"Where is she?" I scream at the cat who looks just as distressed as me, hair rising on the back of its neck as it keeps up its pacing.

"Sir Purrington, I swear—" I don't manage to finish my sentence as Sir Purrington darts out of my study and races down the hallway. I chase after him, searching the wards and finding the answer I fear.

I'm out the front door faster than I've ever moved, instantly soaked as I run for the edge of the clearing that Florence favors. The icy rain intensifies with every breath that saws in and out of my lungs and I will my limbs to move faster.

Another bolt of lightning splits the sky and illuminates the grounds, helping me spot her white dress through the sheets of rain pummeling down on me.

The wind whips against me and harsh drops lash me from all sides as I fight my way across the clearing toward Florence, rumbling thunder urging me hurry.

When I get close enough to her that my voice can carry above the downpour, I shout, "What are you thinking being out here?! It's a storm!" I'm furious and I don't care about sounding nice. She can get hurt.

Florence's clothing is plastered to her skin, her long hair clinging to her face and arms as she bends forward to cradle her embroidery to her, doing her best to keep it dry.

"My dress... is snagged... on something. I'm... trying... to untangle... it," she stutters with chattering teeth while tugging gently on the skirt.

"Fuck your dress!" I shout.

"But—"

Florence doesn't get to finish her sentence as I bend down and fist the fabric, ripping it free from the underbrush.

"Your life is more important than a fucking dress."

Lightning flashes again and thunder follows way too soon, mimicking my racing heart, intensifying everything I'm feeling, as Florence stares at me in shock. Before she can say anything else, I surge forward and kiss her.

I kiss Florence with everything I've got.

All my frustration.

All my passion.

31

Florence

Adelbert is kissing me.
He's *kissing* me!
And I'm kissing *him*.

Adelbert

The rain comes down hard around us but in this moment, everything ceases to exist besides Florence.

I cradle her face between my palms and take a moment to drink her in while her arms wrap around my back, holding me close.

Unable to stop myself, I go back for another kiss, capturing her mouth and letting my tongue slide in. Florence's tongue meets mine and our kisses get greedier.

My hands glide across her wet skin, moving to her shoulders, her arms, threading into the hair at the base of her neck. Little mewls escape from her and my grip tightens, wanting, *needing* her closer.

Florence fists the back of my shirt and pulls me into her so our bodies are flush, as eager as I am to devour one another.

Thunder and lightning go off around us and the rain pelts us with its cold, sharp needles, but I can't seem to tear myself away from our hungry kisses and roaming hands. Yet, with unnatural inner strength and the desire to keep her safe trumping my body's needs, I'm finally able to ease my lips from Florence's and I rest my forehead against hers. Breathing hard, I skim my hands down her neck and arms, moving to her waist, then around to her lower back.

"Let's get you inside, Liebling," I say into her ear, my voice barely audible above the pouring rain.

I hoist Florence up by the back of her thighs and her legs wrap around my waist like we've done this a thousand times before. She throws her head back and laughs with absolute delight as I marvel at how perfectly we fit, how perfect she is for me.

There's no use denying how I feel about her. That this was always going to happen. That I was only delaying the inevitable. I knew she was meant to be mine the moment I saw her on that island, but I fought it every second of the day. Only blaming the bond for my attraction.

Not anymore.

I stride quickly toward the house with Florence in my arms, her breath warm against my neck as she nuzzles into me. Even though I can't see it, I can feel her smiling and it is utterly contagious. I sport my own grin as her sunshine radiates through the rain, warming me up from the inside in ways I long to reciprocate.

Lightning lights up the sky again and I pick up my pace, wanting to get Florence safe and dry from the storm.

When I step onto the porch, I take quick note of Sir Purrington waiting in the dimly lit entryway and it's as if he gives me a subtle nod of approval before he saunters off somewhere.

That cat is smarter than I've been giving him credit for.

"What were you thinking?" I ask Florence when we cross the threshold.

I slide her down my body and pin her to the wall with my hips. Shutting the front door behind us, I blink as we're plunged into semidarkness, unwilling to live without the sight of Florence's face before me for even a second.

Rain splatters against the windows, drumming a sound that rivals the beating of my heart.

"I embroidered something new to the hem of my dress this morning and I wanted to save it," she says sheepishly, arms still slung around my shoulders and fingers toying with the hair at my nape.

"At the risk of your life?"

"It was sentimental," Florence says with a tiny shrug.

"What was?"

Florence bites her lip and traces a button on my shirt, her gaze focused on the movement of her finger.

"Our picnic. I wanted to remember it so I embroidered some cornflowers into my dress."

"I'll sew your cornflowers myself next time. I can't lose you," I say vehemently, grabbing her face so she's looking directly at me and understands how serious I am.

"Okay," she breathes, as if not certain what to make of my declaration.

Florence's eyes are wide as she stares up at me with open vulnerability and she stretches onto her toes to place a featherlight kiss on my lips. My heart ricochets against my chest as emotions I have not ever allowed myself to feel rush through my body, setting off all kinds of reactions.

A tingling sensation works its way from underneath my skin, spreading out from the center of my chest, rippling through my body, all the way down to my toes.

The house's wooden floorboards creak and groan as if in answer and my vision narrows until I can only see Florence.

Beautiful Florence with her flushed cheeks and parted lips, patiently waiting for me.

"You are so enchanting, Liebling," I whisper to the woman who has had my heart in a vise grip for weeks, even though I hadn't allowed myself to fully acknowledge it.

"You're going to have to tell me what that means."

"I will, but later. Right now I want to fuck you until you scream my name."

Florence grins at me with a little mischief dancing in her eyes.

"I'd like to see you try."

Unwittingly, a laugh bursts out of my chest and Florence's

smile grows even brighter.

"There are those dimples. I missed them." She reaches up and frames my face, her thumbs brushing over the indentations in my cheeks.

"Only yours," I say, meaning it.

Florence's breath hitches and she stills. I lean my forehead against hers and time suspends as we breathe each other in. The weight of the moment is almost tangible, enclosing us in our own bubble of safety while the rain continues to pound against the house.

Lightning cracks outside and it jolts us into action.

Simultaneously, our mouths find each other and our kisses become voracious.

Florence's hands move to the buttons of my shirt, her cold fingers fumbling in the dim light with the wet material, sending goose bumps careening across my skin despite the way my flesh burns for her. I reach behind me and pull the drenched shirt off my back and it hits the ground with a wet splosh.

I reach for her sodden dress and tear it up and off her body with quick efficiency, throwing it behind me while I guide her deeper into the house.

The rest of our clothing leaves a trail in the hallway as we stumble toward my bedroom, devouring each other with eager kisses. Mouths almost fused together, our limbs tangle as we caress every bit of flesh we can reach.

I spin, barely feeling the sharp pain that shoots up my hip as I hit the corner of a table. The piece of furniture rattles, then settles as I push us onward.

Florence's breath whooshes from her as I press her to a wall, needing a moment to feel her body fully against mine. With a light nip on my bottom lip, she shoves me back, moving us toward the bedroom.

A crash sounds a second before my shoes crunch on the broken bits of a very expensive vase. I didn't even feel myself hit the credenza it was on.

It doesn't matter. Nothing matters but the woman in my arms.

Needing to get closer again, I press Florence's naked body up against the closest wall with mine and she hikes a leg over my hip, just as needy as I am.

I dip my head and nip along her neck, licking a stripe across it to ease the sting and Florence moans in response, hips rocking toward me, searching for friction I know she desperately needs.

"I don't think I can wait until we get to the bedroom," I rasp out, hands moving over her flesh, caressing, kneading.

"I hope not," Florence pants with blunt nails digging into my back. "If you don't fuck me right now I might combust."

"Take my cock and guide me home, Liebling."

Florence reaches down between us and I groan at the feeling of her soft hand wrapping around my aching cock. She gives my cock a squeeze and my hips buck forward.

"Liebling, please," I grit out and grab her thigh, hitching it higher and opening her up to me.

"Since you asked so nicely," Florence purrs and guides me into her warm, wet pussy.

I drive forward painstakingly slowly but don't stop until I'm fully sheathed. I hold absolutely still, afraid I'll come too soon from the exquisite feel of her, and also to give her a moment to adjust.

Florence's head thuds against the wall behind her, her eyes closed and her chest heaving.

"Adelbert, you feel so good, baby," Florence moans and something in my chest takes flight.

"Say my name again," I demand hoarsely, needing her to say my name while I make her mine.

Florence opens her eyes, her gaze half-lidded and looking just as affected as I am.

"Adelbert." Never has my name sounded so sweet and I'm

afraid there is zero possibility of me ever growing tired of hearing her say it in that breathy tone.

"Whose pussy is this?" I growl.

"Yours."

"Whose cock is this?"

"Mine," she says fiercely and squeezes around me.

"All yours, Florence. Now, let's see how loud I can make you scream."

And then I'm thrusting hard, branding Florence from the inside out the way she has branded herself on my very soul.

I lift her up and bring her hips away from the wall, angling her so my cock can hit her G-spot at just the right angle that is sure to make her scream.

It works perfectly.

Florence rides me just as hard as I'm fucking her, mewling, panting, moaning, and soon she starts tightening around my cock.

Knowing she doesn't like to be edged, I keep my rhythm exactly as it is and encourage her through my own panting, "Look how well you're riding my cock, Liebling. It's like it was made for you. Now, I want you to come and scream my name, knowing you belong to me."

My words have the desired effect and Florence clenches around me, throwing her head back and screaming my name. It only takes two more thrusts for me to find my own release, and I fall over the edge with her, steadying us with one hand braced against the wall and my other arm wrapped around Florence's waist while I come.

It's like my soul is being pulled from my body and into Florence's as pleasure surges through me, twining around every fiber of my being until it shudders out of my cock.

Breathing hard, I collapse against her, resting my head in the crook of her neck as I wait for my heartbeat to return to a sustainable rhythm.

"Good thing I have an IUD," Florence pants.

"I take a tonic too. Double coverage," I reply breathlessly.

Florence's chest heaves against mine, her hard nipples jutting into my bare chest while a hand gently glides through my hair.

"I've always wanted to do this," Florence whispers once her breath is a little steadier.

"What? Fuck in a hallway?"

"No, you silly goose." Florence giggles. "I've always wanted to see if your hair was as soft as I thought it was."

"And is it?" I ask and dare a glance up at her.

She smiles serenely down at me and nods.

"It's even better."

Then, Florence places a gentle kiss on my forehead and my heart just about grows two sizes.

After the most passionate sex of my life, Adelbert takes me to his bedroom where we shower and he dresses me in one of his sweaters, which just so happens to be my favorite one.

"What are those?" I ask Adelbert and point to the gray pants he just slipped on.

"Sweatpants," he answers hesitantly and pauses his movements.

"Adelbert Alberad," I chastise playfully and saunter over to him, "why is this the first time I'm seeing them?"

"Um..." Adelbert looks genuinely confused and I walk my fingers up his naked torso until I cup his cheek.

Staring into his silver eyes, I explain cheerfully, "If you had worn these earlier I think I might have had to do some very naughty things to you." I boop his nose with my forefinger and turn around, leaving a stunned Adelbert in my wake.

"Naughty things?" Adelbert huskily asks the empty room as I make my way toward the kitchen, humming my favorite tune. "Like what?"

"Cook me dinner and I'll show you," I call then giggle as Adelbert rushes after me, his footsteps thudding across the wooden floorboards.

I try to speed away, but two strong arms band around me from behind and I laugh as Adelbert hugs me to him. I turn my head so I can see his face and the joy etched on his features makes me giddy.

"Hi, baby," I whisper over my shoulder.

"I never thought I'd say it, but I like it when you call me that," Adelbert whispers back.

My eyes widen when I realize I said it out loud.

Adelbert kisses my temple.

"It's cute."

"You don't mind getting a cute nickname?" I ask and turn around in his arms so I can fully face him.

"From you, no. I like it. Liebling."

My breath catches at the sound of that nickname again and something inside me unravels when Adelbert stares at me like this. Like the mask he always wears has finally come off and I can see a glimpse of his warm heart that he hides from everyone. Adelbert's brows aren't scrunched up, his mouth isn't turned down, and his jaw isn't tight. For the first time, he looks relaxed. At peace.

I splay my fingers across his chest, tracing invisible patterns and ask, "Care to tell me what that one means?"

Adelbert gives me a soft smile. "Darling."

"That's so sweet. I like that," I sigh in contentment.

With a voice full of affection, Adelbert elaborates, "But it also means 'favorite.' You're my favorite person, Florence Everly."

My heart skips a beat and it feels like a kaleidoscope of butterflies has just been set free in my stomach. I melt in Adelbert's arms and feel myself fall in love with him in that exact moment.

Maybe I've always loved Adelbert a little but never had the guts to really examine my feelings. But this, right here, right now, stamps the final seal on my heart, ensuring that I never want to leave his side.

"You can call me that any day." Then I lean up so I can press my lips against his.

Adelbert walks us backward until we're in his bedroom again. This time we explore each other's bodies slowly and tenderly until we're both sated and boneless.

When we enter the kitchen, it's with ravenous appetites for real food and not just for each other.

I start walking toward my usual seat but Adelbert snakes an arm around my waist and draws me back into him.

"And where do you think you're going?" Adelbert says and runs his nose along the column of my neck, making happy goose bumps dance down my arms.

"My spot, so I can drool over you while you cook," I state, nuzzling back into him and luxuriating in all the physical touch I'm getting. It's like I've been running on empty for so long that I didn't realize how much I needed human contact, but since that first kiss in the rain—which I'm totally going to embroider—he has filled my touch tank to overflowing, yet I can't get enough. If I had it my way, I'd be gluing myself to Adelbert's side for as long as he can stand me.

Adelbert huffs, "I don't think I'll be able to get anything done with you so far away from me."

When I turn my head to look at him, there's an actual pout on his face. He's so cute with his puffed-up lips and knit brows.

"Is my baby feeling a bit needy?" I tease.

Do other elves also secretly crave touch and affection? I might need to secretly plot how to surprise the next elf I meet with a cuddly hug, just in case they don't know how to ask for it.

"Very," Adelbert answers solemnly.

"We can't have that now, can we?" I step out of his hold. Spreading my arms, I add brightly, "Show me where you want me."

"How about right next to me at the counter? I want to teach you how to make *Kaiserschmarrn*."

"I have no idea what that is, but it sounds great to me. Every single thing you've made so far has been absolutely delicious."

"I'm glad you like my cooking. It's the one way I can show you that I care when my words fail me." In a softer voice, he adds, "If you haven't noticed, I'm not very good at expressing my feelings."

"You don't have to worry about being perfect around me or saying the right words. I can see your heart and it's beautiful. That's enough for me."

"I want to be more for you."

"You're enough. You're perfect."

"I'm—"

I cut Adelbert off with a kiss, not wanting him to argue any further, hoping my words will seep into his brain and marinate until he believes them as much as I do.

Before the kiss can deepen and we end up in the bedroom again, or perhaps the kitchen floor, I take a step backward and beam at Adelbert.

"I can get used to kissing you."

"I hope so."

My legs turn to jelly and I make a conscious effort to lock my knees before I fall on my butt.

Am I swooning? I think I might be.

"You can't just go saying things like that," I scold lightly. "You've got to warn a girl."

"My apologies," Adelbert says but the dimples in his cheeks give his amusement away. "Do you know how to divide eggs?"

Tilting my head to the side, I give that some thought then ask, "Divide? Won't they break if I divide them?"

Those delectable dimples deepen as Adelbert's smile stretches.

"I see we're going to be spending a lot of time going through some basics."

I prop my hands on my hips and tilt my head to the other side.

"Basics?"

"Dividing also means separating, as in removing the yolks and setting them aside so we can work with the egg whites first."

"If that is a basic cooking thing, then yeah, assume I know nothing."

Adelbert walks over to me and tips my chin up with a finger until I meet his sincere gaze.

"I like taking care of you, so there's no need for you to learn to do any of this. If you want to, I'll be happy to show you but there's no pressure."

"I want to learn. A little. With you," I say meekly.

"Only if you promise to teach me how to sew cornflowers," Adelbert barters. "I owe you for the dress I ruined."

"Deal." Sighing dreamily, I add, "It was worth it, though."

"I'd like to think so." Adelbert's gaze heats for a second before he shakes his head and replaces the look with a focused one. "Let's learn together."

Adelbert places a kiss on the tip of my nose then takes out a bottle of alcohol from the cupboard behind me.

"Okay. I'll start soaking the raisins in rum and you can gather the rest of the ingredients."

My mood shifts back to excitement and I tell my heart to slow down on the swooning. Food first.

"Teamwork. I like it."

Using his mage hand in combination with his two physical hands, Adelbert sets out bowls and measuring cups and calls out ingredients for me to get out of the pantry.

I set the eggs, flour, sugar, and vanilla on the counter and gather the butter and milk from the fridge.

"Has anyone ever told you that you're really good at multitasking? That's rare for a male," I jokingly state the obvious. Also subtly recalling in the back of my mind how he was able to make me come with that magic hand while stroking himself to completion.

"Not that I recall. Why?"

"Well, you have bowls floating through the air with magic, and your own two hands are doing something completely different, and you're also telling me what to do."

Adelbert shoots me a smirk.

"Hmm... I like the idea of telling you what to do. But you're also a bit bossy in bed. I like it."

My heart stutters at him stating that so plainly and a blush races up my chest and burns my cheeks.

Fingers fidgeting, I mumble, "I don't know why, but it seems that's the only place I can find my backbone and ask for what I want."

Adelbert pauses what he's doing and steps in front of me. Grasping both my hands in his, he says earnestly, "I really like that. I hope you will grow to trust me enough to always tell me what you want, in every aspect."

I offer him a half smile.

"I'm working on it."

"I have a lot to work on too," Adelbert admits.

"Like with your magic? Since the picnic you haven't really used it on me." Then I quickly add, "Not that I've noticed."

Adelbert chuckles lightly and skims his hands up my arms until they're settled on my shoulders. He waits for me to look him in the eye before he speaks with utter sincerity.

"It's actually quite strange, but I haven't really wanted to. When I finally gathered the courage to kiss you, I wanted it to be all *me*. *My* hands touching you. *My* mouth kissing yours. *My* tongue tasting you. *My* cock fucking you," he adds in a sultry tone. "I was greedy. Still am." Adelbert shrugs nonchalantly like this truth didn't just rearrange my brain and everything I thought I had figured out about him.

"You've wanted to kiss before today?" I ask, focusing on that one specific thing.

"For so long."

"Really?"

"Really."

"I didn't know."

Adelbert's smile is a little wistful.

"In a way, I didn't either. Everett gave me a bit more perspective when we were in Vegas. That certainly helped. But when I saw you out in that storm and the thought of losing you, it made me feral. Everything that had been holding me back until that moment was as good as gone. I had to have you."

"No regrets yet?"

"Not a single one."

Adelbert folds me into his arms and hugs me close, swaying softly from side to side. He places a kiss on top of my head and I snuggle closer to him, the way I've wanted to since I arrived in the Black Forest.

I can't help but feel like I'm home. This house. This kitchen. This male. It feels right. It feels like mine.

Meow.

"Sir Purrington!" I exclaim, carefully extracting myself from Adelbert's arms and making a beeline for the cat. I fall to my knees in front of my fluffy friend and stroke his fur as he rubs against me with a contented purr resounding from him

"You must be hungry. Let me get you something to eat."

"Don't worry, I'll get it. I think Sir Purrington deserves a special treat tonight," Adelbert says with a soft smile as he looks at the cat.

I flick my gaze between the pair, picking up on the new energy between them, then do a double take.

"You just called him by his name. Not 'cat.' I'm not complaining, but did I miss something?"

Adelbert's expression turns melancholy for a second, his eyes focused on the cat as he says, "Sir Purrington is the one who alerted me to your whereabouts during the storm. I was so busy wallowing in my study that I didn't notice that you weren't in the house. I'm so sorry."

"Is that true, Sir P? Did you help Adelbert find me?"

Sir Purrington rubs harder against me and I take that as confirmation.

"Thank you, my friend," I whisper to him and scratch under his chin in the exact way I know he likes.

Adelbert places a bowl of salmon in front of Sir Purrington and I swear the cat looks at him with approval before wolfing it all down.

"Where did the salmon come from?" I ask Adelbert, knowing I haven't seen any in the fridge or freezer before.

Adelbert clears his throat and the apples of his cheeks pinken in the most adorable way.

"I, um, may have, um, placed a special rush order with Pixie Parcels as a special treat. To say thank you and all." He rubs a hand through his hair and the pink spreads to the tips of his pointed ears.

"Babyyyy." Butterflies return to my stomach and warmth spreads through my chest. The fact that Adelbert is showing this unguarded side of himself to me makes my eyes prickle and I blink furiously to will the evidence away.

I place a peck on Adelbert's cheek and wash my hands.

"What's the next step?" I ask him and pretend I'm not falling deeper in love with him with every second that passes.

Adelbert bends and places a kiss against my temple and guides me through the steps.

Together, we make the most delicious torn pancakes. He teaches me how to beat egg whites until they're stiff, or until my arm gets so tired that his mage hand has to take over. I marvel at how Adelbert uses his magic to whisk those egg whites until they're stiff enough that he can hold the upside-down bowl over my head and nothing falls out.

We talk and laugh and touch. We share kisses and cuddles and I know I'll never grow tired of doing this exact same thing every day for the rest of my life.

We don't talk about the bond and we don't talk about his presentation. I also don't allow myself to look too far into the future, choosing to revel in the present and getting to know this unencumbered version of Adelbert.

Arms coming around me, Adelbert helps me sprinkle confectioner's sugar over the pulled-apart pancakes.

I feed him the first bite and go to lick some of the stickiness off my finger, but Adelbert reroutes my hand and puts my finger in his mouth instead, licking it clean.

"Delicious," he purrs.

I return the favor.

Soon, we're feeding and licking, until Adelbert decides he's had enough of the *Kaiserschmarrn*, and hoists me up on the counter, drapes my legs over his shoulders, and eats me instead.

It doesn't take long until I come undone and Adelbert's name echoes off the walls as I scream in pleasure, trembling with waves of bliss rolling through me.

When my soul returns to my body, I find Adelbert hovering above me, gently brushing stray hair from my face.

"You're so incredibly beautiful," he mutters.

"So are you," I slur, drunk off orgasms and blissed-out with life.

"Let's get you to bed." Adelbert scoops me up and I sling my arms around his neck.

After a couple of steps I lift my head and point out, "My room is that way."

"Liebling, if you think I'm not keeping you with me then you are sorely mistaken."

"Okay," I sigh contentedly and snuggle closer.

34

Adelbert

I wake up with Florence's naked body curled around mine, her head on my shoulder, arm slung across my waist, and leg draped over my thigh. I glide my fingers through some strands of her pale blonde hair fanned out behind her, admiring how it glows in the morning light streaming in through the gap in my curtain. She looks utterly ethereal.

"Morning," Florence croaks and burrows into me. My heart swells at the move and I realize how natural it feels to have her in my bed, to wake up with her. I swallow around the unexpected lump in my throat.

"Morning, Liebling," I rasp back, lacing our fingers on my chest.

Florence beams up at me with bleary eyes and a strange sensation takes root deep in my gut, setting loose a swarm of butterflies.

She's pure radiant sunshine and I can't help but fall a bit deeper in love with her.

"I like waking up with you," Florence whispers and bites her lip. A faint pink stains her cheeks before she tries to duck her head.

I reach out with my mage hand and tip her chin up so she can see the truth in my eyes.

"I like having you in my bed. Waking up with you. Cooking with you. Living with you." And not knowing if it's appropriate to say it but needing to utter it regardless, I add, "And I really like fucking you."

Florence repositions herself onto her side so she can look at me more directly and I mirror her move.

"This is really fast, isn't it? Two days ago we were in Vegas and acting like polite acquaintances, and now we're here. Sleeping together. Are you still okay with everything that's happened?" she asks, and bites her lip.

I free her lip from her teeth and rub my thumb along the plump flesh, gathering my thoughts before I speak, not wanting to fuck up my explanation or hurt her ever again.

"Please bear with me as I try to explain this. I've been up for a while trying to logic my way through the past twenty-four hours, but I can't. Too many emotions. And for the first time in my life, I don't mean that in a negative sense."

I take a deep breath and rub at the back of my neck while Florence lies absolutely still, patiently waiting for me with a soft, encouraging smile. My heart hammers in my chest at the thought of saying this the wrong way and her misunderstanding me.

I sit up and card my fingers through my hair. Florence copies my move and drapes a sheet over her naked chest. Good thing too, or I'll get distracted by her lovely breasts and then have to lavish them with attention.

Florence reaches out her hand and grips my clammy one.

"Take your time. There's no rush."

My smile is faint but true, bolstered by her kindness.

"The moment I saw you in that storm, the moment I thought there was a chance of losing you, I let go of everything that was holding me back. You have to understand, from the first time I saw you on the island, you felt like mine. I never allowed myself to pursue anything that would be considered selfish or would take me off the course that has been set for my life. Relationships, love, those are—no, were—concepts meant for others. Not for me.

"Since you've moved into this house, I've had the opportunity to get to know you. Not as the person bonded to me by the fates, but as Florence—the amazing, caring, kind, funny, playful, thoughtful person that you are. With every moment spent together in the kitchen, and every conversation, I liked you more. And then there was the picnic."

I pause and inhale slowly through my nose and exhale my nerves with a loud sigh.

"It was like my brain shifted at that point, where I saw the potential of us being together. But I didn't—still kind of don't—feel good enough for you," I admit sheepishly.

"Baby—" Florence tries to interrupt, most probably to comfort or encourage, but I can't let her derail me from admitting my truth. It's time to come clean about it all.

"Hold on," I cut her off. "Let me get this out, Liebling. I think you deserve so much better than I can give you, but I want to try. I want to see you happy and I want to be the reason you are happy.

"Communicating is not my strong suit, as we have established," I say with a wince and rub at my chest. "I beg you to be patient with me. I have spent my whole life wearing a mask and suppressing my feelings. If I say anything that makes you upset, please tell me and give me the chance to fix it, knowing it was a mistake."

I shift so that I'm fully facing Florence and I lace our fingers together.

"I always feel like a dark cloud and you are the brightest ray of sunshine in this world. I don't want you to lose your shine because of me. But when I'm with you, it's like a weight gets lifted off my shoulders, like you somehow pierce through all of my layers and give me a chance to just be me. I like the way I feel when I'm with you and I want you to like the way you feel with me. Please give me a chance to make you happy."

"You know what?" Florence asks and moves to sit cross-legged, tucking the sheet under her arms before taking both my hands and looking me straight in the eyes, a righteous fire burning in her blue pools.

"What?" I ask nervously, my heart doing its best to beat its way out of my chest.

"I wish you could see yourself the way I see you. It may feel like there's a cloud around you, but you aren't a cloud. To me, you're a rainbow. And on days when the cloud gets too heavy, I'll be your umbrella. There's no need to wear a mask around me. I like you cloudy, rainy, as well as the sunny version I got yesterday. I like you, Adelbert. You make me feel seen. I'm so used to taking a back seat to bigger personalities, and I'm totally fine with that because I don't like being the center of attention. But somehow, you make me feel important, like I matter, and you always listen to me."

Florence sits up straighter and squeezes my hands for emphasis. Her brows scrunch up with passion and her words ring with veracity.

"The way you make sure my mornings are perfect. The pastries. The sweaters. The teapot. Cooking dinner for me every night. All the conversations we've had over the months I've been here. The way you show me you care. All of that has added together to show me a version of you that you don't show the world. I feel incredibly lucky," Florence finishes fervidly.

"I'm the one who is feeling lucky," I admit. "Things between us have been building over a long time."

"They really have."

"I do have to say, though, I think the bond is facilitating certain aspects too."

"Yeah? Like what do you think?"

"I think it enhances our connection. Once we acted on our feelings, things moved much faster than they would have for couples without these bonds. It has happened with the other bonded pairs, like Sadie and Everett, too."

"That's true. I know you warned everyone not to have any physical touch in case it strengthens the bond. Looks like all that research was very accurate. There's no way Dede would've just moved in with someone like a week after they met, but with Everett, she said it all felt very natural."

"This is what I want you to understand, Liebling. The bond might be expediting our relationship, but I fell for you all on my own. Without physical contact. Without the bond influencing me. Over months of conversations and getting to know you as the lovely person you are."

I reach over and touch the symbol on her side, tracing the sun, moon, and star aligned over each other, the twin to my marking.

"You know, in my family's culture, it's customary to get a tattoo of the family crest when you are appointed as a professor at Alberad for the first time. For the males, anyway. I have avoided thinking about branding myself with a daily reminder of my responsibilities for so long. When this fated mark showed up on my body, it felt like just another burden I have to carry, another choice taken from me."

Florence's empathy is so sharp that it pierces through my mental barriers for a second before I reinforce them again.

"But know, I would choose *you* over Alberad." I enunciate each word carefully, making sure she understands the weight of the statement.

Florence sucks in a breath, her eyes wide and pulse hammering in her throat.

"Me?"

"You, Florence Everly. You've opened my eyes to so many new things and new possibilities. For the first time, I'm thinking about what my life could look like if I made choices for myself. For *us*. And I'd like to. I don't know what life could be like with me, or what kind of options I have in terms of work if I'm not following the expected life path that's been laid out for me, but it's something

I would like to give some consideration to." Hesitating for a second, I add cautiously, "That is, if you would be interested in exploring such options with me?"

Florence frames my face with her hands, her eyes misty but bright.

"Adelbert Alberad, you are so much more than your name and your legacy. You are a beautiful male, inside and out, and I think I'd just about follow you anywhere. Despite our initial challenges and misunderstandings, I really like living here with you. The forest feels like home and it calls to me on some deeper level, if that makes any sense. I'd never ask you to give anything up for me, so if you want to stay, I'll stay. If you want to go, I'll go. Together."

"You mean that?"

"Why would I not mean it?"

"No strings? No conditions?"

"Baby, come on. It's me." Then Florence does the unthinkable—she straddles my waist and starts tickling me all over. Every inch she can reach gets tickled until I'm a squirming, laughing mess underneath her and her joyous laughter fills the air.

Chest heaving and with a genuine smile stretching across my face, my hands still on Florence's hips. We pause the tickle fight and she props her hands on my bare chest. The air grows thick between us as we just take each other in.

"I love you, Florence."

"I love you too, Adelbert."

"Now guide my cock into your sweet pussy so I can show you how much."

Smile turning wicked, Florence shifts back until my cock is wedged against her wet pussy. She pushes against my chest, wordlessly demanding I stay down while she does the work. I happily oblige her.

Florence rubs herself against my hard length, desperately searching for friction, and letting out little whimpers every time she rolls her hips and the head of my cock hits her clit.

"Do you like that, Liebling? Do you like taking your pleasure while torturing me with this dripping pussy?" I ask Florence, trying to keep my composure and not come undone by the sight and feel of her.

Florence looks magnificent, like a queen on a throne ready to be worshiped, and worship I shall.

"Yes," Florence pants. "This cock is mine. I'll ride it how I want to."

I groan as her warm, soaked core glides smoothly over my cock and my grip tightens on her hips, fingers digging deliciously into her flesh. Watching my woman take charge of her body as well as mine is the sexiest thing I've ever seen.

"All yours. Take what you want, Liebling," I grit out.

Florence is a sight to behold with her head thrown back, hips rocking, and long golden hair swaying behind her.

When her strength starts to wane, I take over, gripping her hips and grinding her against my throbbing cock at the same pace she set.

"Baby, I'm so close," Florence whines. "Don't stop."

"Never," I hiss between clenched teeth. "I'll give my greedy woman exactly what she needs."

I reach for her tits with my mage hand and tweak her nipples, making Florence's whimpers turn into desperate mewling. She closes her eyes and her back arches and I know she's one pinch away from fully flying over the edge.

I angle Florence's hips slightly at just the right time and, with a choked grunt, drive my cock up into her slick pussy.

"Adelbert!" My name escapes from her on a strangled sob. Her thighs shake and eyes roll back as her climax rushes through her body.

Florence pulses around my cock, squeezing me so tight I think I might come instantly. But my focus remains on bringing her pleasure, so I keep pounding into her, hitting her G-spot with every thrust, determined to make her come again.

Flipping us over, I drive into her with complete abandon, spurred on by her moans and the way she's clawing at my back.

I need to be closer to her, connected to her, consumed by her.

The sound of my name falling from Florence's lips keeps me present, my heart beating wildly and my breathing ragged.

This time, when Florence comes, she drags me with her. My grunts mingle with her screams as I shoot my release into her pussy and she flutters around my cock, milking every drop from me.

My arms give out and I roll us to the side as waves of pleasure continue to rack my body and Florence trembles with hers. Bodies limp, I hold her close while our rapid breathing comes down.

We lie there in each other's arms for a long time, whispering sweet nothings, exchanging gentle caresses, brushing sticky hair from foreheads, and bathing in our newly declared love until hunger summons us from our bubble.

CHAT LOG

Sadie: You've been quiet since you got back. Did you finally fuck?

Florence: *zipper-mouth face emoji* *winking face emoji*

Sadie: ...

Florence: *fire emoji* *fire emoji* *fire emoji*

Sadie: !!! *clapping hands emoji* !!!

Florence: *purple heart emoji*

Sadie: *Sparkling heart emoji*

35

Florence

So, what's the plan today?" I ask Adelbert who hasn't stopped staring at me with the most adorable grin firmly affixed to his lips. The way those dimples wink at me from across the kitchen table has got me weak in the knees.

"I find myself to be rather attached to you, so I'll do whatever you want to do," he says and places his hand out, palm up on the table. I put mine in his and he laces our fingers.

I think I might literally be glowing. Since Adelbert kissed me, it feels like my world has shifted on its axis. Like my heart, brain, and soul have all somehow aligned and everything points to him.

"How about showing me all your favorite parts in the house? I still haven't explored every hidden corner, and seeing your bedroom has been a revelation to me."

Adelbert's brows scrunch up and he sits back in his chair, acting like I've just said the weirdest thing.

"A revelation? How so? It's a plain, functional room with a bed and a wardrobe."

"That's exactly my point. There is nothing personal in there. No knickknacks. No paintings. It could be anybody's room. In contrast, my room in this house is done up beautifully with its canopy bed and fancy linens. It looks like it's out of some home decor magazine."

"Ah." Adelbert nods and I note the flicker of sadness in his eyes. "The house belonged to my grandmother and she decorated it according to her heart's content. Her lodgings on campus were according to my grandfather's specifications, so this house was all hers. As you can tell, she had really good taste, though perhaps a bit too baroque for me.

"My bedroom was given to me to do with as I pleased. I've been using it for many years and haven't gotten around to, how can you say, finding my own personal style. At Alberad, Everett took care of the dormitory room we shared, but I didn't really care enough to do something to my bedroom here."

I tilt my head to the side and worry my lip between my teeth as all of that information sinks in.

"Wait. So you've been living in the same bedroom that you've had since you were a child? Why didn't you move into the main suite after she died? Made the house your own?" It doesn't come as a surprise to me that Adelbert hasn't made the house a priority, but to have had the same bedroom for so long and for it not to show a bit of his personality blows my mind.

"It was not exactly a priority for me," Adelbert says, mimicking my thoughts. "My reasoning was that I'd be moving to the Alberad campus anyway. And it's not like I needed that. The bed is just somewhere to sleep. My study, on the other hand, is mine. I have taken the time to decorate it according to my own specifications."

"This is making a lot of sense for me now. It has a very different vibe than the rest of the house. Dede would call the house old-money chic, but your study is masculine and earthy. Your desk especially is beautiful and has its own character."

Adelbert grins and pride shines in his eyes.

"That is my favorite piece of furniture. It was custom-made, handcrafted from oak trees that are local to Germany. The company I worked with has an eco-friendly, holistic approach to carpentry and considers their environmental impact. Plus, their craftsmanship is top-notch."

I lean forward in my seat, intrigued by the thought that went into that single desk. Adelbert has rarely shown interest in many personal things, besides cooking, so I find it fascinating that eco-friendly, handcrafted furniture has him this invested.

"You sound very passionate about that. Would you consider getting more pieces done by them for the house?"

Adelbert shifts forward and takes both my hands in his. His throat bobs on a swallow and vulnerability is evident on his face.

"I would love your input on this too. I'd like for us to redecorate the whole house—together. Really make it *ours*. Maybe that was what I was waiting for all along. For us to turn this house into a home."

A warm, tingling sensation starts up in my chest and works its way down my limbs, goose bumps following in its wake as a strange peace settles over me.

"I'd really like that," I admit on a dreamy sigh. "Can we give Sir Purrington a room too? One with cat trees and comfy pillows? And lots of sunshine he can stretch out in?" The whole vision is clear in my mind's eye.

Adelbert's eyes crinkle in the corners with the radiant smile he's sporting. "Of course. He deserves only the best."

Before I get lost with ideas on interior decorating and paint fights—which I'm sure I'd eventually be able to coax Adelbert into—another thought occurs to me.

"But, what about the lodgings on campus? Would I stay here alone and you live there? I know it's not far away. I'm just curious as to how it would work."

"Firstly, I want to say I'm very pleased that you're asking me this so directly. The Florence from a couple of months ago wouldn't have felt comfortable enough to voice all of her concerns so plainly. Thank you for trusting me enough to be forthright with your worries.

"Now, to answer your questions. I go where you go. I told you, if you don't want to live here, if you're not comfortable at Alberad, I'd be happy to follow you elsewhere. *You* are now my priority. Ensuring your happiness, showing you my love, that is my main focus. Jobs come and go, but I am not willing to lose you."

"Can I ask you another favor?" I ask, voice coming out wet as my eyes start to well up at that declaration from my male.

"Anything," Adelbert says vehemently, squeezing my hand while his mage hand wipes away the single tear that escaped.

"I want you to lower those mental barriers you have in place when you are with me. If you're comfortable with it of course. I want you to feel how happy you make me, how much I love you, and that I am not only saying things to keep the peace."

"Are you sure?" Adelbert asks, eyes nearly bulging out of their sockets.

"I'm sure, my noble Adelbert," I say gently. "I'd like to share this with you. I'll tell you if I want them back up."

Seemingly happy with that, Adelbert nods and a small but hesitant smile quirks his lips. I push all my love and excitement for our future toward him, wanting him to feel my sincerity.

A sudden gasp escapes him and a pink flush steals across his cheeks and up to the tips of his pointed ears. A misty sheen covers his eyes and I squeeze his hand.

"I love you, baby."

"I love you too, Liebling."

Shifting gears, I say, "Quick thought, let's redecorate the whole house, but let's not touch the kitchen. I'm kind of sentimental about it."

"It's funny you say that. My grandmother only updated minor things to improve functionality, but this is largely still the original kitchen from when the house was built."

I trace the wood grain on the table and circle a particularly pretty knot.

"It's like there are memories embedded into it," I remark.

Adelbert uses both hands and follows a line on his side too.

"I think you might be right in a sense. The wood in this house has lots of character, especially in the kitchen." Looking up at me, he adds, "I'd really appreciate your ideas on the rest of the rooms throughout the house too. We can tour through them all today and end in the main suite. That's the first place I want us to put our personal stamp on. Then, we can move into it and start claiming the rest of the house bit by bit too."

I wiggle a bit in my seat and my feet tap giddily.

"That sounds amazing. I'm so excited to dream with you."

Adelbert's face softens and he gives me that devoted look with puppy dog eyes I'll never get bored of.

"Me too. I'm looking forward to hearing all your ideas." Blinking suddenly, he adds, "Before it slips my mind again, remind me to get the book of fairy tales from my grandmother's study. I have been toying with a new theory and I'd like to read up on it, see if there's anything in this book that might substantiate my theory."

"Sure. The one about the branches coming out of the elf's head?"

"Horns," Adelbert corrects with mock sternness.

"Horn branches." I wink and giggle at how funny it is to echo a conversation from so long ago.

Sir Purrington makes himself known with a charming meow and I automatically move back in my seat to make space for him on my lap, but the cat passes me by and heads to Adelbert's side. I swear there's some extra swagger in his walk today.

"Why is he coming to me?" Adelbert asks, eyes darting between me and the cat.

"I think he wants you," I say from behind my hand, trying to stifle a giggle that wants to escape at Adelbert's confused expression.

"Me? Why me?" Adelbert asks, a little flustered as Sir Purrington patiently stands next to his chair.

"Cats are very independent creatures and they make their

own choices. Today, you have been chosen," I attempt to explain cat behavior.

Adelbert does not look convinced.

"Chosen to do what?"

"He wants to sit on your lap. Just lean back a little so he has enough space to jump up," I encourage gently, hoping it will lead to more bonding between my two loves.

"Why would he want me when he can have you?" The question is so unguarded and sweet. I know Adelbert really means it, and I melt a little at that.

"Maybe he now approves of you after you listened to him and saved me?" I suggest.

Adelbert's brow furrows but he silently scoots back. Sir Purrington jumps onto his lap, turns in a circle, and settles down into a ball.

"Pet him," I encourage. "Stroke his fur a little."

"How hard should I press?"

"Just go softly, like you're playing with my hair. He'll let you know if he likes it or not."

A hesitant hand raises and barely touches the cat's fur with the first stroke. Sir Purrington lifts his head a bit and Adelbert's hand freezes.

My heart aches for Adelbert who has been so bereft of affection all his life that he doesn't even know how to pet a cat.

Picking up on my emotion, Adelbert's voice is rich with concern. "Are you sad because Sir Purrington came to me?"

I shake my head and smile fondly at him, silently vowing to make up for all that he's missed. "I'm just sad for the little boy that you were, but I'm so very happy to be part of what we'll call your 'affection' era."

"I'm looking forward to learning all I can from you," Adelbert says. The mushiness of the moment is so sweet, I almost giggle.

I redirect the conversation back to an oddly patient Sir

Purrington.

"Try stroking him again. He likes it a bit harder than that."

"I know someone else who likes it hard too," Adelbert quips under his breath.

I raise my hand to my chest in mock outrage and put on a thick accent.

"Mr. Alberad, dost thou jest?"

"I'll let you know, I do have a joke or two saved for a special occasion."

"I'd love to hear them! Tell me one, pretty please," I pout playfully and lace my fingers together in front of my chest.

"You'll have to work for them. They only come out on special occasions."

"Then work, I shall," I declare. In a softer tone I add, "Don't look now, but that is one happy cat."

In the time it took to have that little exchange, Adelbert had relaxed enough to start petting Sir Purrington the exact way he likes it. The resounding purr filling the kitchen is evident of that.

"Are we pet owners now?" Adelbert asks me, his eyes nearly bugging out of his head as the realization hits.

"I think Sir Purrington adopted us first," I surmise.

Adelbert stares at his hand as he keeps up the petting, seemingly entranced by Sir Purrington's response to his touch.

"Cats are very unique creatures," Adelbert remarks. "I don't personally know any big cat shifters, but I might get in touch with Rollo or Sawyer and ask them to connect me to one."

"Let me get this straight…. you want to call Rollo, your wolf shifter friend, and Sawyer, your bear shifter friend, to ask about a cat shifter because you have a cat now?" I try to follow the thread of his thought process, but I'm not quite sure how it's all connected.

"Yes. Is that strange?" Adelbert asks and shifts his hand to scratch under Sir Purrington's chin, eliciting an even louder purr from the cat.

"And may I ask *why* you want to talk to a big cat shifter?"

"I think a lion or tiger, or maybe even a jaguar shifter can give us some insight into Sir Purrington's mind and some guidance as to his care," Adelbert explains like it's the most sensible step to follow.

"That's... really, really sweet. I appreciate you trying to logic your way through having pets, but he's just a cat. A very smart cat at that. But cats tend to be private. And I can guarantee that if you call anyone with feline genes then they'd be offended if you asked them about a pet," I warn gently, not even willing to imagine how his questions might be received.

"What could possibly offend them about it? Isn't it the responsible thing to do?"

His questions give me better insight into his dynamic with his friends and why Everett took over most of the talking on the island instead of letting Adelbert explain the bonds to a bunch of nervous human women.

"Would Rollo like it if you called him about getting a dog?" I ask, trying to get him to see reason.

"Good point. I'm going to have to keep you around if I don't want to offend people."

"You've got me for as long as you want me."

"Forever," Adelbert whispers.

MONSTER FUCKERS CHAT

Sylvia: Florence, you've been holding out on us, girl. Saw your art hanging in Sadie's store *starstruck emoji* You're so talented! I know a gallery who would be interested in showing more of your pieces.

Natalie: Send a pic! I want to see too!

Alice: Sucked that you couldn't come to Sadie's opening, Natalie.

Cordelia: It was so much fun!

Natalie. Sorry I missed it. The Arctic Circle is pretty cool, though. Living the dream up here *smiling face emoji*

Iris: Natalie, do you even have time to breathe while taking care of two males?

Natalie: They're taking care of each other right now *winking face emoji* *fire emoji*

Helena: Glad you don't have to do all the work

Sadie: That question is better asked to Diana. She's got 3 *hot face emoji*

Diana: No complaints from me.

Louisa: And to think, I was happy when I got chocolate.

Florence: @Sylvia Yes! I'd love that *face holding back tears emoji*! Sorry for the slow response, didn't have my phone with me.

Sadie: I think we all know why *smirking face emoji*

36

Adelbert

Walking through the forest with Florence's hand in mine is the most extraordinary feeling. Her sheer joy is so strong it's nearly palpable, making me feel incredibly grateful to her for allowing me access to her emotions. She hasn't stopped humming since she woke up, a fact that hasn't escaped my notice.

"I'm really happy we are going to our meadow again today," she tells me with a broad smile that's been stuck on her face for hours.

Florence's cheerfulness is contagious and I answer her smile with one of my own. My heart has had this odd, full feeling since I've finally admitted my love for her and she has returned it with the same fervor. It is something I have never experienced before and can never do without again.

"I am happy to go anywhere with you, but this meadow does feel special. Plus, the last time we had a picnic here was rather memorable," I tease and enjoy Florence's blush. "Perhaps we could recreate some of that, but this time I'd like to use all three hands and my cock."

"That sounds... promising," Florence says, trying to sound nonchalant but failing spectacularly when her arousal spikes and hits me square in the chest.

I take a deep breath and let that feeling settle into me, then shoot her a smirk so she knows I noticed it. Florence shrugs with one shoulder and raises her eyebrows suggestively.

"You're trouble," I say with a laugh. "And I love you for it."

"Someone's got to keep you on your toes."

"You certainly do."

Not being able to resist any longer, I tug Florence into my arms and drop the picnic basket. Her arms instinctively wrap around my neck as I slant my mouth against hers.

Florence's lips part so sweetly for me when I suck on her bottom lip, and she whimpers at the first touch of my tongue against hers. My fingers dig into the base of her spine and I wrap her long hair around my fist so I can angle her head better.

I groan at the feel of her tongue dancing with mine, writhing, twining like they can't get closer.

The kiss takes on a life of its own. It's hungry yet tender, sealing promises and dreaming of futures.

Our breathing picks up and Florence's short nails scratch at the back of my neck, anchoring me in the moment.

I need more.

But before I lose control completely and fuck her right here, I slow us down and press open-mouthed kisses along her jaw and down her neck. Florence whimpers again and an uncommon growl rolls up from somewhere deep in me for not satisfying my woman the way she needs it right now.

"Hold on, Liebling. Let's get to the meadow and we can continue this."

Florence tilts her neck, quietly indicating her need for more, and I lavish that part of her skin with attention for a little longer.

Pressing a final kiss to her lips, Florence languidly opens her eyes and stares at me with a dopey smile.

"I like kissing you."

"I like kissing you, too," I reply and kiss the tip of her nose.

We right our clothing, which had gone askew at some point, and set off walking again, hand in hand.

Florence looks at me with mischief written all over her face.

"Knock knock."

Without hesitation, I say, "Who's there?"

"Armageddon."

"Armageddon who?"

"Armageddon in your pants real soon."

The sentence hasn't even fully left Florence's mouth before we're both laughing.

"I don't think I've ever laughed this much in my life before," I say, clutching my stomach.

"You've got a lot to make up for. But don't worry, I'll keep the jokes coming."

"That's not the only thing you'll keep coming," I joke and shake my head at my lame attempt.

Florence sputters out a laugh and I chuckle with her. I feel like I must be the fates' favorite male for bringing Florence into my life, and I instinctively pull her a little closer to me.

Once we settle down, I focus on carrying the picnic basket with my mage hand.

With her eyes fixed on the floating basket in front of us, Florence asks, "Is this the kind of experiment you would do in your study too?"

"Yes, there are a couple of other things I'd also like to try once we get to the meadow. The day of our picnic was the strongest my magic has ever felt and I had complete control over it."

"You can test it on me anytime," Florence jokes but I know she means it one-hundred-percent seriously too. "Do you think there's a specific reason for why there specifically?"

"I'm not sure. Even now, my strength is building. This basket is heavier than any of the items I could manipulate in my office." Quirking my head to look at Florence, I continue, "At first, I assumed it was my bond with you. When you are near me, it is definitely stronger. However, that day, it was like it had doubled in strength. It was itching under my skin, almost begging to be let out."

Florence places her other hand on my upper arm in comfort, and a line forms between her brows.

"I didn't know it was that strong. Is it uncomfortable?"

I shake my head and give a reassuring smile.

"Not really uncomfortable, but it's a sensation I haven't experienced before and haven't since. Perhaps there's some magical ley line running under that meadow that I'm unaware of. It could explain the boost to my magic that I get there and not at home."

The forest opens up and the meadow spreads out in front us with the giant oak tree at its center, framed by the blue sky and the rolling hills in the distance. The yellows, oranges, and reds of the early fall leaves enrich the landscape. From next to me, Florence lets out a very satisfied sigh.

"It really is something special, isn't it?" I whisper reverently, feeling something deep within me clicking into place whenever I am here.

"It is. I'll never get enough of this place," Florence says and leans her head against my shoulder.

"It's here for you whenever you want. I am, too." I place a kiss on top of her head.

Feeling silly for the first time in my life, I utter words I never thought I'd say, "Last one to the oak is a rotten egg."

I take off, and Florence's laughter skitters through the air behind me. Soon she's catching up, giggling the entire time and I slacken my pace to lace our fingers together and run alongside her. Strands of golden hair glowing in the sun stream out behind Florence, and a carefree smile is painted on her face. I take a mental picture of her like this, wanting, needing to remember this image whenever I have a hard day.

Florence is my purpose.

My hope.

My future.

My grin is stupidly big and there's a lightness within me that makes me feel like I'm floating.

When we get close to the oak tree, I grab Florence's hand and slow us to a stop. I bend down and band my arms under her butt to lift her up. She slings her arms around my shoulders and, cautiously at first, I spin us in a circle, then go faster and faster.

"I'm flying," Florence sings and throws her arms out on either side of her. She tilts her head to the sky and laughs giddily with every twirl. Her pure delight permeates the air, and I fall a little deeper for her.

This feeling right here, this unencumbered gleefulness when I'm with her, is something I never want to lose.

I carefully bring our spinning to a halt and slide Florence down my front. Leaning my forehead against hers and with goofy smiles plastered to our faces, we take a moment to drink each other in and get our breathing regulated.

"That was fun," Florence whispers.

"You make me want to have fun," I whisper back.

Florence leans back, cups my jaw, and trains her fiery gaze on me.

"Good. You deserve to relax. To play. You're not a robot programmed to jump when someone tells you to. You don't have to carry everyone else's burdens and responsibilities," she says with such utter passion it makes my eyes sting.

I sigh sadly and lace my fingers with hers, bringing them to my chest. Florence's compassion and empathy wrap around me like a warm embrace, viscerally easing my burdens and motivating me to communicate my feelings clearly.

"I have never been given a choice before, Florence. I have been conditioned to serve others, and to put their needs before my own. To not feel, to only think. To not be self-centered and to only make decisions that will benefit my future as the sole heir of

Alberad. It has been my whole identity until now. Please be patient with me as I unravel the beliefs I once held dear. I want to reevaluate my priorities as I discover this new side of life—with you."

"I understand that your father, even your name, has placed an incredible amount of pressure on you," Florence says and a dab of anger glimmers between her words. Not anger at me, I realize, but anger at my father and the situation. "But I'm telling you, with me, you have a choice. As long as I'm around, I'll always give you the freedom to make your own choices. I want you to be selfish and ask for what *you* want."

Like shutters lifting off my eyes, my brain and my heart come into alignment. The fates, the island, the research, everything has led me to this moment. Right here, in the middle of my favorite meadow—the meadow that appeared in Florence's dream—my soul is calling me to recognize its mate.

I know what I should do.

Staring intently into Florence's captivating eyes, I ready myself to say the words that will alter my future forever.

"Florence Everly, *I choose you*," I say passionately, enunciating every word with all the love I have.

Florence sucks in a breath. The weight of my words—my choice, my decision—reflects in her eyes and her emotions change so quickly that I find them hard to track. There's surprise, elation, and affection, before finally settling on determination.

Florence squares her shoulders and fixes me with a soft but unwavering smile.

"Adelbert Alberad, *I choose you*," Florence says confidently with tears brimming in her eyes.

I lean down and cup her face.

"My mate," I whisper against Florence's lips.

My lips skim over hers and Florence's tongue darts out in response. Granting her entrance, I meet her tongue with mine in a soft, languid kiss. Our tongues stroke and twine lazily, echoing our commitment and sealing our love.

My body heats and a prickly sensation spreads across my skin. It starts in the center of my chest and radiates out toward my fingers, my toes, even up my neck to my scalp.

Florence pulls away slowly and breaks our kiss.

"Baby."

The concern in her tone has me on alert, growing more worried when I see her wide eyes and mouth parted in shock.

"What is it?" I ask and look around us, searching for the threat. But something doesn't feel right and I lift my hand to inspect my head.

"You've got horns," Florence says tenderly and lets out an excited squeal.

31

Florence

Blinking rapidly, Adelbert reaches up with shaky hands, and walks his fingers along his new horns from their base to their highest points.

Jutting out from behind his temples on either side of his head, the taupe-colored horns twist and curve about eight inches high, splitting into two leaders.

They're marvelous and my hands are already itching to capture them with thread.

"You look dapper," I tell Adelbert affectionately. "They suit you."

Adelbert doesn't seem to hear me, lost in thought with the deepest frown I've yet seen on him marring his brow. He tilts his head from side to side, seemingly getting used to the horns' added weight.

"Careful! Don't strain your neck. It might take some time to get used to them," I say and hover my hands in front of him, not sure if he'd welcome my touch right now.

"I've... but... they're..." Adelbert grabs both horns, then lowers his hands again. He starts pacing, pauses, and then paces again, hands flexing at his sides.

I step in front of him and lay two hands on his chest,

hoping to catch him before he spirals.

"It's okay. We kind of knew this could happen, right?" I suggest gently.

Adelbert looks at me like I'm the one who has grown horns and shakes his head slowly.

"How could we have known?" he asks, genuinely oblivious.

"Baby, let's sit and talk this through," I coax, feeling like someone trying not to spook a wild animal.

"I can't sit now. I have to... to..." Adelbert picks up his pacing again, his hands waving animatedly through the air as if they're the ones who will give him the answers. "Do... something."

"You don't have to do anything right now. Let's figure this out. Together." I smile warmly at him and push comfort, peace, and love toward my anxious mate.

Adelbert closes his eyes as he receives my emotions, then takes a deep breath in through his nose. On his exhale, his brow relaxes and his shoulders loosen.

"Okay," he croaks out with a half smile. "Help me make sense of this, please, Liebling."

The vulnerability in Adelbert's voice pinches my heart. For him to lower his guard like this for me, is a gift I do not take for granted.

I give myself a second to mentally thank the fates for putting us together. For allowing me to be the strong one and support Adelbert the way he needs right now.

I walk closer and frame his face with both of my hands.

"It's going to be okay, baby. I'm here and I'll be with you through anything and everything. I choose you, with or without horn branches." The final words have their desired effect and Adelbert huffs out a single laugh. I give him a quick but firm kiss on the lips and go to fetch the picnic blanket.

"What did you mean when you said 'we kind of knew this could happen'?" Adelbert asks as he grabs the other side of the blanket and helps me spread it out under our favorite tree.

Adelbert sits down opposite me and I lace our fingers together.

"During one of our earliest conversations in the kitchen, you explained all your research about the fated bond and how it becomes a mate bond through genuine feelings and choice." I try to prompt him, hoping he's not too overwhelmed to connect the dots that have become increasingly clear to me over time.

"Yes." Adelbert drags the word out, and a line forms between his brows. "Are you saying that this is how the bond manifests for elves? That we grow horns?" He skipped a few integral details, but he caught on quickly.

"I don't know about *all* elves, but for woodland elves, yes," I confirm, nodding my head emphatically. "That's your basest being. That's what you are underneath all your layers. Just like the portrait of your forefather."

Adelbert goes completely still and his mouth falls open. He blinks blankly at me as it all sinks in. Sitting quietly in front of him, I brush my thumbs over his limp fingers, linking them with mine, and give him time to process this information.

"A woodland elf," Adelbert says slowly, eyes still not focusing on me but scanning the forest around the meadow. "That could be why I'm drawn to this particular spot and why my magic is strongest here. It's not because of a ley line. It's my connection to the forest."

I nod furiously, happy Adelbert's following the thread.

"Yes!" I lean forward and squeeze his hands, my stomach a fluttery mess of excitement as it all clicks into place. "And all your favorite places, the places where you feel most comfortable, they have an abundance of wood."

Adelbert's eyes brighten and a lighthearted laugh bursts from him.

"The kitchen. My study. The library." Each place is said with more enthusiasm. "It seems obvious now."

"Your desk, the kitchen table…" I add, naming his favorite pieces of furniture too.

A genuine smile settles on Adelbert's face, eyes crinkling in the corners.

"They're all made from oak," he says reverently, then his hand shoots up to inspect the bark.

Wanting to get everything out in the open and not lose momentum, I quickly add, "There's a chance that there might be some more woodland elf characteristics."

Adelbert's eyes narrow with curiosity. He tilts his head to the side, then wiggles it a little as he experiments with the weight of the horns.

"How do you know all this? How did you connect it so fast?"

"Firstly, because I always pay attention when you speak." I wink and Adelbert smiles indulgently at me. "And also because of that portrait of your ancestor," I explain. "I loved the horns and wanted to embroider a version of them, so I studied the portrait in detail. I noticed he had some bark on his skin, around the collar of his shirt."

Adelbert reflexively pulls his collar away from his neck and peeks down.

I started the piece so long ago, but I've not been able to complete it. Now I know why. I'd much rather prefer recreating Adelbert's horns instead.

Adelbert's mouth turns down and his throat bobs on a swallow.

"You don't mind patches of barky skin?" The shadow of insecurity in his voice hurts my very soul. This male has no idea how much I love him or how handsome he is to me.

I better remind him.

"Not one bit. Can you lie down for me?" I ask gently.

Adelbert nods and lies stiffly on his back, hands at his sides. I kneel next to him and roll his sweater up slowly. I stop when I find an inch of raised bark on his smooth abdomen.

Leaning down, I place a tender kiss on top of the new skin.

"How does the bark feel for you?" I ask.

Adelbert runs a finger over the patch I just kissed. "The texture feels smoother than I thought it would, similar to my horns. But it's as if it's more sensitive to touch than my elf skin."

I repeat the process on the other three spots I find scattered across his torso.

"I think this new look makes you even more attractive," I say honestly as I lower his sweater again and boop his nose.

Adelbert exhales sharply and as the stress visibly leaves his body. A soft, slow smile tugs on his mouth, and he sits up. His fingers tunnel into my hair and he looks me in the eye with so much affection that my heart will be full for days to come.

"I love you, Florence. Thank you for being here with me. For seeing things I wasn't ready to see, for speaking them. I am ashamed to admit that I might have underestimated you in the beginning. Never again."

"I love you too, Adelbert. Just because I'm more reserved to speak my mind, doesn't mean I don't have a mind to speak. I'll give you a reality check whenever you need one," I joke but also really mean if I'm spending the rest of my life with this male. "Now, are you ready to talk about the horns?"

Adelbert raises a hand to his temple and glides a finger along the curves of the horn.

"Can you tell me what they look like?"

"I'll do you one better. I'll sketch them for you," I say brightly and reach for my supplies.

Adelbert rotates his neck, getting used to the weight of his horns, while keeping his eyes on me as I stretch a new piece of fabric over a hoop and tighten it.

"Thank you. I should've brought my phone but I've gotten into the habit of forgetting it lately," Adelbert says as he presses his fingers against the tips, testing how sharp the ends are.

With my erasable pen, I sketch out Adelbert's face and attempt to draw his stunning horns. "That's a good thing, isn't it?"

Forearms propped on his bent knees, Adelbert looks out across the meadow. "I think it might be. I used to be anxious about not being able to be reached. What if a friend needed me? Or if my father had to contact me?"

Adelbert trails off in thought and my heart pangs at how he's always putting others first, even in his small actions like keeping his phone on him at all times.

Gaze shifting to me, Adelbert says, "When I'm with you, it feels like other things don't matter as much. The cloud of worries and stress that's always present just kind of dissipates. It's like you're a ray of sunshine piercing through it all. Just like now. For a second, I was ready to rush to the Alberad library or scour the books I have at home, but then you, my mate, were simply here for me, and your sweet, calm demeanor brought me back and kept me from spinning out completely."

Goose bumps race across my skin at Adelbert's unguarded honesty. I appreciate how hard he is working at communicating with me, ensuring there aren't any more misunderstandings and that I know how much he values me.

I pause my pen and blink the moisture in my eyes away.

"I'll always be here for you, just like you are for me. And I do love me some cloudy weather," I add and wiggle my eyebrows, then finish the last couple of lines of the quick sketch.

"Only you could crack a joke and make it sound endearing," Adelbert says fondly with his mouth curving into a grin.

I hold the hoop to my chest and take a fortifying breath.

"Are you ready?"

"Yes. No. Maybe?"

Adelbert worries his bottom lip and the need to comfort him propels me forward. I put the embroidery face down on the blanket and I crawl over his legs, straddle his lap, and place my hands on his shoulders to look him straight in the eye.

"Baby, these horns are so sexy, it makes me want to sit on your face and use them as handles so I can ride your mouth," I say bluntly, feeling like a boss for speaking my mind so succinctly. My nipples pebble and my pussy grows slick as the image roots itself into my brain.

Adelbert's pupils dilate and his face morphs into something between amusement and desire.

"Oh, really? I think you might have to test them out, then," he says with a feline smile that sends a shiver down my spine.

Note to self—use sex to distract him from anxious thoughts.

"You'll have to see them first," I counter carefully, pausing my lusty thoughts and shoving all my love and support toward him.

Adelbert gives me a singular, definitive nod and I reach behind me for the sketch.

"I'm ready."

I turn the hoop around and Adelbert stares at it, tracing the lines with his index finger.

"You're really talented," he says, awe and admiration thick in his tone. "This sketch is so lifelike."

"That's your first comment?" I laugh, then ask more insistently, "What do you think about the horns?"

"They're not completely unattractive," Adelbert says slowly and brushes his fingers from his temples up to the highest shoot. "They're quite similar to that portrait back home."

"They are. But yours are longer. And thicker," I purr and swallow down some excess saliva.

Adelbert laughs, then grows serious again.

"Thank you, Florence. I wouldn't have been able to handle this without you."

Taking extra care not to graze me with his horns, Adelbert tilts my head and kisses me sweetly. He trails soft presses of his lips along my jaw and neck, activating my horniness again.

Horny!

"Can I touch them?" I ask. My fingers are longing to

explore this new part of him.

"Please do," Adelbert says earnestly and rests his hands on my waist.

I start at the base protruding from his right temple and run my fingers up the stem. The bark is thick and rough, but with a smoothness to it that doesn't make my fingers snag.

"Mmm, that feels good," Adelbert says on a groan and slips his hands under my sweater—*his* sweater. "A little harder."

I shift on his lap and add my left hand so I can study both horns. I map every inch I can touch, experimenting with light skims of my fingers and stronger grips. The moment is intimate, delicate, but an undercurrent of lust flows between us. Feeling daring, I fist the horns a little more roughly.

The effect of my touch is evident in the increasingly hard length pressing into me from below, causing my own arousal to seep into my panties.

Adelbert lets out a manly rumble from deep in his chest and tightens his grip on my waist. He pulls me harder against him and I rock my hips in search of that delicious friction.

My mate knows what I need.

Adelbert pops the button on my jeans and pushes two magic fingers into me.

"Yes," I cry out and arch my back, rolling my hips into his mage hand, feeling grateful that this is the male I get to spend the rest of my life with.

Adelbert shoves my sweater up and mutters, "Off," before carefully angling his horns and lavishing my tits with attention. I momentarily let go of his horns to chuck the sweater out of the way, then grasp them at their base so I can direct him where I want him.

They really are like handlebars.

The brisk fall air against my skin wars with the pleasant warmth of Adelbert's mouth as he laves my nipple. He sucks the nipple into his mouth and flicks it with his tongue, making me mewl with pleasure. My other breast is kneaded and he toys with that nipple too, rolling, pulling, pinching it—all while fucking me with his phantom fingers.

Panting and whimpering, mewling and moaning at the symphony of pleasure Adelbert is conducting in my body, I come so fast and so hard, it catches me off guard.

"Adel-baby," I scream before my orgasm robs me of my voice and seizes every fiber of my being.

When my spirit returns to my body, I find myself laid out on the blanket, staring with hazy vision at the beautiful mustards, ambers, rusts, and gingers of the oak tree above me.

"Oh... my... goodness," is all I manage as a very self-satisfied Adelbert stares down at me with an arrogant smirk adorning his face.

"I think you blacked out there for a second," he says and brushes some hair from my forehead.

"Holy shit." I blink lazily. "That... has never happened before." A grin creeps its way across my face, and I roll my head to the side to get a better look at Adelbert.

"Wow. You really are something," I mumble. Even my mouth feels sluggish.

"Something special, I hope." There is zero insecurity in Adelbert's voice.

"Very," I affirm. A mental switch flips inside me and I summon my strength to sit up. "Now, lie down so I can show you just how much I appreciated that."

"You don't have to—"

Before Adelbert can finish that sentence, I press lightly against his chest and he lets me push him down onto his back. The desire to give him even an ounce of the satisfaction he gave me burns under my skin. I want my male to have his own out-of-body experience and I'll try my best to make it happen. But first, I need to get him out of his head.

"You just lie back and enjoy this. It's about time I tasted you," I say as I climb on top of his thighs, my damp crotch making me very conscious of the massive orgasm he wrung from my body.

"Taste? You—"

I cut Adelbert off with the fiercest look I can muster and he grins sheepishly back at me.

"Let me rephrase," he starts. "Can I hold your hair?"

"That would be lovely." I smile sweetly before returning to my wanton hussy state and slowly undoing his pants.

Adelbert gathers my long hair away from my face and keeps his eyes fixed on me while my sole focus is his cock.

I tug at his pants and he lifts his hips for me to pull them down enough to free his erection. I fist him through the fabric of his underwear, then pause.

"This is new."

Adelbert picks up on my intrigue and raises himself up on an elbow.

"What is?"

Carefully, I lower his underwear enough to let his cock pop free.

His bark-covered cock.

I t's magnificent," Florence says with genuine awe in her voice. Her warm breath wafts over my cock as she leans down to study it from all angles, causing it to twitch.

"This too?" I ask no one in particular, staring at the thick branch-like erection and trying to make sense of having a body part that's very much mine yet foreign at the same time.

I run a hand over the warm-brown shaft, feeling it out and... Is that a knot? The texture is similar to my horns but more intricate. Where my horns are rough, my cock is smooth but deeply ridged and furrowed. I can't help but think how good it would look with Florence's arousal dripping between the grooves.

"I don't know how many more surprises I can handle today," I say honestly, and thumb the knot midway down my thicker-than-before shaft.

Thank the fates for that. I guess.

"Baby, I'd really like to put your cock in my mouth. Can I do that?" Florence asks and audibly sucks some drool back.

Deciding to live in the moment and push my worries aside—not like they're going anywhere—I lean back on my elbows and drawl, "This cock belongs to you, Liebling. Show me how much you want it."

Florence wraps first one hand, then the other around my girth. My eyes roll back and a grunt escapes from me as she twists her hands gently around it, exploring the new feel of my cock.

"Your cock is gorgeous. And this knot over here on the front, it's going to hit my G-spot perfectly. And this texture—" Florence leans forward and licks a stripe from the base up to the tip "—it's going to feel so good inside my pussy."

Her words have precum leaking from me and my breathing picks up. I gather her hair into my mage hand again and wrap the length around my fist, not to take control, but purely because I don't want to miss one expression from her. The fact that I can *feel* her emotions—how turned on she is, how much she's enjoying this, and how much she loves me—makes me feel invincible.

"Ready?" Florence asks seductively and opens wide before enveloping my cock in her warm mouth.

The sensation is incomparable. Her silky tongue massages around the head of my cock and her moans vibrate against it. Florence swirls her tongue and sucks, while applying pressure to my base with one hand and fondling my balls with the other.

This must be nirvana.

My breathing turns ragged and groans and grunts fall from my lips as I try not to buck and force my thick cock down her throat.

Florence bobs her head up and down, taking me deeper with each pass, drool slipping past her stretched lips and into the ridges of my shaft.

The weak grip I have on my control is only going to last so much longer. The need to fuck Florence and claim her with my new cock screams from the deepest part of my basest being.

I'm riding on pure instinct as I lurch up and tear her jeans from her body. I throw Florence onto her back and shove my pants down further before impaling her on my cock in one hard thrust.

I pull her legs open wide and bend her in half until her

knees meet her ears, my actions urgent with the need to get my cock as deep into her cunt as possible.

"Hold your knees," I growl with a voice full of gravel, more beastly than I've ever sounded.

Florence obliges, and I'm just conscious enough to check in on her emotions and find her very much enjoying this.

I pin her to the blanket and drive into her in long, hard thrusts, rolling my hips to ensure my knot hits that spot inside her that'll make her scream.

"Don't hold back," Florence pants with ruddy cheeks and wild hair underneath her.

"Feel how good your mate fucks you?" I growl, watching my cock enter her dripping cunt. "This will be the only cock for the rest of your life."

"I'm yours, mate. All yours," Florence moans between crescendoing cries.

The words make me feral.

I collar her neck with my mage hand, and Florence's eyes roll back in her head, her arousal hitting me from all sides and compelling me to keep going.

I rut into her, barely conscious of anything but us coming together in this primal act.

Florence comes with a scream, her cunt gripping my cock, trying to suck it into her body with each spasm around it, triggering my own release.

"My mate!" I roar as I come, exploding into Florence's warm cunt, coating it with my seed as I mark her from the inside.

Claiming her.

Bonding her.

Mating her.

Chest heaving and head spinning from how hard I just came, I loosen my mage fingers around Florence's neck and gently lower her legs onto the blanket to rest on either side of me. Florence stares up at me with a satisfied smile, her chest rising and falling rapidly as she comes down from her climax—a mirror to my own state.

I slowly ease my cock from her cunt, causing our combined releases to trickle out.

It displeases me.

Using my fingers, I gather some of it and try to shove it back.

"Give me a taste," Florence rasps, and my brain registers that she must be hoarse from all the screaming.

I lean over her and offer her my fingers. Florence sticks out her tongue, gaze firmly fixed on my eyes. I slowly push my fingers into her mouth and her eyebrows raise a fraction, daring me to go deeper. I push in further, past the first knuckle, and keep going until she wraps her lips around almost the full length and sucks.

I withdraw my fingers and linger a moment on her lips, tracing the bottom one.

"You taste like oolong tea," Florence whispers, "but there's a hint of something else I can't quite place."

"You'll have to try again," I say huskily, with the image of Florence enjoying the flavor of my cum igniting that feral part in me that I didn't know existed.

I press the same two fingers into Florence's warm cunt and swirl them around, causing Florence to clench and whimper, and I grunt in satisfaction at making my mate so sensitive.

Bringing the fingers back to her mouth, she swallows them clean and gratification blooms around her. We repeat the process, quietly watching each other as she swallows everything down.

When I'm satisfied that she has had enough, I can't resist any longer and pull her into my arms, kissing her until we're both breathless and the taste of myself has transferred to me.

"That would be oak tea mixed with the oolong," I say and lean my forehead against hers.

"Oak?" Florence asks, fingers toying with my hands, lacing our fingers.

I nod against her.

"Based on overwhelming evidence, I'd venture to say that I'm a kind of woodland elf especially connected to oaks."

Florence leans back and looks up at my face, my horns, then at the trunk of the oak tree behind her.

"That makes a lot of sense."

"Now, let's get you clothed before I go feral again. You have no idea how my sanity is hanging by a thread when you're looking so tempting."

Florence shimmies her shoulders, making her tits jiggle in a way that has me reaching forward, but she quickly grabs her sweater and slips it over her head, following it with a wink.

39

Adelbert

"Baby, look!" Florence says breathily. Her hands cover her mouth and her eyes sparkle with absolute delight.

"Are those...?" I quickly button my pants and stand up.

"They are!" Florence exclaims as she runs toward the closest flower that has sprouted up around us. Crouching down, undiluted joy radiates from her as she gently traces the bioluminescent blue petals before hopping to the next flower and repeating the motion. Giggles chime from her like the sweetest song while she makes her way around the oak tree, greeting the numerous flowers and acknowledging their unexpected presence.

My heart nearly stutters to a stop with my sheer love for Florence, and I marvel that I get to call her mine.

The golden rays of the setting sun dance between the tall branches on the edge of the meadow and all around us, the trees sway on a light breeze, making the leaves rustle in applause. Goose bumps dot my arms and reach into the nape of my neck at the magical scene.

I walk over to Florence and wrap my arms around her. Not even tempted to mask my emotions, I let her read it all on my face— my joy, my love, my gratitude for her.

"These are the exact same flowers from the island that led

me to you," Florence whispers with glassy eyes darting all over my face. "The fates really think of everything, don't they?"

"Surely, this is their way of acknowledging our mating," I say, fairly certain I've figured out how they've orchestrated the events that led us to this moment.

I cradle her face and brush my thumbs across her cheekbones.

"I'm sorry if I was a bit rough back there, but I didn't have much self-control. I did check in on your emotions when I had enough self-awareness, though the rut quickly took over and I had to claim you in a very primal way."

Florence splays her fingers across my chest and pushes a hoard of emotions toward me. She patiently waits for me as I sift through all of them until I can identify surprise, arousal, fascination, marvel, and satisfaction.

"The way you fucked me back there was the hottest moment of my life. Your cock. Wow. The way you moved. Wow. If this is what it means to be mated to you, I can't wait for the rest of our lives. I like feral Adelbert. You were a beast. And I wouldn't change a second of that," Florence says with total candor, reinforcing the emotions she sent me. The mere picture of her pinned beneath me has my cock twitching again.

I blink my lustful thoughts away, then trail a hand up one horn.

"Isn't it ironic that my whole life I've been focused on looking composed and elegant, upholding the image that's becoming of an Alberad. And now, I've turned into a beast with horns and a barky dick."

"First of all, I love your barky dick. That thing is an A-plus penetration machine. Not that there was anything wrong with your previous one, but this one—" Florence gives me a pointed look, then looks at my crotch before looking into my eyes again. "That bumpy knot. Mm-hmm. The ridges. Yum. You didn't even have to touch my clit before my orgasm barreled into me. I'm going to have to drink so much water tonight. Not that I'm complaining," she quickly adds. "Also, oolong tea cum with notes of oak. There's nothing better. You might just make me addicted to drinking straight from you instead of a cup in the morning."

"Stop." I laugh and lean my forehead against Florence's. "You're going to make me hard again, and I know you must be sore. I plan to have you soak in the tub while I prep dinner before I can even think about touching you again."

Florence skims her fingertips along the skin above my waistband, taking extra care to caress the raised patches of bark. She leans back to look at me. Her brows knit, and her voice turns serious.

"Thank you for sharing your fears and worries with me. For verbalizing your introspection and bringing me along your emotional journey. It gives me insight into where you are at emotionally and mentally, and I appreciate how hard you are working to communicate clearly with me."

My mouth tips up into an easy smile for my mate.

"I know I have much to learn about communication, but I am trying my best to be open and honest about everything I'm feeling. I am so grateful that the fates brought you into my life and that they gave me enough time to get my head out of my ass before I lost you. I'm also grateful for friends who gave me a reality check when I needed it."

"The fates really knew what they were doing, matching us up. Do you think the distance limit is gone now that we're mated?" she asks and tenderly caresses the base of one horn.

"I'm certain it is. We can test it on our way back home."

"Home," she sighs delightedly.

"Home," I echo.

Florence's nose does that adorable wrinkling thing and a hint of nerves tinges the air around us.

"Is now a bad time to tell you about your eyes?"

My brows climb up my forehead.

"What about my eyes?" I ask, feeling curious and less worried than I would normally be.

Florence's voice is full of tenderness as she says, "They're the loveliest hazel-brown eyes I have seen in my life. They're this rich, honey-brown color with a mossy-green ring around the edges. If you look closely, there are flecks of gold at their center."

"Do you like them?" I ask.

"I love them," Florence says earnestly. "There's so much warmth in them."

"That's all that matters to me. You're the one who spends the most time looking at them. As long as you're happy, I'm happy." I shrug one shoulder, not feeling too bothered about the new eye color after everything that has happened today.

Reaching up onto her tippy-toes, Florence throws her arms around my neck and presses a firm kiss to my lips.

"I'm very happy," she whispers against my mouth. "I love you. No matter your shape, form, horns, or eye color. I loved you long before this and will love you long after."

"I love you too, Liebling. Forever."

Taking a step back, Florence says, "Now, please excuse me. I don't know if you've recognized it yet, but this is the exact forest from the dream the fates sent me. I need to dance in this meadow. Come join me, if you want."

Florence glides through the bright blue flowers, taking care not to step on one. My feet remain rooted to the ground but my eyes stay firm on her, not wanting to miss a moment of her recreating the scene from the embroidery piece she showed me. I gasp and stumble back a step as it hits me.

Her dream, this view right here, was from *my* point of view.

The way she described it. The scent, the foliage, the crisp fall air.

Everything has come full circle.

"The forest is fond of your mate."

I twist and turn, searching for the source of the deep,

rumbling voice, but find no one else in the meadow besides Florence and myself.

"Who said that?" I ask.

"I am Lebethron Nordo. I am the leader of the trees of the Black Forest. I speak on their behalf." A chorus of leaves stirs behind me and I turn slowly, not ready to face what I'm sure is an ancient oak tree talking to me in Elvish. I swallow hard and incline my head respectfully toward it.

"Please accept my most humble apology," I say in Elvish, addressing the thick trunk. "It is an honor to talk to you." I mentally cringe that I had fucked Florence so brutally in front of this sentient tree.

"Do not fret for reverting to your basest nature. We have waited a long time for your kind to return to us." His tone is warm and has a dash of humor lacing it.

"Are you able to sense my thoughts?" My heart thumps violently in my chest at what this all could mean. I almost lift my hand to shield my head, but realize the action is futile.

"Your emotions, Galadh."

A strange calm blankets me as the name settles into my soul, my deepest self recognizing it as its true name.

Galadh. Tree of the forest.

"How can I assist you, elder?" I ask the tree that I'm guessing to be more than a thousand years old.

"Your mate has unlocked your true nature. Thus, you are henceforth able to access the intrinsic parts of your soul. It allows you to once again commune with nature the way your forebearers had, the way it was intended for your kind."

"And Florence? Can she hear you too?" I turn my head and find her still frolicking through the meadow in nothing but the sweater she had commandeered from my wardrobe. She's breathtaking.

"Ah, your dear mate," Lebethron says with affection apparent in his voice. *"I find it unfortunate that it is a gift only woodland elves*

have the honor of. However, her pure heart has granted her the ability to sense the soul of the forest. We are deeply connected to her and call her Lótë."

"Flower," I whisper to myself, feeling Florence's Elvish name out. It's perfect.

My lips quirk up. Trust Florence to not only enchant this elf but also the whole forest.

"*The fates have foretold of you, Galadh,*" Lebethron says in his grandfatherly voice. "*You are the first elf in hundreds of years to have opened your heart so fully. It is time for woodland elves to return to the forest. To access their true magic the way you have. To open their hearts and listen to the deepest parts of their souls.*"

"I want to help. I want other elves to experience what I have, to be set free from the cage that has been placed around us. To feel, to truly live. Can you teach me more?"

"*We only require you to make woodland elves aware of their nature, which has been hidden for too long. Let them leave their stone castle and bring them to the forests they are native to. We will guide each elf who is willing to learn, as we did with you. It will be their decision if they choose to listen.*"

A plan takes shape in my mind and I stand up a bit straighter, a smile settling onto my lips. I can already imagine what my father's response will be, but I will fight for this forest, for elves, no matter what.

"I can do that."

THE BRETHREN CHAT

Adelbert: I am happy to report that Florence and I are mated.

Erik: Happy?!

Jamie: Who is this?

Harvey: Jamie, are you prank messaging from Bertie's phone?

Rollo: Told you! Who had October?

Sawyer: I had September.

Jamie: Now I feel stupid for betting it'll take a year.

Adelbert: You guys bet on me?

Edmond: Of course. We saw the way you looked at her on the island. Was only a matter of time until you let your heart do the talking.

Harvey: Congratulations to both of you. What did your dad say?

Adelbert: I'm telling him tomorrow. At the presentation.

Jasper: Double whammy. Nice. Can someone take video footage?

Everett: Anyone else have anything to report?

Daehan: Who's gonna be next?

Adelbert: Whoever is waiting for some big sign, don't. Pull your heads out of your asses and tell her how you feel. It's worth it.

Everett: I second that.

40

Florence

"A re you ready?" I ask Adelbert as we walk through the forest, retracing our steps toward Alberad School for the Supernatural, just like we did the morning after I first arrived in Germany.

Adelbert pulls me closer to him and tucks me under his arm.

"With you by my side, I'm ready for anything," he says and kisses my temple.

"I'll remain just out of sight, but within hearing distance," I promise, heedlessly reminding him of the plan we've gone over at least a hundred times already.

Since our mating a week ago, Adelbert and I have visited the meadow every day to hang out with the trees before they rest for the winter. We made plans for our future and talked about our goals and dreams until we had a rough idea of what we wanted it to look like.

Under Lebethron's branches, we laid out our picnic blanket. Adelbert read his grandmother's fairy tale book while I embroidered the sketch I did of his horns. He also learned to braid my hair—apparently something he had wanted to do for quite some time—using one physical hand and one mage hand. Adelbert practiced his magic every day and had long conversations with Lebethron about how to best help the forest.

Then, we'd make love. Or I'd ride his face. Or he'd go beast mode on me until my legs got all wobbly and I struggled to walk back.

Yay for piggyback rides.

I lift my hand to Adelbert's resting on my shoulder, and trace the enchanted emerald in the ring he's wearing on his index finger. For the first time since we left the island, he had to put on his glamour ring to hide his horns, bark, and hazel eyes from the other elves who are attending today.

"I can't wait to see your father's face when you reveal your horns and magic," I say, thinking how shocked that male will be when he sees elvish horns in person for the first time.

"Is my mate feeling a little diabolical today?" Adelbert teases and chuckles lightly.

"Perhaps a little." I giggle, then scrunch up my nose. "Am I mean?"

High above us, the branches sway on an invisible breeze and the leaves rustle in a way that lets me know they support my scornful thoughts.

"Never," Adelbert says. "I like all sides of you."

We walk in comfortable silence for a stretch, both lost in thought as we mentally and emotionally prepare for this day that will redirect Adelbert's future—*our* future.

"We're almost at the wards. You should be fine, just like last time."

"Need me to punch through them again?" I ask. I jump into a boxing stance and wiggle my eyebrows.

Adelbert bellows out a laugh and takes my hand as we start walking again. I tilt my head to study his profile and the smile that's just about a permanent fixture now. A lilting melody reaches my ears, and it takes me only a couple of seconds to place it.

"Are you humming my favorite song?" I ask Adelbert,

recognizing the tune.

"I think so? I've never heard the original version, but the melody has been stuck in my head since I met you. You were always humming when you first arrived and it annoyed me because it was so pretty and wouldn't make me stop thinking about you."

"I'm sorry?" I say hesitantly, not sure what to make of this confession.

"Don't get me wrong. I was only annoyed because of how much I liked it. How much I liked you. It's entirely my own fault for being so obtuse for so long."

Adelbert pauses and cups my shoulders. Dipping his head, he looks me square in the eyes with his once-again silver ones.

"Loving you has always been inevitable, Florence."

My knees weaken and I blink the instantaneous tears away that threaten to spill over.

"You can't say things like that to me before the biggest presentation of your life," I choke out and wipe at the happy tear that managed to escape. "You're going to make it hard to concentrate on what you're saying when I have all these mushy feelings from your ooey-gooey sweetness."

Adelbert brushes a tear away that's tracking down my other cheek.

"Good. Hold fast to that feeling. I will amplify my barriers so none of the other elves can sense you. My father might not be very nice today and I don't want you to focus on him," Adelbert says. "Remember, today is just a formality. I'm doing it for the Black Forest, for Lebethron, and for all the woodland elves who deserve to know the truth. But most importantly, I'm doing it for *us*."

"Okay. Because if that male says something mean to you, I can't promise I won't say something mean to him, too."

Adelbert gives me an indulgent smile that says a lot more than his words would and takes my hand again before we cross into Alberad.

Hidden behind a thicket of trees, I peek through the leaves at the high-back chairs set up in a semicircle in the center of the manicured garden and the ten elves mingling about.

Adelbert mentioned he will present to the "top scholars of the supernatural community," but it's curious that the only "top scholars" here are elves. It's something he hopes to change one day.

Adelbert stands in the center with relaxed shoulders and an easy grin when two elves approach him. He shakes hands with the haughty males who give his hair and clothes judgmental glances.

Since Adelbert's horns appeared last week, he's stopped constantly sweeping his hair back and just lets the strands fall where they want. He's now got very sexy ruffled hair that flops across his forehead in the yummiest way.

Adelbert has also swapped his sweaters for flannel shirts. After struggling with sweaters and stretching out their collars around his horns, he's had to find alternate clothing options that are easier to work with. Plus, the material catches less on the barky portions of his skin. He had to contact Sawyer for recommendations for durable fabrics without fully revealing what has happened yet. The bear shifter had a lot of fun on that phone call and the fact that Adelbert called him for fashion advice when he wears what Dede calls "lumberjack-chic clothes."

"Scholars," comes the clipped greeting of Nithard Alberad.

My lips instinctively pull back when I catch sight of him as he strides into view like he's the MVP of the day. In his mind, he probably is.

"Please take your seats for the presentation to commence," Nithard says with a voice that matches his icy eyes. Even though Adelbert's eyes were silver before, they were never cold like his father's.

There's some rustling as the other nine elves sit, but no one speaks.

Nithard stands slightly in front of Adelbert and addresses the group.

"Firstly, I would like to apologize for this highly unusual setup. It is at the request of my son to have today's proceedings outside."

Oh, this infuriating male.

Nithard's little indirect jabs are so cruel, they make me want to say something. But I'll wait. I'll let my Adelbert have his moment. Though, if his father dares to take it too far, I won't be held responsible for my actions.

A leaf stretches toward my face and comforts me with a brush against my cheek. I always knew I loved this forest, but since knowing I'm connected to it, it feels even more alive to me. I smile and take a deep, calming breath in, thankful that the whole forest is working to keep me obscured from view, and supporting me emotionally too.

With his gentle smile still in place, Adelbert moves next to his father and shoots me a surreptitious glance before meeting Nithard's eyes.

"Thank you, *Vater*. You may also take your seat."

Nithard's eyes flare and the way his muscles in his jaw bunch is evident of what he thinks of the dismissal, but he turns on his heel and takes the center seat.

Adelbert looks at each elf in turn, and says warmly, "Thank you to all who have traveled from far away to be here today. I promise to make the trip worth the effort."

Heads turn to their neighbors and brows crease at the statement. They're probably wondering if it's arrogance or sincerity talking, no doubt trying to read Adelbert's emotions.

Adelbert puts his hands in his pockets and the female elf on the left bristles in her seat at the gesture. The male next to her notes it too and his chin lifts in distaste.

"When it came time to pick my topic of research, I scoured

the library for an idea of which direction I wanted to take my studies. I read tome after tome, finding a multitude of interesting topics about woodland elves and elvish magic. Until one day, I stumbled upon a passage in one particularly old book." Adelbert pauses for effect, then says, "A passage regarding mage hands."

A scoff emanates from the right of the circle, but Adelbert ignores it.

"Once thought obsolete, even a myth at most, I am pleased to say, is an actual fact very much alive."

Nithard crosses his arms over his chest. Mouth turned down, he says, "Prove it."

Adelbert smiles warmly at him, perhaps even enjoying this moment of distrust.

"I already have. Please check your bags."

A female elf leans forward and rummages through her handbag.

"Whose is this?" she asks and holds up sunglasses that don't match her look.

"How did that get there?" a male with a thick accent asks and stands up, only to trip over his own feet. The moment Adelbert uses his mage hand to catch the male is apparent in his shout of surprise.

Absolute chaos descends as everyone checks their tied shoelaces and searches their bags, all while shouting over each other for answers. Adelbert imperturbably stands back with his hands in his pockets and that cute little smile still curving his lips.

He's having fun, making up for the mischief he missed out on when he was at school.

Nithard's voice booms across the others', "That's enough."

Silence descends on them again, and they take their seats.

"Explain," Nithard demands and brushes lint off his shoulder, even though he never moved a muscle during the chaos.

"After reading about mage hands, I had to find a way to connect to it," Adelbert says and I almost squeak as his mage hand comes to rest on the back of my neck. "Discovering the way was purely accidental on my part. I got so frustrated one day that I swiped a hand through the air and a book moved on the opposite side of my desk."

One of the haughty males with the judgy eyes scoffs, "That does not make any sense. How do you expect us to master this? That behavior is hardly becoming of an elf." He rolls his eyes for extra effect and my blood boils.

My patient mate—grin in place—looks patiently at him and says, "Finding that my emotions are tied to my magic was a good start."

"Emotions?" asks one female elf, utter disbelief in the single word.

"Emotions, yes," Adelbert affirms. "That's the tip of the iceberg. It only gets better."

I note two of the elves who have stayed reserved throughout Adelbert's speech sit up a bit straighter in their seats. Perhaps they're open to learning and could be in Adelbert's corner when he makes his request later.

"You see, I spent years practicing my mage hand, only able to manage small experiments. However, this summer, my abilities strengthened." Adelbert pauses and makes sure he has every elf's attention.

There is absolute silence and it's like even the forest is holding its breath, waiting to see how they'll take the news.

"This summer, I fell in love," Adelbert states matter-of-factly while gently massaging my nape.

A stout elf on the right side of the semicircle shakes his head and waves a dismissive hand through the air.

"What would that help? You got your dick wet and suddenly your magic is stronger? No, boy, it doesn't work like that," he sneers. "You've cast wards. It takes concentration, discipline, and many hours between the books to get the enchantments memorized. It's not puppy love helping you. You sound absolutely delusional."

I stiffen at the remark and Adelbert senses it. He cards his phantom fingers into my hair then glides them down the full length, similar to how I'd normally comfort myself. I relax into Adelbert's touch and decide to ignore the stout elf's crude comments.

Two seats to the left of Nithard, a female elf inclines her head, attention riveted on my mate.

"Did love strengthen your magic? Is that what you are saying?" she asks with narrowed, calculating eyes the color of moss.

Adelbert nods. "In short, Monika, it did. Opening my heart up and letting my emotions to the fore has aided my magic."

Nithard crosses his arms over his chest. "What are you not saying, Adelbert?"

"There is much more I have to tell you. What I have found can change the course of our future as woodland elves, possibly other kinds of elves too."

The stout elf scowls at Adelbert and leans back in his chair, spreading his legs wide and resting his arms on his stomach. "Spit it out, boy. You got our attention with your little party trick. Now, let's see if you can impress us with the theory behind it."

The leaves of the trees around the semicircle stir with irritation and I send them calming energy, because I know what Adelbert is going to say will shut that rude male up.

Nithard side-eyes the elf and his lips press into a thin line before he raises his brows at Adelbert, indicating that my mate should proceed.

Adelbert's voice comes out steady as he starts his speech he practiced. "When I discovered my magic, it was in anger at first. Accidental. I tried to learn it, control it, and my skills grew over time. Yet, I was only able to pick up small objects and move them around my study, turn them upside down, or spin them around.

"I was ready to present on mage hands alone today. To reveal this magic that has been lost to us for hundreds of years. The theory behind it, originally, was that elvish magic is limited to warding and our empathic abilities, but we have forgotten the deeper well within us.

"We have spent far too much time sitting behind desks, pouring over texts and gaining knowledge that way, instead of practicing magic and pushing our abilities.

"When I fell in love, a part of my soul was unlocked and my magic flowed freely through me. I was able to do more intricate movements, lift heavier objects, and feel things as if I were using a physical hand.

"It got even stronger when I spent time outside, in the forest—the place woodland elves are meant to charge their magic.

"For too long, we have been locked inside stone castles, suppressing our magic. For too long, we have forced arranged marriages for status and prestige, instead of allowing the free choice to love. For too long, we have ignored our basest natures, denied our instincts, and suppressed our innate beings to surrender to a fabricated image of what elves should be."

Nithard opens his mouth to interrupt but Adelbert coolly holds up a hand, indicating he's not done.

"Mate bonds are relevant. Mage hands are relevant. Nature is relevant. Favoring emotions over book knowledge is relevant. If you remember these elements, there is so much you can do. So many you can help."

This time, Nithard can't help himself. He stands up and steps in front of Adelbert with a murderous look in his eyes, then calms his features before turning to the scholars.

Through clenched teeth, Nithard says, "I must apologize for my errant son. I am not sure what has preceded today's presentation to cause this tomfoolery. An appropriate reprimand shall be meted out."

Monika shakes her head and my shoulders sag that no one is hearing him out.

Surprising me, Monika scolds, "Sit down, Nithard. This isn't your presentation. We came to hear Adelbert speak. Let him."

I do a little wiggle and quietly high-five the closest leaf.

We've got one elf on our side.

Nithard's jaw drops to an almost comical degree, but he quickly rights himself and wordlessly stalks back to his seat.

"Go ahead, Adelbert," Monika encourages gently. "We're listening. They won't say another word until you invite us to." She shoots a look at the other elves and a couple sink down in their seats, while others give her nods of approval.

Adelbert's chest rises on a deep inhale and he rolls his shoulders back. Clasping his hands in front of his body, his thumb strokes his glamour ring.

"I am a woodland elf," Adelbert announces. "I have been chosen as the elvish representative for the Black Forest. The forest is alive and wants to help elves connect with nature again. They want to help us strengthen our magic. In turn, we can help them too in the ways of old. The way it was always meant to be."

Adelbert removes his ring and gasps echo through the semicircle. Deciding to hit them with a one-two punch, Adelbert gives me the sign, and the thicket opens up to let me through. I graze a finger along one of the leaves in thanks and glide over to my mate.

Reaching out his hand for me, I place mine in Adelbert's and he envelops me in a warm embrace.

"I'm so proud of you," I whisper into his neck, feeling everyone's eyes on us. "You're doing great."

A muttering of voices starts up as the elves talk amongst themselves, sharing theories, while Adelbert and I hold each other. Eventually, a throat clears and we untangle our arms to lace our fingers, ready to face them together.

Monika asks, "Is this the summer love you spoke of?"

Adelbert nods and has the most serene smile I've yet seen.

"Everyone, I would like you to meet Florence Everly. My mate."

Nithard nearly loses his balance as he jumps to his feet.

"Mate? No. No, no, no, no, no. Now that you have given

your presentation, you will take a mate approved by me. And she will definitely not be a human. I already have contenders in mind that will be befitting of the Alberad name. It is my legacy at stake here. Your legacy," Nithard thunders, voice ripe with indignation.

Monika tuts disapprovingly and rolls her eyes at Nithard's outburst. "Oh, shut it, Nithard," she scolds. "Can't you see how happy the boy is? And he's already mated. You can't break them up." She shrugs, making me like her more by the second.

"I certainly can," Nithard counters.

Not able to stay quiet any longer, I lift my chin and infuse all the sass I've been saving over the years into my voice when I say, "I'd like to see you try, Nithard."

Adelbert chuckles as Nithard's mouth opens and closes like a fish out of water. My heart pounds at having all the attention on me, but with Adelbert at my side, I steel my spine and let them look their fill as they discuss us.

When everyone has calmed enough again, Adelbert addresses the group.

"We wondered which would shock you more, sprouting horns or announcing our mating. Interesting to see where your priorities lie." Adelbert laughs but there's censure in his tone.

"Now, to sum up what has happened. Florence and I discovered that we had a fated bond and had to remain close. Fated bonds occur once every thousand years or so, depending on if the fates deem it necessary. We developed genuine feelings for each other and decided to pursue a relationship. Once we made the choice to be together, we became fated mates. A concept that has not been heard of in many years but is now relevant to us, along with nine other couples around the world. Each couple consists of a human woman and a male of a different species, and in some situations have an addition of one or more mates.

"Our matings see our species return to our most intrinsic forms, and in my case— as a woodland elf—I have features that have not been seen in hundreds of years. Horns, bark on my skin, hazel eyes, and some other, um, features too." Adelbert avoids telling them directly about his new cock, and I don't blame him one bit. To those that it concerns, he'll probably reveal more later.

"After our mating became official, I was able to communicate with Lebethron, an ancient oak in the forest. He welcomes any and all woodland elves to learn about their inherent magic and is offering to guide those who are willing to learn.

"It is my personal mission to travel around the world, visiting different schools, and teach them about the use of mage hands, to reacquaint woodland elves with forests, and ensure that this knowledge is widely accessible to anyone who desires to learn."

I glance around the semicircle and note those with bright eyes and keen interest, but a few remain skeptical. The rude elf from earlier hasn't said a word for a long while and his face is completely drained of color. I try to grin at him but he just looks away and studies his feet instead.

Looks like he's not ready to make friends any time soon.

Monika places her hand on her heart and her lips curve in a genuine smile. She looks at us with warm approval and I feel a special kinship with her.

"Adelbert," Monika says, "I would love to learn more, and to meet this Lebethron. You are welcome to teach at my school anytime that suits you. You are both welcome to visit us in the Great Bear Rainforest and stay as long as you'd like in Canada."

"What about your place at Alberad?" Nithard asks, voice coming out high-pitched and no longer looking very composed.

Adelbert looks at me and I give him an encouraging nod.

"The Black Forest is home. Florence and I will keep our house as our main base here. I would like to teach classes at Alberad when our schedule allows. My first priority, though, is my mate. Her artwork on the Black Forest has been curated for an exhibit at a well-known gallery in California. We will travel there first to prepare for the exhibition. Then I am open to teaching some classes at the local monster school there." Adelbert gives one of the males a pointed look, and the male nods enthusiastically.

Good. Another one on board.

My mate continues, "We will repeat this pattern with other schools around the world, depending on Florence's exhibition schedules. We will return to Germany to rest at home between trips. If your school is open to hosting classes, I would like to discuss options with you. But first, I'd like to take those interested to meet with Lebethron. The forest will enter their winter rest soon, so it's best we start the process. Any questions?"

The elves are eager to learn more about their heritage, Adelbert's magic, and our mating. They pepper Adelbert—even me—with questions on the walk. The stout elf looks to Nithard for cues on how to act, but I don't miss how they're both hanging on every word we say even when they're both pretending to be disinterested.

Hand in hand, Adelbert and I lead the elves through the forest, ready to usher in a new era for all.

"Morning, Liebling," I say to my mate as she glides into the kitchen. I instantly put down the knife I'm using to cut slices of the *Hefezopf*, and gather her into my arms.

"Hi, baby." Florence's breath is warm against my neck as she hugs me back. I squeeze her a little tighter and thread my fingers into her hair at the nape of her neck. I tilt her head up and press a sweet kiss to her lips, then go back for two more.

"You let me sleep in," Florence says with a slightly accusatory tone but her eyes hold no fire. Her fingers reach up to caress one of my horns and I melt into her touch.

"I know you've either been too nervous or excited to sleep well lately, so I wanted you to rest a little longer before Everett and Dede got here," I explain and skim my hands down her back to rest in the back pockets of her jeans.

"Have you heard from them this morning?"

"Everett messaged when they landed, but I haven't felt them cross the wards yet."

Florence pulls me down for another kiss before we reluctantly part and go about our morning routine of preparing breakfast together.

"I still can't believe they're flying to Germany to pick us up," she says while grinding enough coffee beans for Everett, Sadie, and me.

"Can you blame them?" I ask and finish buttering the pastry slices. "I know they've been so curious to see the house now that it's done."

Florence and I have spent the last year painstakingly furnishing our house, searching for unique, handcrafted pieces that spoke to us. It's now a beautiful combination of natural wood and colorful fiber art.

"I know, but it really is a very long way around the world to pick us up here and then go to Seoul. If they flew to Korea directly from Vegas it would've taken half the time," Florence explains as she preps the coffee machine.

I can't help the smile stretching across my face. "Stop trying to logic your way through this. They're coming because they love us."

Florence pauses and her jaw slackens. "Oh my goodness, how the tables have turned. Did I seriously just try to logic my sister, and *you* reminded *me* of emotions?"

I wink at her. "It's been quite a year of growth for us."

"You can say that again." Florence giggles.

Besides teaching mage hand magic, I work with local companies who want to pursue more holistic carpentry. Over the past year, Lebethron has helped me learn how to identify which trees are ready to bid their woodland homes goodbye and I act as their intermediary.

"Good morning, Sir Purrington. I was just about to search the whole house to find you," Florence coos, bending down to run her hands down our cat's fur. He nudges against her, leaning into her touch, before sauntering over to me.

"Hey there, big boy," I say affectionately and lower onto my haunches to scratch under his chin and behind his ears. "Do you like your new window perch?"

Florence perks up. "Oh! It arrived?"

"Lindsey dropped it off this morning. I assembled it already and stuck it in the living room window. When I looked earlier, Sir Purrington was stretched out on it, basking in the center of a sunbeam. Weren't you, boy?" I ask him as I pick him up to cradle in my arms for snuggles. Florence huddles close and we lavish our boy with love.

Despite basically having his own room dedicated to him, Sir Purrington goes where he wants. On cooler mornings he's in the living room with Florence, but he also likes to lie in the special bed I bought him when I'm in my study.

"Lindsey left you a note too when I said you were still sleeping."

Florence pouts. "I'm so sad I couldn't say bye."

"You literally saw her two days ago for that exact reason," I state with a chuckle.

"I guess that's true." Florence's shoulders slump and a trace of despondency trickles through the air. "I'm going to miss Sir Purrington. It's never easy leaving him when we travel."

With my free hand, I tilt Florence's chin up to look at me and cup her jaw, with Sir Purrington still a cozy bundle between us. Florence's one hand automatically sneaks under my shirt and splays across my abdomen, tracing my sensitive bark.

"I know it's not easy," I say, "but Sir Purrington is so smart, I know he understands. And, I am absolutely certain that he's happy that you're being recognized for your talent. We are all very proud of you for everything you've accomplished. This new exhibition in Seoul is going to be even better than last year's in San Francisco."

Florence's eyes turn glassy and her voice is breathy when she says, "I never thought I'd have an exhibition in South Korea. Is this real life?"

Sir Purrington chooses that moment to let us know he's had enough cuddles for now. I set him down and he prances back toward the sunny living room.

I run my hands down Florence's neck and cup her

shoulders, ducking my head so we're eye level. "I love that I get to follow you everywhere. Plus, this time, we get to take Everett and Dede with us too." I smile at the beautiful woman before me who is still astounded that so many people around the world appreciate her art.

Florence turns the conversation to me. "Are you ready to teach your first classes in the Far East?"

I think about it for a second before answering. "Yes. Though, I am a little nervous too. Daehan said the students are very knowledge hungry, and might ask difficult questions. It will be interesting to see how they'll respond to my lesson on accessing emotions when they're used to theory-based teaching. But what I'm most excited about is the school's location in Hallasan Forest and meeting some of their trees. Each forest we've been to has felt completely unique to the others."

"You'll be fantastic," Florence says and her eyes glimmer with her belief in me. "Luckily all the trees speak Elvish so you don't have to worry about language barriers. While you teach, I'm going to try to convince Dede and Everett to hike up the volcano with me."

I laugh, unable to imagine Sadie enjoying the hike up Hallasan. "You might have to negotiate with her for that. Maybe ask Alice to take you shopping in Seoul together before we head to Jeju?"

"That's actually a really good idea," Florence says and narrows her eyes in thought. Stepping away to boil the kettle for her tea, she says, "What time will Sylvia and Edmond get here?"

I collect the variety of jams we have and place them on the table along with the *Hefezopf*. "I think they'll be here in time for lunch with everyone."

Florence sets the table with breakfast plates and cutlery. "Have you spoken to Nithard?"

Things have been different between my father and I since my presentation. Now that I'm free from his hold—and he's desperate to master his mage hand, which he's finding incredibly difficult—he's not been sure how to deal with me. I won't go as far as calling him "nice," but he's certainly been more amenable to my requests.

"He's apprehensive about Edmond teaching a class at Alberad," I say with a light scoff. "I reminded him that Edmond went to school with us and actually did better than me on tests. But I guess as the first non-elf professor at Alberad, it's going to be an adjustment, even if he's just guest lecturing."

Florence boosts herself up on the counter in front of me and I automatically gravitate to her, parting her legs to stand between them. Her hands go to my nape and play with strands that I've been wearing longer since I got horns. Haircuts and looking neat and tidy are not really a priority for me anymore.

"The age of nepotism is over," Florence declares melodramatically. Then adds, "Or getting there. Point is, progress is being made. You said he's going to teach flying lessons too, right?"

"Yes. Flight Physics will be offered to all winged species. He'll also teach Magical Architecture as an extra credit for those interested in learning how magic is used in the building process."

I twist Florence's hair around my mage hand and angle her head as I kiss and nip along her jaw.

Relaxing against my body and leaning into my kisses, she says, "I'd love to listen in on one of his classes, even if I don't have magic or wings."

"Me too. Since they're staying here for so long, let's take Sylvia with us and attend a class when we're back from Korea. I'm not sure if she's sat in on one before."

"I don't know if she'd want to. Big groups and unknown situations don't pair well with her anxiety," Florence says breathily, scooting closer to the edge to rub against my hard length.

"I'll chat with Edmond and see if we can come up with something."

My fingers dig into Florence's butt as I pull her body

against me. I claim her mouth in a fierce kiss and her hands drift toward the button of my pants.

I groan and reluctantly break the kiss.

"Everett and Dede just crossed the wards," I tell her when I feel them passing through the farthest barrier.

"Yay!" Florence squeals and hops down the counter. "I'm going to wait by the door." She starts skipping out of the kitchen, then pauses to look at me.

"You coming?"

"Not the way I want to right now," I grumble with a slight smile and readjust my throbbing cock.

Florence giggles and holds out her hand, waiting for me to follow her.

I always will.

Curious about Jasper, Natalie, and Cole? Join them on their adventures in the Arctic Circle in **Courting the Krampus**, the next book in the Monsters of Alberad world.

If you want a little more from my monster couples, you can sign up for my newsletter to get sneak peeks and exclusive content. You can read Sadie and Everett's story in **Tempting the Dhampir**, or download their bonus scene on www.ellesterling.com

Acknowledgements

From the bottom of my heart, thank you for reading Enchanting the Elf and going on this journey with me. Florence and Adelbert had to work hard for the HEA, but wasn't it worth it?

If you haven't done so already, please consider leaving a rating and review for this book. They're the lifeline of indie authors and will help me get a foothold in the wonderful world of funny, smutty books.

Each book in the Monsters of Alberad world can be read as a standalone and in any order, and will feature a different monster pairing (or pairingS). Who are you looking forward to reading about next? Drop me a line and tell me your thoughts. I love hearing from readers!

To everyone who helped me get this book ready to share with the rest of the world, thank you.

Adrienne, the Florence to my Sadie. Thank you for listening to my early ideas and helping me expand on them, for not frowning at my corny jokes but laughing with me. But mostly, thank you for holding my hand when I got frustrated and all the encouragement when I needed it.

Colette, thank you for your impeccable designs. You understand me so well and take my visions and elevate it to a higher level every time. I love having you in my corner <3

T.B. Wiese, your advice always takes my early drafts to such a higher level. Thank you for being the best beta I could ask for!

Steph, your input has been invaluable. You took Adelbert and Florence's story and pushed me out of my comfort zone to represent them more accurately. This book wouldn't be what it is without you. Thank you!

Mon Reyes, this cover is everything. Your ability to capture my characters and bring them to life with your art astounds me. You're such a pleasure to work with.

Rhea Fox and Monika, thank you for helping me keep the German elements as accurate as possible in this book. Each time I messaged you with random questions, you were so thoughtful with your advice and ideas. Thank you for keeping Adelbert authentic with his cooking and culture.

My street team—Lindsey, Michelle, Erin, Micheala, Katie, Monika, Josie, Mel, Katie B, Mckayla. You ladies are the best! I love our community and look forward to our daily chats. Thank you for loving Sadie and Everett first, and coming on this journey with me as we get to know the other monsters too.

To my husband who is the ultimate pillar of support. Thank you for encouraging me, motivating me, and believing in me. I love you.

And finally and most importantly, thank you, dear reader, for picking my stories. Your love for my characters fuels me. I appreciate you more than I can say.

—Elle

About the Author

Elle Sterling is a monster and paranormal author based in South Korea.

Her stories are fun and flirty, filled with heart and spice. HEAs guaranteed.

Much like her own life after emigrating from South Africa, she enjoys writing characters crossing cultural barriers and loving without restraint.

You can usually find Elle in her writing cave with coffee within reach at all times. She also enjoys grilled kimchi-and-cheese sandwiches and hibernates during the humid summer until the weather has cooled.

Elle loves connecting with readers, so visit her on social media, or email elle@ellesterling.com

Elle Sterling